OVERWHELMING PRAISE FOR
DEEPAK CHOPRA

"Deepak Chopra has done more over the last decade than any person of whom I am aware to help ordinary people understand extraordinary things."
—Neale Donald Walsch

"Few thinkers have done as much as Deepak Chopra to allow millions to embrace the project of personal and social transformation."
—Oscar Arias, former President of Costa Rica, and 1987 Nobel Peace Laureate

"Deepak Chopra has emerged in the last part of the twentieth century as one of its most original and profound thinkers."
—Dr. Benjamin Spock

"Deepak Chopra is one of the extraordinary and creative minds of our times."
—Jack Canfield, co-author of
CHICKEN SOUP FOR THE SOUL

DEEPAK CHOPRA'S

THE ANGEL IS NEAR

*Created by Deepak Chopra
and Martin Greenberg*

St. Martin's Paperbacks

This work is published with the permission of Harmony Books, a division of Crown Publishers, Inc.

DEEPAK CHOPRA'S THE ANGEL IS NEAR

Copyright © 2000 by Boldergate, Ltd. LONDON FILMS

ISBN: 0-312-97024-2

Printed in the United States of America

St. Martin's Paperbacks edition / August 2000

St. Martin's Paperbacks are published by St. Martin's Press, 175 Fifth Avenue, New York, NY 10010.

10 9 8 7 6 5 4 3 2 1

The author wishes to acknowledge with gratitude the assistance given in the preparation of this book by Rosemary Edghill.

DEEPAK CHOPRA'S

THE ANGEL IS NEAR

Ground Zero...
May 8, 1999

"The bare facts are more incredible than anything I could invent. The world's first capture of an angel is imminent. Only a few citizens are being told in advance. I have this upon highest authority. Not from God Himself, admittedly, but if—"

The man, whose name was Marvell, pushed the button on his tape recorder with a long tapering finger, and the machine stopped. There was a short whir as he erased a few inches of the cassette tape. He punched record again. He spoke more carefully this time, less excitably, with frequent halts to make sure he was making himself clear.

"June fifteenth, page one, paragraph one: In some obscure corner of the world, a miracle is about to occur. For centuries men have credited the existence of angels on the basis of faith and visions. In the past this has been proof enough. Faith and visions have been the only way to prove the existence of God or the soul or even Christ, if we are to be brutally honest—damn!"

His fingers fumbled and stabbed at the buttons again, missing the one he wanted. The tape started whirring crazily. Rhineford Marvell was exhausted; the thrill of his ecstasy had combined with the terror that he might be deluded. His forehead glistened with sweat, and there were damp rings under his armpits. He didn't turn around when he heard a faint tap at the door.

"Ford, darling?" It was his wife, Beth. Her voice sounded faint and timid. "I don't mean to disturb you, but—"

"If you knock and enter while I am working, isn't that the very definition of meaning to disturb me?" Marvell said flatly.

There was an embarrassed pause before she tried again. "You have to eat something. I've gone out twice today and come back, and this door hasn't been opened the whole time. Are you sure you're all right?"

"I told you, when I need to eat, you will be the first to know."

His tone of voice left no doubt that he wanted his solitude back. Still not turning around, he heard the door close quietly. He felt oddly refreshed and punched the Record button again.

"The great event will not be stopped. Be alert, await the signs. Soon everyone will be tested. We are about to share a visitation so epic that the rise and fall of empires will seem but a tiny wavelet lapping on the shores of eternity."

He started to feel stronger now, and it was all falling into place. The messengers had something incredibly important to tell humanity, and that was why they would be appearing soon, making themselves known in some spectacular way. A surge of bliss welled up in Marvell's chest when he thought of how privileged he was. They wanted him to know all their secrets, and he was ready. They hadn't made a mistake in singling him out. He smiled at the secret part he was playing. Would Beth believe it when everything came out and a thousand reporters were clamoring to interview him? It would be satisfying to prove to his wife beyond a shadow of a doubt that she was married to one of the chosen.

1
The Capture

"This place gives me the creeps, big time," Krause muttered, shifting her M16 rifle from one shoulder to the other.

"Maybe it's the land mines," her patrol buddy Linville remarked. His voice was matter-of-fact. "We could call you Stumpy."

"Bite me," Krause said. The sweepers had done a good job clearing the ground when the Allies rode in. She looked down at her feet nervously, unable to see them in the dark. You never knew.

It was raining in Kosovo. The landscape of this tormented place was the rugged rolling stuff of the northern Mediterranean, a green and fertile land with a wild beauty.

The terrain looked like home to one of the two soldiers slogging through the mud—Staff Sergeant David Linville of Mendocino, California. His buddy, SP4 Jan Krause, was from Kansas, and the craggy hills cut with narrow valleys made the wary farm girl nervous: She kept seeing snipers' nests in the black treetops.

Spotters from Seventh Air Cav flyovers had sighted suspicious activity in the area and reported it to their superiors. *Activity* was the wrong word; it was more like a glow, too big for a house fire, too small to be a forest fire. It was centered in a small bombed-out village listed on the maps as Sv. Arhangeli. The film in the plane's cameras had been fogged, and that was incentive enough to send in a foot patrol.

Krause and Linville walked in silence for a time. Between them they carried cameras and radiation detectors; Krause was outfitted with a device to detect the common chemicals used in assembling bombs. The odds were against any incident turning into something major. All that either one of them wanted to do was get to Arhangeli, do their job, and get back safe again to barracks.

"Hey," said Krause without a preamble, "you know the Virgin Mary's from around here?"

Linville didn't slow down. The darkness around him was soft and pleasant. Deserted. Almost safe. "You're making that up."

"No lie. Tompkins was telling me the other

night. She's been showing up to a bunch of kids."

"Lucky them," Linville said absentmindedly. "Why don't we wait here for a while?" The road had crested a small rise, and the village had to be below them, with no more than a few scattered farm lights around it. The remaining cluster of houses had been bombed, burned, shelled, and dynamited until nothing was left except a lumpy plain of vaguely geometric rubble. The church, they knew, was in the distance, a gray stone building that had once been white, and nearly invisible in the hazy night.

Krause grunted noncommitally, dropping her heavy pack to the ground and sitting on it. She dug a small pair of field glasses out of her pack and began to inspect the terrain, which was clearing now as the moon broke through melting clouds. She finally got a good look at their objective.

"Looks all right," she said. Linville gave the nod and reached for his pack. They had just gotten to their feet when they heard the sound.

It was a low rumble, a deep remote foghorn sound that seemed to echo off the sides of the surrounding hills, as if some buried music was crying out from beneath the ground.

"Weird noise, man. Some kinda truck horn?" Krause said after a long frozen moment.

"Sure it is," Linville agreed ironically. "You ever heard a truck that sounded hungry? Or perhaps it doesn't mind scaring off its prey."

"Is that supposed to spook me? The sound's definitely coming from that direction." Krause pointed at the church.

"What makes you so sure? It sounded a lot farther away," Linville said cautiously.

"Maybe." Krause was poised, listening to the unearthly echoes.

"Let's go find out. That's why we get the big bucks, right?"

The last echoing notes died wheezily into silence. The two soldiers advanced slowly; it took nearly half an hour to reach the churchyard walls. Just as they approached the gaping doorway of the sanctuary, the wailing began again, higher and more hypnotic.

"Take cover," Linville ordered tightly.

The two flattened themselves against the plastered walls, looking at each other.

"Go on, Sarge," Krause whispered. "I'll cover your flank."

"*You* go on," Linville shot back. He wondered if Krause was making fun of him for acting like they were under attack.

"I just remembered something," Krause said, her voice normal now. There was an odd look on her face.

"What?"

"Organs. This is an old church, it's gotta have a honker organ. Maybe a cat got into it."

Linville shook his head. "Don't they run on electricity? Where are they getting electricity around here?"

Krause looked toward the blasted village. "Good question." The hooting sound died away into silence again. Perversely, the uncanniness of the situation reassured Krause. "C'mon, let's go."

Linville followed his buddy inside. There was no pipe organ that either could see inside the ruined church. Rain dripped from the shattered timbers of the broken roof. The sanctuary smelled of wet and decay. Hesitantly, Linville started toward the pulpit as Krause turned to cover him. Their combat instincts told them that something ominous was going on, despite the hush.

"There's nothing left in here," Linville said, relaxing slightly. "Anything that could burn is ashes already." He pointed to signs that small fires had been built here, as soldiers or refugees took what shelter they could find. The murals of robed saints had been defaced with graffiti scrawled in dried blood. Linville flicked on his flashlight. Over the altar he could read the word

HATO, which was Cyrillic for NATO. But you could read it either way.

Krause was sweeping the walls with her chemical detector, hoping for some evidence that suspicious activity had been occurring. Linville opened his StarTac and punched in his commander's number.

"C'mon, Loot. Answer the friggin' phone so we can all go home."

Krause turned and shrugged, palms up. There was nothing here to find, no trace of radiation or chemical precursors to explosives. She began repacking her equipment.

"Churchill."

"Lieutenant, this is Linville. We gained the objective at around 23:00 hours, but so far we got—"

Just then the sound came roaring over them again, a vast, organlike thrumming that filled the violated space like an ocean wave. In the same instant that the two American soldiers registered this fact, the air was suffused with light, a light that grew and swelled.

"What's going on, sergeant? You're breaking up," the lieutenant's voice squeaked faintly in Linville's earpiece. Linville tried yelling into his instrument, but the roaring noise made him cover his ears with his fists. Now the light grew until it was intolerably bright, brighter than a thousand field flares.

Linville could make out Krause screaming in protest, a wordless outcry that might have been awe, fear, or simply recognition that they were woefully unequipped to face whatever force was toppling over their heads. Krause turned to run. Linville, closer to the source than she was, could not do even that much.

This isn't what I expected, he thought lamely in the brief interval before he began to black out. Sharpness like a knife blade pierced his retina, and he was alone in a white blindness as terrible as a black one. *Not what I expected at all.*

"Can they see us?" the general asked, looking through the grayish square of glass into the hospital room.

"No, sir," his aide answered. "From their side it's a mirror. And I think they have some residual blindness. The doctors are keeping the room dim."

"I see." The general peered at the bandaged faces of the two men—make that two soldiers, since once was a woman. Until that morning they had both worn thick eye bandages; now the swathed white faces wore a layer of thin gauze. They looked spookily like pale racoons in the faint light that filtered in through the blinds.

"Can they talk?" the general asked.

"Limited communication has been possible, but they came out with some strange ideas." His aide coughed apologetically, as if to show that this hitch wasn't his fault.

"When the hell can they be debriefed?"

"No one knows, sir. The thing of it is—"

"They don't make any damn sense when they do talk. That's the thing of it, right?"

"I suppose so, sir."

Tom Stillano had been put in command of Task Force Gabriel exactly a week before—rotten luck. The viewing room off the isolation ward left just enough space for a side chair and table; a digital sound recorder stood by blinking red and yellow signals that meant nothing to the general.

He had every reason to be worried when he saw the field reports. "So what does this all mean—we should sell ringside seats to the end of the world?" he barked when they hit his desk. If there was any sanity accidentally floating around the Army field command, the fat manila folder would never have gotten that far, would have dissolved in the murk of "channels." What next? Maybe the DOD was testing dinosaurs for cavalry games.

Walter Reed Army Medical Center is the military's largest health-care delivery system. The main installation, a swarm of mostly low bunk-erlike buildings, occupies 113 acres in northwest Washington. As with any entity so close to the corridors of power, secrets as well as truths lie hidden here.

Ten days ago, two GIs had been picked up by their unit in eastern Kosovo. They were raving and blinded, suitably terrified after stumbling in the woods for at least twenty-four hours. They had made pitiful attempts to avoid enemy scru-tiny, digging holes in the forest floor with their hands and covering their bodies with leaves. If Linville hadn't been in contact with his com-manding officer at the moment the incident had occurred, both of them would be dead by now, and the United States might have no idea of the magnitude of the threat it faced.

Krause and Linville had been found near a tiny village the maps called Sv. Arhangeli. What had been found there with them had been the reason that Stillano was plucked from his small outer-ring Pentagon office to Walter Reed's central core. Aerial photographs were the first to confirm that the entire rear wall of the Orthodox church had vanished—not burned out or bombed but simply vaporized, leaving no debris behind, not even ashes.

Through the open roof, already destroyed by the local strife, the camera caught an amorphous image that at first appeared to be only a bright light. Brilliant as a ground flare by night, it retained enough luminosity by day to show up easily on the eight-by-tens that lay scattered across General Stillano's desk. No one had seen a light from such a source; it was not feeding off electricity or any kind of fuel. In no way did the scarce farm population have anything to do with the phenomenon, other than to stand around and gawk.

The locals began to gather the morning after NATO lost track of its patrol unit. At first it was a matter of three or four old peasant women, who had probably never abandoned the church despite its devastation; they summoned the nearest priest, and then small crowds of farmers and children began to swell. By the time NATO armored vehicles made it into the area, pilgrims were standing constant vigil on the perimeter of the sanctuary. Their candles looked like fireflies at night, flickering glimmers against the total blackout of the town.

The peasants assumed that the light came from God. The local NATO commander, a Bavarian tank officer named Hopf, decided to take nuclear spill precautions, as if a second Chernobyl were blowing its core reactor. He cleared the area for two miles around, imposed a curfew, travel ban, and media blackout. These moves were resented by the locals, but NATO had no choice. In the end, the outside world—except perhaps for Russian spy satellites—learned nothing about the phenomenon.

The brilliant light had no definite shape. It was approximately three meters across, according to Hopf's communiqués, and hovered over the ruined altar about four meters in the air. With protective shielding and welder's goggles, it was possible to approach very close to it. Technicians detected no measurable increase in gamma or X rays nearby, ruling out the assumption that this was a nuclear incident.

"It's a damn quark or something," the Army major on the ground reported to Colonel Burke. "Only it's not hot, sir. I mean, the ground and air temperature don't vary within a hundred yards."

"So you're telling me it just hangs there and glows like a Christmas tree?" Burke demanded. Stillano's aide was not an imaginative man, and after the first whistle of amazement, this whatever-it-was became a nuisance—you could pull the troops out and give it back to the peasants as far as he was concerned.

"No, it's not exactly a Christmas tree, sir," the major on the ground muttered doubtfully. "You'd have to see it for yourself."

By the time it was determined that Krause and

Linville were in a state of religious hysteria, Stillano had come on board, and quickly the decisions were kicked upstairs. "If Christ returned to quarterback for the Redskins," the general grumbled, "they'd find a way to make it a national security priority." The whole mess was a logistical nightmare. Funding had to go through totuous routes that made it seem like the ultimate black ops fiasco; NATO had to be shrugged off (an easier task than you might suppose, because their heavy responsibilities in Kosovo didn't leave much room for the paranormal), and eventually the President was sure to want hourly briefings.

"I wish those two grunts nothing but good," Stillano remarked in private, "but it would have made the situation a whole lot simpler if they *had* been radiated."

Where the hell is Carter? Stillano now thought, glaring at his watch. At that moment the door down the hall opened, and a tall man in civilian clothes walked through carrying a black valise. He wore wire-rimmed glasses, his hair was cropped short enough to expose his skull. The tall man held out his hand, shifting the valise as he did.

"I got here a couple of minutes ago—Marty Carter." He was in his early thirties, a good twenty years younger than Stillano.

"I think they might be too tired for us right now," said Stillano, disguising his resentment that a civilian contingent had been called in.

Carter smiled without mirth. "Let's check on them and see. It never hurts to try, right?" He walked ahead of the general and entered past the Marine guards without asking Stillano for a by-your-leave.

"Hello, gentlemen," Carter said cheerfully as he entered. "You awake in there?"

"Yes, sir," Krause croaked. Her voice was slurred by the morphine, but the gauze over her eyes was thin enough so that she turned her head in Carter's direction.

"Sorry there—I should have said gentleman and lady," Carter corrected himself. He stood between the two beds; both soldiers looked warily toward him. He hoisted the valise onto Linville's bed and began rifling for some papers. Linville was half sitting now.

"I can give you ten minutes," the general said from behind him. Carter didn't look around or give any sign that he had heard.

"Good, so here we are," he began, opening a thin folder pulled from his valise. He picked up a chair resting next to the wall and sat down, not bothering to take notes. He realized, Stillano told himself, that every sound made in this room was being recorded on the other side of the mirror.

"My name is Marty. I'm from the government, and I'm here to help you." He smiled faintly at his own private joke. "Sorry to be bothering you fellas, but we really need to know what happened out there."

"We've already told the commander—" Linville began to say.

"Roger that," Carter interrupted. "Whatever you've said up to now, a lot of people are going to want to hear it again. I'm just the first." He shut the folder, not needing to consult it.

"They say we're . . . stateside," Krause mumbled, her voice soft and hopeful. "Are they going to send us home?"

"They're sure not going to send you back to Kosovo," Carter replied firmly, telling the truth where he could. "As for going home, we'd better get you patched up first. I think I've answered enough of your questions. Tell me what you saw at Arhangeli."

"We were on recon, checking out a lead passed to us by the War Pigs," Linville said slowly, using the nickname for the Seventh Cavalry. Of the two, he suddenly became the more verbal. "We got to this old church. There was an organ playing."

"It wasn't no organ, sir," Krause corrected. "It was . . . I don't know what it was."

"Did you go inside the church?" Carter asked, his voice even and low.

"Yeah," Krause said, "we went inside. The whole place was a mess, but it was clean. No tangos." *Tango* was military slang for terrorists, Carter knew. As if anyone could tell exactly who the terrorists were in this particular war.

"So what did you do, then? Linville? You called Lieutenant Churchill, didn't you?"

"I can't really remember . . . it got so bright, and there was a blast," the sergeant replied.

"You were thrown clear, though? Because neither of you shows any kind of injury from explosive impact."

Linville had nothing to reply. Carter chose not to point out that there was no structural damage to the building consistent with a recent explosion, either. He said, "And the brightness, where was it coming from?"

"Everywhere, sir."

"You can't be more specific?"

Krause spoke up. "It came from heaven."

Carter turned to her. "From the sky? Like a bomb or a meteor?"

She shook her head. "No, from heaven."

"I see." Carter nodded. He kept a benign expression on his narrow face, even though he was ready to sell both of them upriver. He was the original Teflon boy, Stillano noted. Nothing would stick to that shiny manicured surface. No blame, certainly no guilt.

"You agree with that, Sergeant?" he asked Linville.

"I don't know. . . . Like I said, it seemed to be everywhere."

Stillano's mind began to drift. It was clear that nobody was going to learn anything new, no matter how many times Carter took them over the jumps. Stillano knew that the next steps on the ground in Kosovo had been unprecedented. After two days of quarantine, the hovering light had not moved or disappeared. The U.S. observers were caught in a time crunch, since the secret couldn't be kept indefinitely. Also, some peculiar things were happening psychologically, it seemed. The technicians who got too close to the light behaved erratically afterward; several refused to enter the church again. Some flavor of the religious mania that Linville and Krause had exhibited was affecting them.

Although she tried to hide it, Krause still mumbled to herself constantly. At first some sort of post-trauma psychosis was suspected, until it was discovered that she was praying. When asked why, she declined to answer. If Linville was also praying, he disguised it better; the evaluation from the psych officer contended that he might be returned to active duty in time.

The Army drew a cordon around the light and cut off further tests. "Pursuant to getting this thing in a cage or shooting it out of the sky," the local commander reported, "we aren't touching it." Now what? NASA had developed prototype "catcher's mitts" to be used on the space shuttle, long-handled mesh enclosures to retrieve satellites that had floated out of orbit. Some blue-sky thinking had envisioned the possibility of using these to capture bits of comets or meteors one day.

"We're not talking about snagging kryptonite in the outfield, for Christ's sake," Stillano had said witheringly when the idea was proposed to use such a mechanism to cage the hovering light. "I need to know what's inside. There has to be a thing in that church, get it? Light doesn't appear from nowhere."

"It's like a laser, sir," Burke had explained after scrutinizing the scientific reports. "Only it's not focused into a beam. I don't get it entirely, but one thing's for sure—it's not sunlight or any kind of light from a star that has been seen from earth."

That settled it. The Army decided to deal with the thing as alien, debatably a life-form, but possibly a tear in the fabric of the universe that had shot an enormous dose of unknown energy into our little wrinkle of space-time. Although this conclusion added little to anyone's knowledge, it settled the question about blowing it out of the sky or caging it: The cage won.

Half the observers began to call the thing Kong, but those who were less whimsical called it *the capture.* It felt decidedly alive, some claimed, if not our conception of any life-form met on earth. A stubborn minority, pure techno-geeks by disposition, argued that giving it a personality was ludicrous; they held on to the possibility that the thing was a wandering white hole emanating force from beyond the known cosmos.

"We're gonna bag it, sir," the ground commander reported on the third day of observation, "but we might have to take the whole damn church with it." Between the Seabees and the physicists who were dropped in, a plan was devised. They had to assume that the capture was there voluntarily, and although powerful and unpredictable, it wasn't hostile. One could assume with some certainty that therefore it wouldn't resist being moved.

You couldn't lead it out on a leash, but if the capture was cooperative, you could envelop it lightly in such a way that it would be disguised from view. No restraints would be necessary (not that anyone had the foggiest notion what kind of straitjacket would conceivably hold it). In the end, it came down to floating their prize out in a blimp.

An Army weather blimp was dismantled and reassembled inside the walls of the church, piece by piece. As the last sections were refitted and the seams sealed, there was the delicate question of filling it with helium, but the capture didn't act disturbed. Its luminosity appeared to decrease whenever the operation brought anyone too close, as if it knew what was going on. Enclosed inside its silver sheath, the capture was hauled through the opening that had once been the back wall of the church, then dragged on tethers behind slow-moving Apache helicopters by night. The nearest airport at Pristina had been repaired sufficiently to allow a mammoth C-5a Galaxy transport to land, a plane big enough to carry a small army and all its equipment. The blimp was slipped into the huge interior, and forty-eight hours after the military had cordoned off the scene, the capture was on its way out of Europe.

All these details were contained in the folder on Stillano's desk, and he had to assume that Carter was just as privy to them. Then why the hell was he badgering these two white mummies in the hospital? The general found himself getting hotter at the CIA's game-playing.

"That's it," he said loudly. "Time's up."

Carter looked around in annoyance, but he saw

that Stillano meant business. "Very well," he said
with a smirk. "I think we did some good here
today." Stillano was almost certain that this
wasn't the case.

"Sir? When can we see our families, sir?"
Krause asked plaintively. Carter didn't answer,
shoving the chair back against the wall and closing his valise.

"We *are* going to see our families, aren't we?"
Linville echoed.

Stillano was halfway out the room when he
heard Carter's reply. "I certainly hope so, Sergeant. Now you fellas really have something to
pray for, right?"

Night came early in the ward, too early for
Krause, who usually lay on top of the sheets feeling the ache of her traumatized body. Now that
it was healing and now that the interrogators
were gone, she sank into her dreams. There really
wasn't a word for them, because Krause couldn't
cause a dream, not just by wanting one, but she
could summon back the light whenever she
wanted. It had kept her going through the pain
and blindness; it had told her, as sheer panic sent
her stumbling through the woods, that rescue was
at hand.

How did it tell her? She couldn't remember
that it spoke, and she wasn't receiving telepathy,

because wouldn't that mean words in her head?

"Sergeant?" she half whispered.

"Yeah," Linville's voice came in the darkness.

"Are we crazy?" It was a subject Krause brought up a lot.

"Maybe, but it's the right kind of crazy."

"Yeah." He always gave the same answer, and still she wanted him to repeat these words each night, as a form of reassurance. The charge nurse would be in every two hours to take their vital signs, but for now the room was dark enough that Krause felt intimate with Linville. When she drifted out of one of her dreams, she even imagined that she loved him. Strange, she hadn't had the slightest hint of that before. Linville wasn't like the strong, unspeaking farm boys she had been used to and one day expected to marry.

"What's God going to do next?" she asked. There was no answer. Linville's silence reminded her that everything they said was being taped. "I think He's going to do to everybody what He's done to us," she said.

"Ssh, go to sleep."

"I'm not dragging you in, Sarge. If anyone's listening, I'm just speaking for myself. Anyway, we already babbled like nutcases, you know? So who cares? It would take an idiot to believe that they're gonna let us back into ranks again. We're out, Sarge, you know that, don't you?"

"Shut up and go to sleep. Please." Linville's voice held a note of pleading.

She did shut up, but not for the reason he wanted her to. Linville was afraid, and he didn't want to give away what the light had done to him. He thought he could play it close to the vest, and maybe he could. That wasn't Krause's tactic. She didn't care who knew that God was coming back to earth. He was coming back through simple people like her; that was how she figured it. She closed her eyes and tried to see the light again. It started to appear, very faintly, and she held her breath. Her great fear—her only fear—was that it would abandon her. She knew that Linville, even if he played it close to the vest, feared the same thing.

But it was dependable tonight, the faint comforting glow that appeared as if in the back of her eyes, like the afterimage of a flashbulb—faint blue and swimming in mild waves and blurry edges. At times the shimmering took on form, and then it looked like a slim lady in a pale blue gown. Krause lay back and let the silence gather around her. She loved the light even more than she loved Linville. Fifteen minutes later, when the charge nurse came in, the soldier in the left-hand bed was asleep. Her vitals were normal. The nurse wrote done the blood pressure, pulse rate, and temperature on the chart. She walked out and turned off the overheads. It was the same every night, but if Krause had managed to remain awake, she might have taken a chance and told the nurse that she loved her, too.

The Angel's Voice

Testing . . . testing . . .

I'm not sure how much of this is coming through. We try to cut through the smoke and the haze around you. You'd be amazed how thick it is. We're lucky to find a landing strip at all. I speak as "we" because there is no "I" for us. That is part of the problem—speaking as "we" cannot be helped, but you do not receive us. You are attuned to small messages from "I" to "I." This problem has been thought about for millions of your years. Many new ways have been devised to get through. We have stood outside you and put on wings and glowed with light and even voyaged inside your minds. These are strange conditions to us, for God recognizes no inside or outside. You are as transparent as glass to Him, as air. We, the angels, look at you and we see through you, too. To us it is very strange that you can barely stand to look at yourselves.

You call us the "messengers." We call ourselves the "watchers."

Now, as we watch, we want to help you, but long ago you forgot us. Our way is not to amaze you. Although not invisible, we might as well be. Being afraid to see yourselves, how much more terrified you would be to see us. So you don't. You are ashamed to be watched, and yet you crave it, too. Like a child who feels loved because his mother's eyes are on him, you will feel loved only when God's eyes can rest upon you.

Now you know the problem. The question is, who will help us to find the solution?

The Mirage Hotel and Casino on the Las Vegas strip is home to Siegfried and Roy's famous white tigers, a time-release volcano at its entrance, a small exotic zoo directly off the lobby, a shark tank, a gourmet pizzeria in the midst of the slot machines, and a row of lurid gift shops flanking a marble corridor. If water makes an oasis, the shark tank counted; everything else only contributes to a swanky kitsch American dream.

Ted Lazar didn't really give a damn about tigers. He'd been working his way methodically down the strip for the last thirty-six hours, heading east to west, spending a few hours in each casino at the blackjack tables. He neither won nor lost—the fluctuations in his finances tended to even themselves out. Deprived of a streak, Lazar moved on when he got bored with the neo-trash decor or made the casino management too aware of his presence.

There was a certain reason for them to notice. Lazar was tall, well over six-foot-two, with a cranelike awkwardness, a creature of knees and elbows and sudden collisions with the world around him. His skin was the sallow putty color of a man who never saw the sun, and his straight jet-black hair hung down past his shoulders. He wore a much-rumpled white linen jacket, black Nikes, and a pink and gold vintage Hawaiian shirt.

Ted Lazar was also fortune's fool, a compulsive gambler. Once he got started, no matter how moderately, no matter how reasonably, he would play until he was thousands of dollars in debt. He didn't own a car or a major credit card, and no sane bank would loan him money. What he did have was a government-level security clearance slightly higher than the moon, a pocket full of comp chits from the leading hotels in Clark County, and a federally paid minder who followed him around, keeping close track of his bets. It wouldn't do for Lazar to fall afoul of either organized crime or an opportunistic mugger. His employers couldn't change him, but they could keep him from getting hurt.

"We're even," said the minder, whose name was Philips.

"I've seen it run this way. It ran this way just before I won a quarter of a million dollars," Lazar remarked. His brilliant mind had no trouble recognizing that his luck would soon go plunging down the rabbit hole where fortunes and sanity are lost. He didn't have either to lose, luckily. In the bizarre reaches of plasma physics, the potential applications of Lazar's work were enough to destroy any normal man's sanity.

"You wanna play a hand?" Lazar asked Philips. The minder shook his head. Philips never played a hand, and Lazar didn't ask in order to coax him; there was a certain symmetry to posing the same question every half hour, and that pleased Lazar's peculiar type of mind.

A beefy man in Army uniform appeared in Lazar's field of vision without warning. He approached and held an ID folder out. Lazar ignored it.

"Go away," he said cordially. "There's one chance in seven that a red queen is going to appear in this hand." The blackjack dealer turned up the queen of hearts in front of herself. "Foiled again," Lazar muttered as his chips slid away.

"Dr. Lazar, my name is Major Seldon," the beefy man said. "I have to take you to—"

"A better place? Stronger men than you have tried and failed. Philips!" The minder, who had taken a break to stare at the sharks and the braless women, appeared at his elbow.

"Is there a problem here?" Philips asked in his flat midwestern tone. Seldon flashed his credentials again, and the minder backed up with a stiff-necked apologetic nod.

"Sir?" Seldon said.

"I'm busy," Lazar snapped. "I'm on vacation here."

"I am authorized to use compulsion, sir," the major said quietly.

"You've got a bazooka and backup down your pants?" Lazar said. "What's the deal, Major?"

Until Seldon had dismissed the minder and gotten the scientist into the back of a white rental Cutlass with tinted windows, the deal wasn't made evident. Its official name was Area 23. Unlike its famous Nevada cousin, Area 51, Area 23 wasn't even a rumor on the Internet. It was ensconced somewhere in southern New Mexico in the heart of a military reservation that covered hundreds of miles of desert. Its personnel called it, prosaically enough, the Twilight Zone, and nobody was cleared to print anything about what went on there.

"They need you to come and look at something," Seldon explained.

"That's special. Can you give me a clue?" Lazar asked languidly.

"It's some kind of capture," Seldon replied.

"Like me. And I'm the sole competent nerd to assess this particular highly exotic capture?"

"Apparently."

"Tasty," said Lazar. "And it's still around? Usually these captures happen in high-speed particle accelerators and last a few microseconds."

"I'm not competent to amplify the situation, sir—and there are security issues," the major said without apology. He had no interest in Lazar's mind-set or its peculiarities. Now that he had accepted the hard news that his gambling fever wouldn't be allowed to run its course, Lazar curled up on the backseat and tried to repair the rigors of the previous two sleepless days. His elbows didn't fit anywhere, and even through tinted windows, the harsh desert sun stung his arms and neck. It made for a fitful nap.

Lazar wasn't the only scientist feeling fitful. Another in the government's endless supply of white GM sedans with tinted windows was heading toward Area 23 by a different road. Simon Potter had been given plenty of time to think on the tedious drive from White Sands, where they had spent the night rechecking his security clearance, and his thoughts were not comfortable ones. When the military yanked someone like him out of the cloud-castle world of R&D, it generally meant something baleful from the realm of weapons that glowed in the dark.

But bad for whom? He turned over the possibilities in his mind. The former Soviet Union had been quiescent of late, managing to continue the ongoing drudgery of disarmament without too many diversions of fissionables in the direction of private sales. Even at that, several dozen so-called "suitcase bombs" had gone missing some years before and never surfaced. And then the heat moved toward bioterrorism; once the government realized that the Soviets had created twenty tons of pure smallpox virus in a remote Siberian lab, Simon and his crew were moved back into the shadows again.

The turbulent Balkans weren't a nuclear problem anyway, and God willing, the participants would continue to restrict themselves to guns, knives, bricks, and conventional bombs. In Kabul the Taliban seethed but was staying within its own borders for the most part, and the rest of the Middle East was continuing on at its usual fast-then-slow simmer. Simon wasn't sure what that left, but whatever it was must be nasty.

The partition that separated the backseat from

the front was tinted the same smoke gray as the windows, and through it Simon could barely make out the back of the driver's head. Sitting in his dark compartment was very much like being smuggled somewhere inside a piano. Simon amused himself by hitting on the analogy. He reached into his jacket pocket and retrieved a flattened ham and cheese sandwich. Now, where was his bloody mineral water?

"Hello?" He knocked on the partition. The driver didn't react.

Typical military robot. A funny thought coming from someone in the computer-savvy world of the new post–Cold War DOD. Visions of overintelligent teenagers with first-strike capability filled Simon's vision. Being British by birth and transplanted to Stanford, he took an outsider's jaundiced view of nuclear stockpiling. It was payback time for the greediness of the past for the superpowers. If you could get your hands on a little plutonium, which was easier than it used to be by a factor of ten, you could buy everything else you needed to build a dirty little nuke from your local Western Auto. Maybe some prankster just had. Simon hoped it wasn't one of his friends.

Simon was thirty-eight years old. He had blue eyes, short blond hair, a deceptively youthful face, and co-workers he faintly despised. He

spent his life migrating between Palo Alto and
the government's defense labs in Los Alamos.
He'd never married because, frankly, setting
aside his intellect, nothing about him could be of
interest to a wife. This assessment, made late in
adolescence, had stuck. He believed in decency,
order, practicality, and an entire catalogue of Au-
gustinian virtues. He had worn a gray suit, ma-
roon rep tie, and white button-down oxford shirt
to work every day for the last fifteen years, and
with very few exceptions he had eaten the same
thing for breakfast and dinner—coffee, two
slices of unbuttered toast, and a soft-boiled egg—
for the same duration. Simon would no more
have considered making a spontaneous gesture
than stripping naked and shooting someone from
a clock tower.

To be scrupulously fair, Simon might have
been an entirely different person if he had ever
paid much attention to material existence, but he
never had and never would. For him the material
world was only a fueling station that allowed the
mind to range through the cosmos unchecked. He
only had the length of his own lifetime to find
the answers to the questions that obsessed him,
and in the moments before sleep he agonized that
a lifetime would not be enough, that he might die
with his questions unanswered.

He was almost dying of thirst when they ar-

rived. A Marine in chrome helmet, spats, and ai-
guillettes opened the door. Simon climbed stiffly
out, finding himself inside an enormous hangar.
The air was oven-hot, and thick white desert light
streamed through every opening.

He was not alone. There was another sedan
parked a few yards away, and another Marine
extracting its passenger, a gangly man who
looked like a heron after his prey.

When their eyes met, Simon recognized him:
Ted Lazar, one of the privileged few on earth
who might possibly be able to follow his conversation. Lazar had met him once, at a conference in Los Alamos. He didn't like snotty Brits
very much, which was almost positive considering the source. But he liked the fact that he
was here—wherever here was—even less. What
was so bad or so big that the government had to
turn over two rocks and call in both of them?

Simon and Lazar had entered the Twilight
Zone now. They could not see where they were
going, but even if they had been able to, each
man's security clearance was high enough that
the exposure wouldn't matter. In the background
pulling the strings, Tom Stillano had been able
to learn from their dossiers that if anyone could
unravel the mystery of the captive light, these
two came closest.

Simon glanced around without acknowledging

his counterpart. He surmised that he had been taken to one of the secret military bases that had proliferated in the five decades after the big bang at Alamogordo.

No possible good will come of this, he thought, gazing balefully at Lazar as if at a bad fortune cookie.

"Wow," Lazar said, spinning in a slow circle as he approached. "An aircraft hangar somewhere in the American Southwest. The military mind is nothing if not original."

Simon allowed himself an inward grimace. Lazar was borderline unstable, if first impressions counted, someone who fit the comic-book conception of a pop-eyed physicist. Simon handed him the tinfoil that had wrapped his sandwich. "Here, souvenir of Roswell," he said. For a second he considered demanding to be returned to Palo Alto, but hesitated. He didn't think the Army was interested in coddling anyone at the moment.

Lazar resisted making the foil into antennae to stick on top of his head. The major who had brought him on board now acted as escort. At the back of the hangar they came to a door flanked by a set of Marine guards. On the other side was nothing but a small room with equipment racks on each side and another set of doors beyond. The major selected a set of goggles for himself before handing goggles to each of the scientists.

Simon inspected them skeptically. They were heavy welder's goggles, designed to block intense light but no serious radiation. In the days when the government had still been doing above-ground nuclear testing, observers in the bunkers had worn glasses like these to shield their eyes from the blast, disregarding the greater damage that would be suffered by standing so close to a nuclear explosion.

Simon glanced over at Lazar, catching the same expression of wry puzzlement on the other man's face.

"You'll need these, too. They're just temporary—we'll get you ones with your ID on them later." The major handed each of them a familiar lead-foil packet.

"What do we need dosimeters for?" Simon demanded abruptly.

Lazar was already ripping open the foil and clipping the small plastic square to his rumpled lapel. Dosimeters were worn by people who worked with radioactive materials on a daily basis. The devices measured the rate of radiation the wearer was exposed to in order to prevent cumulative contamination. It seemed to confirm Simon's worst suspicious.

"General Stillano will explain everything, gentlemen. When you're ready, please go through those far doors."

Unable to see any other course of action, Simon unwrapped his dosimeter and clipped it to his jacket. The major opened the door and ushered them through.

The air had the scrubbed and filtered scent of laboratories the world over. The walls and ceiling were thick and heavily reinforced, reminding Simon of the sort of place where incendiaries are tested. Movable dividers had been set up to block the view from the doorway and to baffle sound. The room should have looked dark, but despite the goggles over his eyes, Simon could see perfectly well, as if the chamber were lit by arc lights. Taking the lead as if by right, Lazar strode into the light, leaving Simon to follow. The major brought up the rear—rather reluctantly, Simon thought.

Lazar zigzagged unerringly around the dividers, and after a few minutes reached the source of the dazzling light. At the far end of the room was a large curved tank. There were three concentric walls of glass forming the tank walls, each more than two inches thick. As they angled away, the color of the glass walls shaded to a Coke-bottle green. Seen straight on, however, it was as if the glass didn't exist, so bright was the thing contained behind it. It was a thing without form. All that could be seen was the luminosity, blazing like a caged sun. No source was visible. It was as if the tank contained pure light.

There was another man in goggles standing about ten feet away from the chamber. Simon guessed that this was probably Stillano himself, temporarily given command on the base and the contact for his own involvement.

"What is this?" Simon asked with forced flippancy. "Cold-fusion home movies?" Gazing into the light, he felt, not afraid but strangely self-conscious. Whatever was in that tank, it was not an everyday item.

"It's an alien," the general said. Against the brilliant radiance he was a dark silhouette; there was no trace of humor in his voice.

"I think that deserves an unconditional wow," said Lazar. "Was there a ship?"

"No." Stillano shook his head. "Not that we know of. It vaporized a chunk of a church when it appeared. We're figuring it came through some kind of space-time warp."

"And you want us to, like, learn to talk to it? E.T. phone home?" Lazar asked. Simon looked over at him, worried that his double could absorb such an unspeakable phenomenon without a hitch, just like that. It seemed abnormal. Simon himself still hadn't found any words, barely any thoughts, for what was before him.

"We want you to tell us what it is first," said Stillano.

"Where did you get it, exactly?" Simon finally spoke up.

"Kosovo—helluva place to find such a thing, huh?" the general said shortly. "Gentlemen, I want to be here as little as you do. I know this isn't physics, but we don't have any security-cleared Ph.D.s in ufology. You're the men on the spot—we have to know what it is and how it works, and we have to know as soon as possible."

Simon shook his head. "It's an alien, you just said so yourself. If it can get here, maybe it can communicate, I don't know how."

"Why not ask it?" Lazar offered. Ignoring Stillano's authority, he walked up to the glass and put out his hand to touch it. As he did, Simon noticed a line marked on the concrete floor. The general was standing on the far side of the line, away from the tank. Lazar had just crossed it.

At that instant—Simon couldn't tell whether Lazar had actually touched the glass—the light flared intolerably brighter. There was a deep peal of musical sound, like a fog-horn or the lowest note of an organ. Simon only reconstructed these impressions afterward. At the moment of the event itself he recoiled, flung backward by an invisible hand. There was a crash as Lazar, more forcefully impelled than either of the others, struck one of the movable dividers. He had been thrown almost thirty feet.

Violent as the force had been, the whole thing lasted less than a heartbeat. A moment later Simon could see again, and the room was silent. Lazar got slowly to his feet and brushed his long black hair out of his face. He didn't seem to be hurt, only shaken up by his violent repulsion. He looked down at his hands as if he expected them to show scorch marks.

"Why not ask it?" the general echoed Lazar's question. "That's why."

The Angel's Voice

Only one kind of person will be of great use to us in the near future—those who know who they are. Do you? I am allowed to move ever so lightly into your mind, and there I see both the light and the darkness. Those who know who they are have more light. It is their clarity and our hope. In awareness is the salvation of the world, yet we are not allowed to change your awareness.

Until now.

God does not feel sorrow, but He can feel your sorrow, and then His love moves Him to bring about change.

He is not willing to alter his whole creation to save you. He has decided not to force you, because one thing He loves most about you is free will. Nor will He drive the darkness to the outer edges of creation— even though He could easily do this—because the only cosmos that you know and accept is made of light and darkness, good and evil, together. For you to see beauty in the light, it must cast a shadow.

What does this leave? God has decided to use the most powerful agency he has at his command: He is going to wake you up. This way is pleasing to Him because it is the way of love, the gentlest way. The angelic host knew it instantly when He hit upon this plan—but I am forced to speak as you would understand it. God does not recognize the passing of time, so we cannot truly say that He saw a problem and thought of a solution. No, the truth is more like this: When you arrived at the point where you began to forget who you are, you also forgot the true nature of God. You were left only with pieces and fragments. As these grew smaller and you forgot even them, there were merely passing moments of grace and in each person's life a few glimpses of the divine.

The rest was emptiness.

You cried out in this emptiness and no one answered. God cannot return to you because He is already everywhere. This means He cannot be gone from you. There is no distance for Him to close. You call out to Him and your words are already God, your thoughts are God, your suffering, pain, joy, hope, despair, and victory are all God. What makes the difference between a world that is nothing but God and a world that is nothing? Only you.

Therefore God's power to change the world is dependent on your will. If you will yourself to awaken, then God will be everywhere. You will see that He has never left you. If you turn your will against the light, God will continue to be absent, a void bathed in a thousand outworn legends.

Even if you decide to be among those who are awakened, you cannot do it all at once. The process would kill you. God can enlighten you in thirty days, but it would take thirty men to hold you down. Angels could make themselves visible to you at this instant, but the sight would be worse than blindness.

So we have pondered on ways to give you a glimpse. And some new ones have occurred to us. Now we will see if they work.

2
"The Angel Is Near"

The insistent ringing dragged Michael Aulden out of his sleep. He drifted into wakefulness like a diver climbing up through warm water.

"Hello?" he mumbled, fitting the phone to his ear. The bed shifted as his wife moved sleepily beside him.

"Is this Dr. Aulden? I must speak to him." The woman's voice was high and frightened. Michael turned on the light.

"Yes. Who am I speaking—"

The voice pierced into his ear even more shrilly. "Oh, please, come quickly. This is Beth Marvell—I think my husband's having an attack. He's dying!"

"Beth?" Michael was groggily certain that he knew nobody who went by— no, his head was clearing now. "From down the road?" he asked.

"Yes. *Please, you have to come now*."

"I'll be right there, just don't move him." Michael gulped in a deep breath. All at once adrenaline had rinsed his sleep away; he got to his feet, tossing the portable phone on the bed and grabbing for his pants.

"What is it?" Susan murmured, beginning to sit up.

"You stay put, try and get back to sleep." Michael needed to remember where he'd left his medical bag. Downstairs, in the entryway closet. He could grab it on the way.

"What's happening?" Susan asked insistently. "I'll get you some coffee." She leaned forward in the dark, the first blue light of dawn coloring the gauze drapes. Her long blond hair tumbled about her face and her voice was hoarse. "What in God's name time is it, anyway?" She squinted at the red digital numerals flicking softly on the clock.

"Just after five. Listen, it's an emergency just down the road," Michael said shortly, anxious to get going. He kissed her and pulled the covers up again. "Stay put, okay? I'll call you."

He was backing the car out, throwing gravel up under the tires, before he had his next thought. *Paramedics*. Had Beth Marvell called the paramedics yet? Probably not if she was in a state of advanced panic. Michael swept out of the long rutted driveway to his house and onto the narrow county road. He tried to recall Beth's face, unable to put a clear picture to the voice. Her husband struck a blank, too, not even a first name. Something weird. *Rheingold?* They were probably lucky she'd had the presence of mind to call him, lucky that she'd remembered that her nearest neighbor was a doctor.

The irony was that he was in the slow process of slipping out of being a doctor. Michael had performed his last surgery across the Syrian border in a refugee camp. He loved being a surgeon because it required two things missing from other kinds of medicine: courage and originality. He had never been a technician, although he had great hands, and he never forgot that his hands were reaching into a person, not just into a body.

His love of medicine might have slipped away on its own, because surgery is like taking ego vitamins, and for some reason the doses weren't working as well as before. When he walked away from operating on a cancer patient who had come in with an ovarian tumor the size of an orange, his assistant would sometimes say, "Don't you feel great saving that woman?" Michael was finding it hard to feel victorious anymore. His mind was nagged by what that woman was going through even after she was "saved"—the lingering fear, the specter of death that would dog her steps, the sense of no longer being a normal member of a normal world. How do you save anyone who has journeyed to the underworld? Part of them always stays there.

These strange thoughts on his part led to even stranger moods. He slipped out of medicine gradually, and he wondered how much longer he could cling to it, like a man holding on with white knuckles to the edge of a cliff. Shouldn't he have the guts to let go? Where would he land after he fell? Or did his ego just need a bigger dose of vitamins? All of this questioning had a secret underpinning, but there was no time to uncover that right now.

In the distance Michael could see the lights of the Marvell house, white clapboard easily visible in the faint dawn. Marvell was some kind of writer, a recluse. But who wasn't? The county was clogged with urban escapees minding their own business. The played-out farms were mostly for show now, a rustic whim for anyone prosperous enough to bid for them. Michael had read somewhere that many New York kids didn't know where milk came from, except a carton. On principle, he and Susan avoided the gentry, so they had seen the Marvells just a few times at most.

And what about himself? To all appearances Michael passed for an admirably quiet citizen, settled in his marriage, more than competent as a physician. He was modest and had backed away from more than one lucrative offer as a surgeon. You could say that he was one of the genteel hermits, too. He still looked young, his brown hair curly and ungrayed, his brown eyes intense under strong brows.

If you mounted a video camera on his shoulder and followed his every movement, nothing unusual would show up. That was just it—the invisible elements in his makeup, the very things no camera could capture, were secretly stirring. That he had certain inner ferment didn't detract from the admiration other people felt. But this ferment was implacably working its way to the surface. It kept interrupting his life like heartburn, a nervous colon, or a broken heart.

He wondered if something drastic was about to happen.

Driving up to the house now, he saw the wife, Beth Marvell, standing anxiously on her front porch. She may have been twenty years younger than her husband, but at the moment the petite brunette looked old, her narrow face crimped with fear. If she gave the impression in normal life of acting rather grand, that had disappeared, too. She waved Michael on and immediately ran back through the door. He took the stoop two

steps at a time and followed her, barely noting
that the interior of the house was new and lavish,
a far cry from Michael and Susan's semi-tottering
Victorian. Designer security lighting flooded the
landscaped lawn with harsh white light.

"Where is he?" Michael asked, breathing fast.

Beth Marvell pointed mutely down the hallway. Michael pushed past her, not waiting for
directions. No doubt her husband was a night
owl, like most writers. He would probably be in
his study.

The door was open as Michael stepped in. A
smoky haze of incense hung in the air, heavily
floral. A dim, flickering luminescence emanated
from the floor, and he saw that the study was
ringed with lit candles, dozens of them, in votive
cups. The room looked like a Mexican church on
a saint's feast day. It felt more profane than holy,
though.

*What the hell, country squires don't belong to
cults,* Michael thought, groping automatically for
the light switch. He found it and flipped it on.

Marvell's body was lying on the floor of his
study. Its position was peculiar. He'd been sitting
on the floor in the lotus position—this was Michael's quick surmise as he turned the corpse
over—and had fallen backward, knocking over
some of the dozens of candles that surrounded

him. Luckily, they'd gone out instead of setting the entire room on fire.

Too late, Michael heard his inner voice say as he felt for a faint pulse and made the inevitable assessments.

Marvell's eyes were sunk into his head and his skin had already settled into the blue-gray undertones of cyanosis. His smooth, pudgy face was contorted with the death agonies consonant with a massive heart attack. Despite what Beth had indicated in her frantic phone call, her husband had been dead for at least half an hour, possibly longer. Michael knelt beside him, feeling for any sign of life, though he knew they were already gone, long gone. The rictus of fear on Marvell's face did not shock him; he had seen too much of these things.

Marvell's wife must have mistaken the time badly, but perhaps she had been asleep. No doubt hope and a desperate need to believe made her phone Michael as if there were still some chance that her husband could be saved.

Go with God. Peace be with you.

For just a moment Michael allowed his attention to wander away from the body to the room surrounding him. When he realized what he was seeing, his mind recoiled.

There were arcane symbols, figurines, charts, and diagrams filling every corner. It looked like occult trash: Two wax effigies of a naked man and woman were tied together with twine, belly to belly. A beaker of reeking liquid was on Marvell's desk. A deck of tarot cards lay scattered on the floor around the body, as if someone had thrown them deliberately. The Hanged Man and the Fool were next to Marvell's head. Whatever the scene was, it wasn't poker night with the gang. Michael stood up, wondering where Beth was.

"Hello?" he called out. He vaguely remembered that Marvell wrote spiritual self-help books, but the toys Michael saw here hinted at something far beyond that. Had Marvell been dabbling in black magic, that baneful stepchild of superstition, even in these enlightened days?

His eye fell on a crumpled piece of paper in Marvell's hand. Once clutched tight, the fingers had loosened their grip upon dying, but the note hadn't fallen. Michael gently pried it out, unfolded the lined yellow sheet, and read the short message: *THE ANGEL IS NEAR.* The letters were block caps, scrawled by hand, but neatly. They weren't the scribbling of a man fighting off death. Suicide? Suicide notes are not mystical; they almost always accuse the living or offer pathetic apologies. This was a note of hope—or maybe just a random revelation from a dying brain. Absently Michael refolded the paper and stuffed it into his pocket. He heard the wife come back into the room.

"How deeply was your husband into the occult?" he asked without looking at her.

"Don't move!" a loud male voice barked. There was the unmistakable sound of a gun being cocked. "Put your hands on the back of your head."

Michael obeyed automatically before he could be either shocked or confused. It came into his mind that bad luck ran in threes—it was the baddest kind of luck for Marvell's house to be burgled on the same night he dropped dead.

"Now turn around, slowly. Don't move your hands," the voice said.

Michael complied and found himself facing two men in the tan and green uniforms of the Columbia County Sheriff's Department. One of them was Tyler Peabody—Michael had seen him in Carbonek a few times, treated his wife for a feared miscarriage. The other deputy was somebody he didn't recognize. Both men were holding guns pointed at him, their faces grim. From behind them Beth Marvell peered in from the hallway, her face flushed and red with weeping.

"That's him!" she shrieked. "He's the one! He killed Ford—he's hated us ever since we moved here,[cf4] he wanted our land—" She broke down in fresh tears, unable to continue.

"Beth," Michael said, taking a step forward.

"Don't move, sir!" Peabody barked. "Morgan, cuff him so we can move him away from the body."

The other deputy stepped forward, holstering his weapon. He pulled out a pair of handcuffs.

"Beth, come on now. You called me," Michael said with forced calm. His mind was starting to go blank with shock. "She said her husband was having an attack."

Michael turned to look at Marvell again. What he saw held him stark and silent as his hands were cuffed behind his back. Rhineford Marvell was lying face up on the floor of his study, just as he had been a moment before. But now he was covered with blood from a stab wound in the chest. The white cotton sport shirt he wore was soaked with it, torn open by the force of the repeated blows.

"You killed him! You killed him!" Beth screamed. She ran past the lawmen and flung herself at Michael, her hands clawing at his face. The two deputies fended her off awkwardly, trying to protect themselves and their prisoner from the grief-deranged woman.

"I didn't kill him," Michael said in total bafflement. The handcuffs were cold and heavy on his wrists. He spoke very quietly, as if he were alone in a hospital room with Beth, beside her sickbed. No one responded to him.

Michael got one last look around as Peabody led him out of the room. It was an impossible sight that he would carry burned into his mind for a long time. Rhineford Marvell lay murdered in a pool of his own blood.

But that problem, strange as it was, suddenly paled next to the big one Michael faced. At one moment he was aware of being led from the room, but then it was as if an invisible fork appeared in time. Part of him, the part that knew he was innocent and would never submit to the preposterousness of what had just happened, split off and stayed behind. This shift occurred somewhere inside himself, and yet it had an immediate physical effect. All at once there were two of him. He himself—the Michael who knew what had really taken place—stood against the wall of the study with his back against the bookcase watching his identical double—a shadow Michael—being led out of the room. There was no doubt of this. Michael looked down at his hands, his shirt, his shoes—he was in the study as before, intact and breathing. This fact, which should cause no shock under ordinary circumstances, staggered him.

"Oh, my God," he whispered. His first impulse was to run after them, to grab Beth or the police and scream at them, "You've got the wrong man!" Only *that man*, the one with his head bowed who left without a backward glance, was part of the murder. Perhaps he was guilty in some bizarre way. Or was that crazy thinking?

Michael ran out into the hallway. He saw the backs of their heads as the small group reached the front door. The shadow Michael stood meekly motionless, waiting for someone to turn the brass doorknob. The Michael who was left behind felt paralyzed. His mouth opened, but at the last minute he stopped himself. They didn't turn around. Michael watched Michael leaving, and that was that, as simple as watching a total stranger depart. Except that perhaps, unless he was fooling himself, the Michael who was going to jail flicked a glance at him just at the instant that the front door closed. Their eyes met for perhaps a tenth of a second. It wasn't a glance of recognition but of total blankness. Michael had no idea, and never would, what was going through his shadow's mind.

Susan Aulden stretched herself out in the middle of the big empty bed, sleepily following the shapes of the cracks in the ceiling while she waited for Michael to come back. She was not worried. The happiness of a woman well loved made her body feel soft inside. The last year and a half had been quiet and peaceful, as the tenor of both their lives settled into a course as tranquil and serene as the path of an underground river. You would never know that they had once been combative lovers, likely to storm off in the night after making love in the desert heat. Deserts were made for them, in fact, the perfect backdrop to melodrama. They tested out betrayal, jealousy, petulant absence, and to-the-death arguments. In the end, it surprised them both that the result was tenderness. But it pleased them, too, and they decided that a relationship could be founded on a soft foundation as solidly as on a hard one.

After coming back from the WHO mission in Syria, she and Michael had married—Susan's second, his first. Michael had said that he wanted to take a few years off to think about the direction of his life, and Susan, although somewhat mystified about his motives and the frequent moods that carried him inward away from her, was happy to get out.

Passing through the security gates of Damascus for the last time, Michael had looked back and said, "We're leaving another world."

"Really," Susan agreed, not thinking much about the comment.

"No, I mean that literally," Michael said. His face was so mysterious as to be comic to her, but the fact that Michael fell silent for the next hour stuck in her mind. Susan felt good about her decision to accept a lateral transfer, surrendering the headaches of being a female senior field administrator in the Middle East. Hers now was the restful life of a writer/researcher. They'd looked around for a while and finally settled on this 150-year-old farmhouse in upstate New York. It had once been attached to a sizable apple farm, but most of the land had been sold off years before. The few acres that came with the house were all that was left of the original orchards.

Old forgotten rugs and sofas, battered desks, and hand-me-down bureaus were hauled out of storage, some newcomers were bought carefully from the antique stores that dotted the Hudson Valley, and slowly their house assumed the air of a home. Almost inevitably they acquired a gray ex-tomcat named Valentino. Michael started up a part-time practice in Carbonek; Susan traveled down to the city about once a month and flew to Switzerland twice a year as a WHO consultant.

She frowned, trying to recall what time Michael had gone out. It had still been dark, she remembered that much. Valentino put his paws up on the edge of the quilt and nuzzled at Susan's face expectantly. She rolled out of bed and retrieved her chambray robe from the back of a chair. Padding downstairs, she turned on the light and flipped the switch that would start the coffeemaker. She went to scoop kibbles into Valentino's bowl. It was then that she saw the woman sitting at the table in the breakfast nook.

The stranger was a little old lady but without tennis shoes; her age could have been anywhere from sixty to eighty. Her large brown eyes were bright and alert in a face seamed with living, and she wore a short flowered skirt.

Susan gaped at the intruder—she would have sworn she was alone in the house. Living so far out in the country, they had lost the urban habit of locking their doors at night. Maybe the old woman had just wandered in.

"Hello, Susan," the woman said calmly. "I'm called Rakhel. I'm an old friend of yours."

"What?"

"I let myself in."

"I can see that. You know me—how?"

"From the past, and other places. We've done a lot together, but I'm not that acceptable. In your mind, that is."

At that moment the telephone rang. The sudden jangling startled Susan into anxiety. "Just stay right there," she said, grabbing for the cordless on the wall behind her. "Michael, is that you? Where are you?" Susan asked.

"I'm at the sheriff's station in Greenport," Michael said. "Look, Suze, could you call up Jack

Temple and have him meet me down at the county jail? Tell him it's an emergency. I've got to go, they won't let me talk long. Just don't worry." Jack Temple was their lawyer, not that he had ever had to handle anything for them. He was more friend than lawyer.

"Wait, tell me what's happened," Susan demanded. "What about the Marvells?"

"He's dead." The answer didn't come as a total shock as the outcome of a medical emergency. She might have interrupted to tease Michael for speeding so fast to get back to her that the cops caught him, but his next words drove all thought of that from her mind. "I've been arrested. They're calling it murder. Get hold of Temple, okay?" The phone went dead.

Susan abruptly realized that she'd been staring sightlessly off into space for several seconds, the receiver lifeless in her hand. Moving slowly, she replaced it on the wall and turned to her unwelcome guest.

"I'm afraid if you've come to see my husband, he won't be back for a while," she heard herself say.

"Longer than you might imagine," Rakhel said imperturbably. "That coffee smells good." She got up from the table, eyed the mugs on the shelf above the sink, and took down a blue and white Japanese one. She came back sipping her coffee.

"Too hot, and too strong—people do that with cheap beans. It doesn't help. All right, now, come sit down." Rakhel hadn't taken her eyes off Susan. "Let's talk about this."

Susan shook her head. "No, I need to call someone. Maybe—"

"I guarantee you Jack Temple's still in bed. It won't do any harm giving him a few more minutes to sleep. And Judge Marshall, who will preside over the bail hearing, won't be in chambers until ten. So you've got time for a little chat, *nu*?"

"What's going on? Are you involved in all this?" Susan hardly noticed that she had crossed the kitchen and was sitting down beside Rakhel at the table. "Who are you?"

"Once upon not too long ago, *mein kind*, I played an important role in your life. You'd remember what it was, except for the fact that you've chosen to forget. Of course, that could change again—life is change, isn't it?"

The hint of a Yiddish accent stirred a vague response in Susan. An echo from Jerusalem that she should remember? But it was ridiculous to imagine that she had encountered and then forgotten the character in front of her.

"Were you in the Middle East?" Susan asked.

Rakhel nodded and asked, "Do you ever dabble in free will?"

"Free will?"

"Two words that I'm not sure belong together. Most people who have a great deal of will rarely have much freedom."

"What are you talking about?"

"They find it very hard to follow the stream of events. No surrender. And so they panic and try to steer the boat. It rarely works out too well."

A haze seemed to be clearing and Susan stood up. "I'm sorry. I don't have time for this right now."

Rakhel sighed wearily. "That's what they all say. You're going to have to make time, you know. We are going to have to learn to mesh our ways, you and I, and on the whole my ways are best."

"I'm sure they are." Susan was no longer listening. She turned and headed into Michael's study, where the phone numbers were kept. *Murder!* The word jumped in her throat, and the blind urgency to save her husband took hold. The office was light and airy, filled with Michael's clutter, books and papers piled together in no conceivable order. As she rifled through one small heap for his address book, her mind began to chatter in a fast, disconnected voice that she barely recognized:

So the time has come. Funny, I always knew we were waiting for something to happen, com-

ing here to live. I'm not really afraid. No, that's not true—I'm scared to death, but something else is happening. . . . I need to connect to it, need to connect. . . .

Sitting down in Michael's wooden office chair, Susan punched the numbers into the phone and waited.

"Hullo?" The voice on the other end was hoarse and groggy.

"Jack? It's Susan McCaffrey. Michael called me a few minutes ago. He's been arrested."

"Arrested? For what?"

"He said . . ." Susan hesitated before she could bring herself to say the next words. "They think he's killed somebody. Our next-door neighbor, Marvell."

"Rhineford Marvell?"

"I guess so. Yes, if that's his name. Marvell. What a stupid name."

"Not stupid, market-savvy. He's a New Age nutcase. He has to attract attention." Temple was awake enough now to sound scathing. "Where is Michael now?"

"At the county jail, I think. I mean, that's where he said for you to go. Jack, I don't know what to do."

"Give me a few minutes to pull myself together. I can't tell you anything until I get down there. I'm sorry."

"No, I understand." Turning around, Susan noticed the old lady standing in the doorway, a bemused spectator to her distress. The sight made Susan want to scream, to drive this noxious intruder from her house. At the same time as the lawyer was speaking in one ear, she could hear Rakhel talking in a loud voice. "He might be able to get Michael out on bail, but that's about it. He won't be able to clear him. Pfft! There goes your good name. What can you do?"

Shut up!

Susan was sure she had shouted out loud, but since her visitor didn't bat an eyelash, she must not have.

"I'm going to the jail with you," she said into the phone. "Don't argue with me, Jack, or I'll snap." He mumbled a grudging agreement and hung up. She turned to face Rakhel, her soft seamed face of age as guileless as a child's.

"So look who's Superwoman all of a sudden—you're going to break down the jail walls and snatch him out with your bare hands, right? *Mazel-tov,* my dear, but that isn't going to happen."

"Look, if you don't mind, you have to leave." Susan ran her fingers through her hair, half desperate to get this annoying . . . *old thing* . . . out of her presence. Rakhel noticed this and added an edge to her words that demanded attention.

"Listen to me, doll. The reasons surrounding Marvell's death run much deeper than you realize—and the man you call your husband did not just telephone you."

Susan's heart skipped a beat. "So he isn't involved?" Bizarre as the old lady's claim had been, it sparked a surge of hope.

Rakhel shrugged. "No, he's involved, all right. He knows this, so he will step carefully. But you need to help."

"How?" Susan asked. "If he didn't call, where is he?"

"Who knows? I can't see through walls. But he will figure out what to do. Right now he might not be able to reach you."

The reasonable part of Susan's mind revolted. "What do you mean? I can't stay to figure out anything you've been saying. I'm going to see my husband right now," she said forcefully, like someone pushing a teetering railroad car back on track. "Do you understand?"

"See him? Seeing is such a strange problem." Rakhel's voice had a bizarre certainty.

"I'm going. Now," Susan said, turning away.

"So, do you need your windows cleaned?" the old lady asked aimlessly. "It's my specialty."

"Are you mocking me?" said Susan, walking away but somehow not losing the old lady, who dogged her steps to the stairs.

Rakhel shook her head. "I'm going to help you, which means forming a conspiracy."

"A conspiracy against what?"

"Oh, come now," Rakhel said with a smile, "it's not as though the other side ever changes. We march against chaos and old night—that's the classy way to put it, *nu*? The bad stuff. The confusion that ruins everything just when we try our hardest to be clear and right."

Susan suddenly felt fed up with the cryptic. "I'm sorry, this is too much. And it's the wrong time. I'm sorry." Susan lowered her head as if fending off a blow and pushed past the old lady. Mounting the stairs to get dressed for the hard things this day promised to bring, she hoped in the bottom of her heart that the house would be empty when she returned downstairs. If the front door closed in the next minute, Susan didn't hear it.

The Angel's Voice

You find places on the fringes of society for the old, the disabled, and the insane. Sometimes you relegate your saints to the same places, but we will let that go for now. God has to worry about the spiritually homeless. I don't mean the empty of spirit but the full. In a world that is descending away from

God, where is He to put those who have stayed with Him?

Are they to wander the face of the earth? God could not allow this, so He had to find a way to tend his most faithful. Again there were choices that could have been made. He could have displayed such favor to His saints that people would bow down before them. But because of free will, God could not force anyone to love His saints; there were many who would persecute and revile them. This made God decide to let the richest in spirit appear quite ordinary to the rest of you. As one of your scriptures declares, "Be not forgetful to entertain strangers: for thereby some have entertained angels unawares." Quite so, but the stranger himself was not an angel, since angels have no flesh and bones. It was the sacred act of hospitality that was angelic: Whoever brings light into this world is feasting with angels.

Yet God could not set aside the most awakened people so lightly. He put them under His grace in a subtle, almost secret way. He allowed them to see not just with the eye of the body and the eye of the mind— although these are also God's grace—but with the eyes of the soul.

Then He said to them, "Do as you please."

Are these miraculous words? Doesn't God let everyone do as he or she pleases? Yes, but what a difference it makes when you know that God has told you so Himself. The voice of God is being heard in you whenever you deeply believe the following commandments:

Be not afraid.
Remember that you are loved.
Regard everyone as a child of God—
   this means everyone.
Appreciate every fiber of creation as
   holy.
Do not see yourself in the world but the
   world in yourself.

* * *

Michael—the real one whom the police had left behind—did not phone Susan. He had tried, but the line was busy. Still badly shaken, he poured himself another scotch from Marvell's best decanter. He had the whole house to himself, and the liquor cabinet was unlocked. His doctor's mind took over. If he was in shock or hallucinating, he wanted to check out what effect alcohol would have. Deep psychosis isn't affected by alcohol.

Here goes, Michael thought. He had taken the liquor into the kitchen and found a water glass. Standing at the sink, he gulped down the second shot and waited. Because his stomach was empty, the effect should wash over him quickly. It did. Michael felt flushed and relaxed; drunkenness would no doubt creep up on him fairly soon.

A raving hallucination would have been much simpler to deal with. Michael left the kitchen and wandered the premises without seeing much. The Marvell house was furnished in fake country manse. The cut Persian carpets were old and frayed, to resemble family heirlooms. The Moroccan leather sofa in the living room gave the impression of being inherited from a nonexistent grandmother instead of bought at auction on the Upper East Side.

Michael plunked himself down on a tufted divan, observing himself through the haze of the liquor. He looked for signs of shock or obsession; he expected his brain to frantically replay the last hour over and over, seeking to ward off total panic by reworking reality until it fit a rational pattern that could be lived with.

But his mind did not obsess or freak out. He saw very clearly that moment when the shadow

Michael walked away. It had simply happened. He had not split down the middle like an amoeba dividing in two; he had not emerged from his body like a ghost, the way we imagine the soul leaves when we die. It was simpler than that, and a lot worse. He was one, then he was two.

For want of anything better, Michael got up and left the Marvell house. His car was where he had hurriedly parked it, at a slant that almost ran off the driveway.

At least go home. That's where you went to bed. Maybe the trick of it is to return before you can wake up.

It seemed like a weak theory, but he got in the car anyway. His hand reached for the key, then fell back. A crazy person could die trying to drive. Psychosis has a strange way of pretending to be sane, but the illusion eventually falls apart. People stop at red lights, then go catatonic, glued into the driver's seat, unable to move until the firemen come and pry them out.

Who's going to pry me out?

Michael started the car and backed out onto the road. If he could think about psychosis, it must mean he wasn't psychotic. Faulty reasoning, maybe, but it would have to do. A measure of calm came over him. He didn't need to figure out the impossible just because it was impossible. But of course that was the alcohol's way of looking at the situation. It would wear off.

He reached his driveway in time to see Susan speeding off in her Jeep. *Hey, wait!* his mind wanted to scream. But his hand didn't reach for the horn. He braked and watched Susan until the Jeep rounded the bend going toward town.

A few seconds later Michael was inside, once again having a whole house to himself. His empty stomach was betraying him now. He felt sick and dizzy; he needed to eat something. Mindlessly he took out the ingredients of a tuna sandwich. Presumably he needed to eat, or if not, this wasn't the right time to experiment.

So, mein kind, you think you are ready to be real? I warn you, it's a tricky business. As long as you trust in normal things, you are buried in unreality. Only going mad—or waking up—will show you what is really real. A voice he had tried to forget came back to him. Michael pushed it back down into the dark part of his mind, under the floorboards of awareness.

He took his plate and a glass of cold milk to the window and began to eat standing up. It seemed that he was himself. So who did that leave to be arrested for the murder of Marvell? Michael stopped himself from going there—first he wanted Susan to see him and touch his skin. That would be the test. Then possibilities would unfold. Susan could possibly reassure him, and normal life would go on. She could see him and not recognize him, or maybe not see him at all. Odd, that one. What if he floated around the premises for a while, only to find that tomorrow's newspaper reported the tragic car crash that killed Dr. Michael Andrew Aulden on a country road in the early hours of the morning?

Michael took the plate and empty glass back to the sink. Sunlight from the window landed on his arm, warm and bright. It was a small thing, a passing sensation, but he stared down at his arm anyway. Evidence of the ghostly was not at hand. If he was alive, he had the same obligations as any other person who was alive. And that meant one obvious thing.

Without a glance backward, he found himself running out the back door. Michael headed for his car and jumped in. The black Saab screeched onto the road and headed for town. Now he knew where to go, and that impulse, so easily taken for granted when you aren't inside a mystery, helped make the mystery go away. For the moment.

The shadow Michael had no opportunity to do anything that might rock anyone's life. It took almost four hours for Jack Temple and Susan, working their way doggedly through the Columbia County bureaucracy, to secure his release. The arraignment itself went quickly; a reputable physician was deemed to have sufficient ties to the community not to be at risk of fleeing prosecution for his alleged crime. Bail was set at $100,000, which the house mortgage covered. There was a possibility, the judge warned him, that bail would be revoked after he faced the grand jury.

"So what happens next?" Michael said grimly as he stood in front of an iron-grated window passing forms back to a blankly indifferent clerk. Susan was by his side with her arm folded into his; he had turned his head back at Temple, who was standing close behind him.

The lawyer shrugged.

"They're going to seek first-degree homicide, because to all appearances you didn't act out of irrational or sudden impulse. You deliberately sought out Marvell in his own home at an unusual hour."

"I didn't seek him out, that's just the point," Michael protested.

Susan felt weak at the knees. She wasn't afraid of life, or at least it hadn't frightened her enough so far to make a permanent reflex out of fear. She didn't marry Michael to make herself feel more safe, nor did they use each other as a haven. Yet the threat of being abandoned was now so thick in her mouth that she tasted its bitterness. She had outfitted herself—maybe *armored* was

a better word—in a man-tailored suit of pin-
striped navy wool. It was what Michael called
her "corporate avenger" look, and it made her
appear formidable, a pale Valkyrie come down
from Valhalla to demand justice.

But the magic had worn off. "Can we just go
now?" she murmured, her throat almost catching.

The two men, still caught up in legal warrior
talk, looked over at her; they both hesitated, then
Michael noticed what was going on. "Sure, let's
get out of here." Susan was grateful to be pulled
away, down the brown-painted corridors lit by
flickering bluish fluorescents and scented with
old wax and trepidation. She had not even fleet-
ingly considered the possibility that Michael was
guilty, but as they made their way through the
morning's proceedings, she gained a vivid picture of Marvell's body, stabbed repeatedly with
his own eleven-inch kitchen knife. Every mark
of premeditation was there; if the wife had not
woken up and surreptitiously phoned the police
from upstairs in a horrified whisper (caught on
tape by the 911 dispatcher), they might not have
caught the culprit red-handed. But she had and
they did.

The prosecutor had rained these damning facts
down on Michael's head, which was bowed with
numbness and exhaustion as he stood before the

judge, and Susan became painfully aware that everyone else but her believed in his guilt . . . including his lawyer.

"Look, Michael," Temple said as they walked down the courthouse steps into the warm noon light, "this is as far as I can take you."

"You assume I did it," Michael said, not accusingly but as if he had assessed the facts and come up with the same rational conclusion.

"Don't try to take me there," Temple said abruptly. "I'm not stating a conclusion. I'm just telling you that I've already gotten too involved with a criminal case—a capital case that I am totally unqualified to handle in your best interests—for my own peace of mind. I'm a little ole country corporate-law specialist who hustles his butt into Manhattan four days a week. You need a good defense lawyer."

Michael stopped and looked at himself. He was still wearing the white T-shirt and khaki slacks he'd left the house in before dawn. His hands were raw and pink with scrubbing, and there were rusty brown smudges on his shirt that Susan recognized as blood.

"I already have a lawyer," Michael said stubbornly.

"No." Temple took a step backward, throwing up his hands. He was a vigorous man with the build of a stevedore, whose thick dark curly hair gave the lie to the fact that he had turned fifty half a decade ago. "This is murder, Michael, not insurance fraud."

The expression on Temple's face was complex, hard to read, but it was almost one of pity. "I already spoke to the DA. You need someone who can protect your rights, get you the best deal possible."

"Deal?" Susan interrupted, a note of panic in her voice. "Why would we need to deal if Michael is innocent?"

Temple ignored her, plowing on. "I can recommend a few names, people with experience. They won't come cheap, but this is your life we're talking about."

"That's blunt enough," Michael muttered.

"It's realistic, that's all." The two men shook hands awkwardly, then Temple headed off in the direction of his car.

''Come on," Susan said gently. They walked to the parking lot in silence. Michael seemed to be turned totally inward, staring out the window in silence as they drove home. Neither of them noticed a black Saab parked at the edge of the courthouse grounds, much less the man inside it who was the exact mirror of the man who had been arraigned inside. This Michael had been staring at them, and when they passed him, the distance separating them was no more than

twenty feet, if that. You would think that Susan
would recognize such a familiar face. But her
head didn't turn. She and the shadow Michael
headed home to ponder their next move. The
man in the black Saab rode off in another direction as unnoticed as a ghost among the living.
Apparently that was how these things worked.
He knew now who to ask about it.

The Angel's Voice

We don't mind changing tires. We have
heard the tales of cars stranded at midnight
on a lonely deserted road, the driver despairing of help, when suddenly a stranger
pulls up and stops just in time. The tire is
changed, and the grateful motorist feels res-
cued, touched by God. In this guise you
think you have seen angels, or in the shape
of other nameless benefactors bringing
Thanksgiving dinner to the homeless and
weary of heart.

We can be these rescuers, but usually we
do not touch you in this way. Other benefactors come from God but more indirectly.
He sends them by "coincidence." Coincidence is just a piece of the divine plan that
surprises you. You assume that you know
how the world works, but how could you?
In order to know how the world works, you

would have to know who you are, and that is part of the great forgetting.

Would you like to know how the world works?

It is arranged solely for you. Every event is woven into a cosmic tapestry, and each thread vibrates in response to every other. God who wove the web and oversees it, His finger touching every tiny part. The angels cannot sing without it having an effect on your life; you cannot weep without it having an effect on ours. The living whole breathes and moves together.

Webs are made to catch their prey. What is God out to catch? Imperfection. You call it sin or karma, but to the Creator the only sin is that which falls short of perfect love and joy. His intention is only to bring perfection. He could decree it. In other universes He has decreed it and allowed no deviation. But there is a game afoot in your universe, and that game is hide-and-seek. You hide from your own perfection so that you can seek it again. This game began from your own choosing. You forgot your choice, which makes you lament your sins and sorrows. But if you look deep in your soul, you would have the game no other way. Why? Because this is the game that allows you to be the creator—your constant creation is yourself. Instead of paint or clay, you use the stuff of experience.

Experience comes in every shade and color. You are fascinated by this. You wake up every day wanting nothing else. That is why you will never permit yourself the luxury of satisfaction, not for long. In the heart of every ending is the seed of a new beginning. Do you realize this? Can you accept it? If so, you are near to God and His ways.

But sometimes you will have to change your own tires.

The conference room at Area 23 had the bland, Sheetrocked anonymity of briefing rooms everywhere. It held a large oval table surrounded by gray office chairs. On one wall was a whiteboard, its surface bare and pristine; on the facing wall was a world map inset with clocks that showed the time across the global time zones. In Area 23 it was one forty-five in the afternoon.

Simon and Lazar slumped in two chairs at the far ends of the table from each other. They were thinking independently, considering the alien possibilities presented by the capture. Neither had offered any abrupt opinions, still feeling wary about the military's motives for bringing them there.

Besides the two scientists, there were three other men in the room. One was General Stillano, in his green dress uniform, his eyes hooded and his expression grim. The man on his left was a civilian with wire-rimmed glasses and a navy pinstripe suit. He was years younger and looked like an investment banker. Stillano did not introduce him, which to Simon was as much as announcing that he was CIA. Stillano called him Carter. On the general's right was his aide, Colonel Burke. He had the ferocious good grooming associated with mind-control cults and the Hoover-era FBI.

"Okay," Lazar said, flinging himself around to face Stillano. "Fun's fun, and you've poked and prodded this thing, yet you've come up with zilch so far as useful data is concerned. What's next?"

"Brainwork," Stillano said, "which is your department." He made it sound as if a specialized weapons division had been called in. "I want you—*both* of you—to give me three viable explanations. Rank them in order, state your conclusions, and support each hypothesis with the best physics you can muster."

"If this thing is alive, maybe we need a biologist," Carter interjected.

"Nix that," said Lazar. "Biologists know one

thing: DNA. You're not telling me a giant light bulb has genes."

Against his better instincts, Simon piped up. "We might have some use for a linguist, however, or a cryptographer. The pulsations emitted by your capture no doubt exhibit some degree of patterning. Any nonrandom emissions could be considered a language or at the very least a code."

"It's trying to talk to us?" said Stillano.

Simon shrugged. "I can't reach such a conclusion without a great deal more evidence. What did the locals on the ground tell you?"

"Essentially nothing," said Burke after glancing over at Stillano. "There have been few sightings of UFOs in the southern Balkans. The locals believed they were seeing an angel."

"Typical," Simon muttered.

"It was actually the most logical conclusion for them to reach, given their culture," Burke pointed out. Simon didn't look impressed.

Lazar was getting more restless. "Start with the facts. It showed up, it frizzled a stone wall into nothing, and then when some Army types come along with a few trucks and guns, it allows itself to be captured. What does that tell you?"

"I'm all ears," said Stillano.

"Volition. It tells you that this entity has a will. It can control its power as and when it wants to."

"Which further implies purpose," added Simon. He was reluctant to be seen as Lazar's egghead twin, but his competitive streak ran deep. "The implication is that it did not choose its landing spot at random—after all, this was a church located in an extremely contentious part of the world, a focus of global attention."

Stillano nodded. "Okay, so you're saying that because it allowed itself to be transported here, this stage could also be part of its purpose?"

"Possibly," said Simon. He glanced over at Lazar, who had slumped farther down into his chair, no doubt his knee-jerk retreat whenever a colleague took the limelight. "I assume Dr. Lazar agrees with me."

"I never object to the patently obvious," Lazar said lazily. "I'm hungry. Does your new pet emit enough microwave radiation to cook a burger?" They all ignored him.

"You say you want three viable explanations," Simon repeated. "How far out do you want us to go?"

"Give me a for-instance," Stillano said.

"All right: Contrary to your skimpy UFO data, sightings of supernatural entities appear to be common in this area. Many believe that the Virgin Mary has been appearing to a group of young people in Medjugorje since June 24, 1981. That's in Bosnia, in case the name didn't ring any bells."

Carter had been gazing up at the ceiling, as though none of the others were in the room. He spoke up. "Medjugorje is a simple rural village of approximately four hundred families, located, as you are aware, in the middle of a fractious area that erupted into a war zone. Despite this, it became a destination for millions of people from all over the world because of six kids who swear the Mother of God showed up there to chat on a regular basis."

"I would say a fat lot of good it did them," Simon replied. "In any event, that sighting or visitation, call it what you will, began with a glow on the horizon seen over the crest of a hill at night."

"This is the Virgin Mary? That's your initial explanation?" Stillano asked, unable to hide his incredulity.

"Not necessarily," said Simon coolly. "The actual form of that visitation is widely debated, even among believers. What appears as Mother Mary to one is just a glow of light to another and a faint change in the atmosphere to a third."

"The government keeps tabs on this kind of anomaly," said Carter. "We aren't particularly worried about the BVM—Blessed Virgin Mary— unless there are defense implications, which means local unrest. These kids lived in a hot spot that's about to blow. Out of the blue they come up with a message from the BVM. Guess what? She wants the whole world to fall on their knees, pray 'round the clock, and reconcile their sins with God. If they follow orders, that will bring peace. Without it, she foresees war and widespread destruction."

"Worked real good so far," Lazar commented.

"What's your point?" Stillano asked impatiently.

"I don't have a point. I'm just giving you a report that might prove relevant," Carter replied smoothly. " "Medjugorje is a heavily Catholic area in what was until very recently a Communist country. Four of the seers are girls and two are boys. Their ages at the first encounter ranged from ten to seventeen. Several have entered the church or still intend to. The Communist regime, as it was at the time, put strong pressure on them not to speak out, and even went so far as to detain some for a while.

"Despite government opposition, internecine fighting among church factions, and the outbreak of war, the visitations have continued from 1981 through the present day. That's close to twenty years, and many of the believers, who number in the millions, are awaiting a disaster or a revelation of major magnitude."

"When is the cosmic bulletin coming over the wires?" Simon asked.

"Soon."

The scientist snorted. "There's always a global disaster to show God's wrath, and it's always coming soon."

"At the beginning of the apparitions, the BVM said that she would give each of the six children ten messages. The information contained within four of these messages would be so-called visible signs to mankind that the return to God must begin now.

"There have been the usual quota of healings, just as at any pilgrimage site. But that isn't the big game. According to the devotees, when Mary stops appearing, a permanent sign will appear at Medjugorje for all humanity. Speculation is that this sign will take the form of a great light or a pillar of fire, similar to the one that led Moses and the chosen people across the wilderness in the Old Testament. When all the messages have been fulfilled, the end of the world will come."

Simon shifted uneasily. To him, America was afoul with strange exotic sects. Despite Carter's flat neutral tone, Simon wouldn't put it past him to be a true believer in this hokum—not a comfortable feeling when the country you are a stranger in can bring the end of the world at will. Maybe to fulfill a prophecy. Was that probable?

Possible? Simon deflected his mind from images of apocalypse; he decided that a hint of paranoia must be creeping into his thought processes.

Carter was winding it up now. "The BVM is particularly down on drugs and television, and while she wants everyone to convert to Catholicism 'before it is too late,' she also preaches tolerance for other religions."

"So you're suggesting that we've got a box full of Jesus here in the bunker?" Lazar asked.

"That's one way to put it," said Carter dryly.

"Could we move on to the next possibility, please?" Simon suggested with cold punctilio. "I asked at the outset how far afield you wanted us to go. If zapping an angel is unacceptable, say so."

"I like the idea of shiny saucer creatures better. *Klaatu barada nikto, Gort!*" Lazar intoned, quoting a legendary bit of alien talk à la Hollywood.

"There wasn't any saucer. No vehicle at all," Stillano reminded him. Lazar looked as if he wanted to argue the point, but at that moment the door opened, and the major who had served as their first escort entered the room.

"Sorry, sir, I think you need to see this," he said, rushing to a television monitor in the corner and turning it on.

The familiar CNN logo ran in a stripe along the bottom of the screen. Grainy minicam footage showed an image well-known to the military around the table: the ruined church at Sv. Arhangeli. But now the area around the church was crammed with humanity. It looked at first as if they had come for no purpose. They didn't shout or demonstrate. They only stood facing the church, waiting. The eerie silence held for a beat longer, then the picture cut to a bright CNN newsroom.

"Uh-oh, cover blown," Lazar cried with obvious glee.

"Christ," Carter muttered.

"That was live footage from our correspondent on the ground in Kosovo," the anchorman reported. "As you can see, the overnight vigil continues as thousands of displaced Serbs, with an uneasy scattering of Muslims, flock to a small village in the southwestern corner of the state. Despite the danger from rebel forces, people are refusing to disperse. UN peacekeepers have been ineffectual in clearing the area, and observers report that the crowd is here in protest to the involvement of American troops in local ground activity—"

"There's a credibility gap for you," said Lazar. The rest of the room was fed up with his gibes— Stillano gave him a glaring look that shut him up for the moment. The TV picture changed to a close-up of a Serbian refugee being interviewed.

He looked grizzled with rage and chronic anxiety. He wore the anonymous ragged outfit that was the uniform of a human condition, the war-ravaged civilian survivor.

"This is not the Americans' fight. They have no business to interfere in our troubles. Now they have stolen from us our most precious possession, the Virgin Mother. . . ." The man spoke in English so heavily accented that it was subtitled, the words boxed across the bottom of the transmission.

"Do all these thousands of people believe that?" asked the offscreen newsman.

"We all have one belief," the man replied, scowling into the camera. It was raining, and the droplets of water clung to the stubble on his unshaven chin like cold sweat. He disappeared, replaced by the tag line *Kosovo in Crisis* and a map with a question mark over Sv. Arhangeli.

"The protest is apparently connected to last week's training exercise conducted in this area by U.S. forces," the anchorman said. "During those exercises, members of the United States ground forces are alleged to have quarantined the church in Kosovo for several days. State Department officials would confirm only that sniper attacks had occasioned an increase of security during that time. Meanwhile, in Iran today—" The major flicked the set off. In the ensuing silence the general regarded the two scientists intently.

"As you see, gentlemen, we have a ticking clock," he said.

"It could be worse. The real credibility gap is theirs," said Simon. "No one's going to believe you kidnapped the Virgin Mary—I mean, the BVM." He nodded for Carter's benefit.

"Not for the time being," Stillano agreed. "But I want that list of explanations on my desk yesterday, if you can manage it." He got to his feet and strode from the room, followed quickly by his aide.

"I suggest you get started, gentlemen," Carter said.

Simon looked down the table at Lazar. For once, the prankster's expression was as blank and unrevealing as his own.

The Angel's Voice

Perhaps you think that we should simply appear en masse, flying in formation over the Super Bowl, to bring humankind back to its senses. But we have never appeared to anyone as we truly are. How can we, since we have never disappeared? Our vibration is as constant as the vibration of an electron or a quark. Since we are as constant as the stars, some cultures have imagined that we *are* the stars.

The only fading away happens inside you. This is the great forgetting. In forgetting yourself, you have cast such a thick cloud that you cannot help but forget God. Since we are part of God, you forgot us at the same time.

How did we react to this lamentable event? As always, we watched.

For a long time we assumed that our ecstasy and our total abandonment to love of God was enough. What else could we do? But as you descended into the empty spaces and began to cry out, we saw you change. In your descent you became much more prey to violence and grief. You became wolves who fed on their own kind. It was unimaginable that such ones could ever see us again—and yet we were wrong. We had overlooked what God always knew. The greater the darkness, the greater the contrast with the light. When you no longer could rely on glimpses of us, you began to look harder. You missed us, and like lost sailors craning in a storm to spy even one dim guiding star, a few of you started to look for us. You are not always the saints or sages. Among you are those of great suffering and much wrong action—but a stray spark of the divine made you want to spy us.

And so you shall.

3
Revelations

Sitting in the roadside diner, Michael stared into a cup of black coffee as if it were a pool of remembrance. He had no trustworthy facts to go on, but after seeing his double again at the courthouse, the territory felt weirdly familiar. Someone wanted to make it seem as if Ford Marvell was stabbed to death. The trap was laid perfectly, yet there was no way to tell how it had been done. Michael's unseen tormentors had the power to bend reality or at least distort perception at will. He knew of only one group with such power, but they were not people he had ever wanted to tell Susan about.

Haven't I turned my life upside down to keep her safe?

He looked up and saw the short-order cook leaning against the stove, facing him as he smoked a Camel. Michael tried not to think about what was happening between his wife and *that man*. Was there any other way to think about the false Michael? Whoever had laid the trap must have created that little touch, too. It gave Michael the incentive he needed to stop hiding in ordinariness the way he had for almost three years.

Fate is that part of yourself that won't listen to excuses, Rakhel had said. It was not her only daunting remark, but it was one Michael didn't like to think about.

He got up and paid the bill. For an instant he wondered if his credit card might not work, but it did. The cashier smiled and nodded. Everyone who knew him still knew him. Except Susan. The fact that she had not immediately sensed his presence at the courthouse had stopped Michael from chasing her. Susan didn't need to be shocked to death unless it was absolutely necessary. Strangely, as the real Michael drove the Saab through town, he found himself talking to her as if she were in the car with him—another old habit, he supposed, but he didn't resist it. He could see the high chignon of her hair. Like her man's suit, which she had been wearing to court, the knot was a gesture of toughness.

"I'm going back there," he told her. "To his house. I need to get a better look at Marvell's study, find out what he was doing."

"Michael, you're talking about breaking and entering." She talked back to him in her sensible voice, and she didn't flinch.

"Yeah, it must sound pretty crazy."

"Reckless, needlessly reckless. What if they catch you?"

"They won't." He had to laugh at that one. Imaginary conversations don't have rules, but it was pretty blatant that the police wouldn't catch him, because they already had. Now Michael started telling his wife what he should have told her long ago. They were now in the kitchen back home—this was the conversation they would have had if his double did not exist.

"Suze, listen to me." In his mind's eye, Michael put his arm around her and looked closely. "Do you remember two years ago when we were in Syria?"

She looked perplexed but went along. "We met, we fell in love, WHO folded the aid station when Syria heated up, and we decided to come back stateside. You were there, Michael."

"What if I told you that wasn't what happened?" He saw her take a breath. "Wait, wait, don't jump ahead." He searched for words. "I've been in a place like this before."

"Meaning what?" Susan's body seemed to want to back away.

"I don't mean in trouble with the law. Look

at this. I found it on the body." Michael handed
her the folded note, and she silently read its few
words: *THE ANGEL IS NEAR*.

He heard himself saying, "Marvell was involved in the occult—deeply involved, so far as
I can tell. He must have uncovered something,
and it's connected with his death."

Susan managed a pained smile. "Are we getting to the part that's supposed to make me think
you're not insane?"

"Here, sit down and listen, okay? How would
you feel if you discovered that what you remembered wasn't what had really happened? That the
true past was something completely different, almost . . . magical?"

"Is that how you're feeling right now?" she
asked anxiously.

"No, I really am talking about you."

"Are you saying I have suppressed memories?
Something like that?"

"Something like that, yes. Reality is stranger—
more *malleable*—than people think. A woman
named Rakhel taught me that."

In his mind's eye she looked startled, as if this
name meant something to her, but he raced on.
"Rakhel was in the Middle East, and she saved
your life once, a part of your life you don't remember. Wait." He held up his hand to block her
objections. "While we were still in Syria, you

took me to Jerusalem to visit a friend of yours, Solomon Kellner, a retired rabbi. You knew him from a human rights conference in Basel."

"Funny, I haven't thought about him in years. You say I took you to him?"

"Yes. The reason isn't important anymore, but what Kellner told us—told me—is."

The mathematical angels. The phrase the old rabbi had used in explaining the mysteries of the Hebrew alphabet still rang in Michael's ears. He remembered how he had resisted believing what Kellner had to tell him. Now he had to tell the same things to Susan and hope she would be more open than he had been.

"What Rabbi Kellner told me when you took me to see him in Jerusalem is that Hebrew is a language of magic. Each letter has a meaning and each letter has a numerical value as well. When a word is written in Hebrew—the language in which the Lord created the world, so Jews believe—it automatically has a numerical value. And each word whose numerical value adds up to the same number is the same word. The number for *life—l'chaim—*is eighteen. Twice eighteen, or thirty-six, is the number of *creation.* In Hebrew, the number thirty-six is *Lamed Vov.* Thirty-six is eighteen pairs: God's chromosomes.

"But there are also thirty-six souls, living people, known as the Lamed Vov. They see everything, and God needs their clarity in order to maintain the world. Without human awareness, the stars and mountains and seas are as faint and shadowy as dreams. To keep this world intact, God needs someone to dream it, century after century. To see it, to experience it, to *be* it.

"Without these special dreamers, everything you see would disappear. The Old Testament records a covenant that God swore with Abraham: If Abraham could find a pure soul, God would spare mankind. According to Judaism, ever since the Fall, man has been defiled by the touch of death, but God spares the impure—which means all of us—because thirty-six pure souls exist. Under most circumstances, none of the Lamed Vov knows who any of the others are, or anything about them. The thirty-six could be anyone: a Russian nun, an Australian shaman in the outback, a Brazilian Candomblé priestess, a Catholic cardinal, a Pentecostal faith healer, a Tibetan Buddhist, a Shinto priest, even an unsuspecting American, strange as that sounds.

"Or there could be no religious affiliation at all. *Pure soul* means much more than someone who is sticky with virtue. *Pure* also means clear, and the thirty-six are totally clear about the nature of everything. They cannot be deceived— they aren't asleep or blinded like the rest of us. And they're real. I've seen them. And so have you." Michael stopped to let Susan soak at least a portion of this in if she could.

Instead of reacting, she made a logical leap. "I don't see why these people, if you believe in them so much, have anything to do with angels."

"Who can tell? Maybe they are in contact with them. I can't see the world through their eyes, but if there are invisible levels and layers outside our five senses, then somebody might be able to reach them," Michael said. "Anyway, Marvell's fixation with angels is our best lead, or only lead, so far."

But Susan's mind took another leap. "This is kind of a creepy question, but have you been contacting this group the whole time we've been together?" she asked.

"No, not since the first time. And you were there, you were part of it," Michael said.

"And that's what I don't remember?" Susan asked. "Why not?" In his mind's eye, she didn't look paranoid or jealous. Her eyes were filled with curiosity and fascination—perhaps she was even regaining memory from wherever it had been banished two years before.

Michael wondered why he felt subtly guilty, as if he had been cheating on her. Was there such a thing as spiritual adultery? But in fact secrecy had nothing to do with it; events had been out of his control all along. The adventure that Michael didn't want to relive had involved an emergency among the thirty-six. The demonic side of creation had sent forth a terrifying adversary who had almost hypnotized the world into believing he was the Messiah. While it was happening, the nightmare of this "false Ishmael" (he had come in the guise of the long-lost spiritual heir to Islam) had threatened to dissolve reality into a nightmarish hallucination. He had clutched at Susan's life directly, but now that he was gone, the nightmare was as nothing, a thing not to be recounted but only forgotten.

Michael said, "You weren't told any of this. The thirty-six found me, but the majority wanted to dismiss me. They don't by nature want to be known for who they are. Only one, Rakhel, insisted that I was a kind of apprentice. I wasn't born a pure soul, yet somehow I had stumbled into the beehive, so to speak. No one understood why, but Rakhel said that they had to improvise—bring someone up from the promising candidates."

Susan whistled. "So I should be impressed." She paused to think. "Did this group kill Marvell to frame you?"

"I don't know. It wouldn't be like them at all."

"But his death is something like that—a 3-D charade to twist things around, like a scary movie?"

"Maybe. Nothing's really clear, and we could be talking about a supernatural cabal. But limits have been set down—that's what I understand. In one sense the Lamed Vov have all the power. They are the glue by which God maintains creation, or a switching mechanism that He uses to reach all human consciousness. Normally the thirty-six are only a passive system. But should they choose to take control of their power, they can literally change reality."

"Pretty wild," Susan said. She usually wasn't so guilty of understatement. Michael could read her mind. *You want to ask me if I want to join them, want to sign up with the cosmic elite.* He longed to tell her that he wouldn't leave, but that was too hard to think about. In some way he had left, hadn't he? He had stepped out of the game into a new game he couldn't understand

But he had to reassure her some way. "I don't know what Marvell's death is about, but I do know that the thirty-six are out there, and I've seen them use their power to bend reality, just as it was bent last night."

Michael had to remind himself that this wasn't a real conversation. Susan did not have the benefit of all this information in real life—she was lost and alone. He wouldn't blame her if she reacted to his story, once he revealed it, as a betrayal or a sign of deep lunacy. Maybe it wouldn't go that way. Maybe she would look again at that note of Marvell's: *THE ANGEL IS NEAR*. It would strike her as the key. She would lean over and kiss him. "My little murderer, doing God's work."

No, it wouldn't go that way. That was wishful thinking. Michael jumped out of his reverie. Susan would feel betrayed. To her, the thirty-six would sound like a spiritual CIA that had crept out of the shadows. Spooks for God. Only one thing was certain. *That man*, the other Michael, would never tell her such things. He didn't know them. He was as blank as Susan herself. This realization hit Michael hard. To the whole world, the other Michael was him. But without this one secret piece of knowledge, it couldn't be him.

His mind was touching the hem of paranoia, and that was pointless. He would have to wait and see. Right now there was only the mission. It was crucial to enter Marvell's house again without getting caught. The suspense of it made Michael feel more alive, and the focus kept him from visualizing the worst thing, that a stranger would that night be sleeping in his bed.

The Angel's Voice

If you want to know God again, here is your first clue: Every day is a new world. Creation happens at every instant. You are not living in an old, fallen world—that is your legend, not God's truth. God keeps Genesis going and going. He is just as present with you as He ever was; there never was and never will be a better time to contact Him.

How do you do that?

God exists on three levels at once, and you must meet Him on all three. Each is like one big piece of a puzzle. The first level is the material world, known as His creation. You feel comfortable at this level and already understand it quite well. This is the level of mountains and stars, rivers, trees, the sea, plants, and animals. In your myths you call yourselves lord over this dominion, but God intends something else. He wants you to appreciate the material world and re- joice in it. This is your playground.

The second level is nonmaterial and therefore best known as the subtle worlds. The subtle worlds penetrate into the material world like air, invisibly but totally necessary to life. From this level God communicates love and truth. Even the animals need love, but you are made to feel much more refined energies of emotion. The prophets of love are prophets of the subtle level. It is also here that angels are met and truth is known. Whereas the material level makes life beautiful, the subtle level gives it meaning. You crave meaning and cannot exist without it. You know God here through your mind rather than your senses. In the eyes of the mind you see yourself as worthy, as a vehicle for truth. You learn trust and wisdom here; you see the value of idealism. When you exhibit violence, however, you depart from the subtle world and betray God's intentions.

The third level is so far from the material world that it has been almost forgotten. This is the world of pure awareness, without thought or desire. To know God here you must leave behind mind, emotions, and the senses. What remains is the most God-like thing of all: being. To be is to know God; it is the purest bliss, the purest intelligence, the purest creativity. Here you meet God as the genius who contains infinite inspiration, the artist with untold paintings yet to be put on canvas. This world is totally silent yet it contains the potential for creating infinite universes. How can I describe what God is like here? Even the angels stand in awe before this world, which your scriptures sometimes call "the Throne." It is the seat of God, yet in literal terms it is infinite awareness moving at infinite speed through infinite dimensions.

All three levels are constantly changing, both in themselves and in relation to each other. That is why I can say that every day is a new world. Your senses are fooling you into believing that even the material world is stable, for it is constantly in flux. Your mind is fooling you by repeating the same thoughts over and over when in truth the subtle world is nothing but change also. And the world of pure Being coordinates everything anew at every instant.

To meet God on these three levels, you must pay attention to what each world means. On the material level you meet God through appreciation of His creation, which means love of nature. On the subtle level you meet God through love of Him, through thoughts of spirit and a desire to live your own deepest truth. On the level of pure Being you meet Him through silence, mediation, and prayer. This is what it means to know God.

Once he got out of his car, Michael circled around to the rear of the Marvell house, avoiding the exposed vulnerability of the front door. The interior looked dark and still; Beth's car was absent from the garage. Michael took a deep, grateful breath for that. He'd expected to have to break in, but when he accidentally kicked the coconut mat outside the back door, he saw a key underneath. It fit the lock, and he went inside.

Down the darkened hallway the door to Marvell's study was closed, sealed off with bright yellow tape. Michael felt a pang of disappointment; at some level he had harbored the wishful thought that the whole incident would evaporate like a toxic mirage. With the door shut, the scene retained the aspect of a serene suburban home, but once he opened the door, the odor of death filled his nostrils. An ugly brown splotch on the pale rug was outlined in white chalk. The position was not where Michael had found Marvell the first time, but it approximated where the stabbed body lay. So this much of the invented reality was still true.

The rest of the room was as Michael had first glimpsed it, including the occult paraphernalia. On the walls he saw depictions of angels from every culture: Buddhist angels, their faces long and catlike, solemn Eastern Orthodox angels, playful and secular French cupids, oracular Renaissance angels. He recognized a drawing of the kabbalistic Tree of Life, colored in garish polychromatic 3-D; other designs looked as if they'd been taken from medieval woodcuts, or perhaps

Marvell had drawn them himself. Michael felt as if he were in some sort of sacred doll hospital.

Most people, because they've been exposed to wings and halos and harps, imagine that angels are oversized devotional candles, a larger-than-regulation fairy approved by God, or else a spiritual armed guard to make sure the demons don't bite. What if the shapes that Marvell was so fixated on didn't mean anything? What if humankind had spent centuries painting the messenger and missing the message, hypnotized by images of winged beings because that's what they had been conditioned to look for?

Michael realized that he knew almost nothing about his eccentric neighbor, although he had seen a splashy ad in the Sunday *Times* announcing the triumph of Marvell's latest, a book called *Other Bodies, Other Worlds,* about parallel incarnations and "space entities." On their few chance meetings, Ford had been gracious and down-to-earth, not at all the gullible purveyor of fantasy one might have expected. Michael realized that he had to stop thinking like either a detective or a wrongfully accused defendant. What had happened to Marvell was an illusion, not a murder. The sole way out was to find the illusionist's motive.

He walked over to Marvell's desk and sat down gingerly. In front of him was a Powerbook, its lid still raised. He tapped the space bar and the screen woke to life. There were icons on the desktop marked "Diary," "Notes," and "Working." The wallpaper on the screen was a scanned image of an occult glyph: a design of concentric circles containing triangles and squares, heavily annotated in Hebrew and Greek. Michael clicked on the icon marked "Diary." The file opened into the middle of a document:

January 16th. I have made the astounding discovery that angels aren't in heaven at all but all around us. Their world is ours, only a higher vibration of it. Their domain is so close I enter it in my dreams and fancies— now I intend to enter it in the flesh. Why should we not rend the veil and merge the earthly and angelic spheres?

"Bad idea," Michael mumbled. Most people were hard put to sustain the fantasy of their own daily lives. To force anyone to confront absolute reality would destroy them. He scrolled down a page on the screen.

I have been favored with my first communications, and the excitement coursing through my body makes it all but impossible to type these words. But at this historic

moment I must. It is only a matter of time
before my private thrill becomes a thrill for
the world, and then they will ask for ac-
countability.

Michael kept scrolling, growing more impatient. If he'd been hoping for a clue to his own
predicament, he was disappointed. Despite the
reassurance he wanted to give Susan, he wasn't
completely certain that the Lamed Vov were not
involved in this. But what good would it serve
to pull him in, even if they had the power to do
that?

Most of the diary entries were written in a self-
obsessed style. It was clear from the frequent ref-
erences to Beth's meddlesome questions that she
had become increasingly concerned about her
husband and had tried weakly to intervene. The
entries painted a sad picture of a brilliant man's
descent into depression and delusion.

Michael knew that this wasn't all folly—the
writer had entangled himself in things that were
real. His diary left no doubt that he was serious.
There was no pretense that he had just been gathering notes for one of his fanciful books.

Michael suddenly realized that he had no idea
how much time had passed. Moving quickly, he
unplugged the computer and tucked it under his
arm. He saw Marvell's Rolodex to one side. It

had fallen open to a glossy pink business card embossed with golden angels. Taking that as an omen, Michael picked up the Rolodex and left the house as unobserved as he had come. He reached the sanctuary of the Saab; an hour later he was pulled off on a side road contemplating his next move. Had Marvell's killer known about his burgeoning fixation? Or did the cause of death, assuming it was stroke or heart attack, hold some key?

Michael hadn't fully comprehended how it would feel to be so alone, with only the frail evidence of his soul to support him. It would be easy, despite all that he knew, to surrender to despair and the lure of inaction. He wasn't a reader of the Bible, but he remembered a taunt hurled at Christ as he was dying: *He trusted in God, let God deliver him.* With a sigh, he opened the first file on Ford's laptop and began to peruse the dead man's diary.

Susan had been too exhausted to spend much time with her husband before going upstairs to bed. The shadow Michael fit into his surroundings with perfect smoothness. After giving Susan a reassuring kiss, he decided to wait awhile downstairs. The phone in the kitchen began to ring. After a brief internal struggle he picked it up.

"Michael? It's Jack. I've got that list of lawyers I told you I was going to put together for you."

"Not interested," Michael said quickly.

"I think you should be reasonable," Temple said carefully. "I pulled a couple of strings and got the autopsy results. You might want to know what Criven's going to say on the stand before you do anything stupid." Criven was the county coroner.

"All right," Michael said. Rhineford Marvell had been stabbed in the chest and torso. There were no injuries to the face, and no defensive wounds on the hands and arms, which the coroner considered peculiar, given the savagery of the attack. Cause of death was severing of the anterior vena cava by means of a sharp instrument, probably the kitchen knife found near Marvell's body. Death was nearly instantaneous once the fatal wound was administered.

"It doesn't look that good," Temple said, "in case you're thinking about serving as your own counsel."

"Did Criven find anything suspicious?" Michael asked, ignoring Temple's implication of guilt.

"Not really. The ironical thing is, Marvell probably wouldn't have been alive by this time next year. He was suffering from a severe aneurysm of the aorta, which could have burst and killed him anytime."

Michael hung up and stared off into space. He knew that he had killed no one. It was obvious that he had been framed, yet that wasn't possible. He had witnessed his own innocence when he saw Marvell's corpse. Dead was dead, and the coroner was capable enough to detect any postmortem wounds, on the chance that Michael had put a knife into a corpse. He hadn't, he knew he hadn't. Beth Marvell's hysteria was madness, yet to the world the only madness here must be his. To deny what was plain to everyone's eyes told of a deeply disturbed mind, or else an evil one.

He went numb, unable to look any deeper into the mystery. Tired as he was, he decided not to join Susan. He would sleep on the couch. Michael got up and walked through the house. He was intensely absorbed in his grim thoughts; therefore he didn't see his wife standing on the landing at the top of the stairs with a strange look in her eyes, the fearful look of a lone woman confronted with a stranger in the house.

"Go-o-o-d Morning, Vietna-a-a-m!"

Simon's shoulders hunched as the braying voice filled the bunk room. Every morning when he rolled out of bed, Lazar announced his presence in the same raucous fashion, and every time it grated uncontrollably on Simon's nerves.

"What have we got for the running dogs of war this morning, babe?" Lazar continued irrepressibly. He leaned over Simon's shoulder, trying to see the computer screen. It was bad enough that Stillano demanded daily progress reports. But the disruption of Simon's normal routine and the complete lack of privacy were worse.

"Has it never occurred to you to bathe before you interact with me?" Simon asked irritably.

"Yes. But it passes."

Their time was supposed to be spent in intense work—Simon on a disciplined schedule of twelve-hour days commencing exactly at seven A.M., Lazar on a more erratic but equally protracted timetable combing the spectral data to find even the slightest clue about the capture's origins.

"Stop that." Simon slapped away a hand that was reaching over to scroll down the page. "I have to be allowed to complete my thoughts without interruption."

"Complete away, old boy," said Lazar. "Your eagerness for this project humbles me."

"I'm not eager, as you bloody well know. My sole aim is to get off the reservation as quickly as possible."

"Super, but playing lackey to the pinheads upstairs isn't going to do it, not unless you produce results. And so far that hasn't been too promising, has it?"

"You mean unless *we* produce results," Simon reminded him. "Now for God's sakes get your stink away." Simon was aware that he had a finicky nose, one that hated all disagreeable odors. Stale food, trash cans, alleyways, sewers, public bathrooms, subways, and crowds of all kinds— he had spent a lifetime detouring around the rank smells of life, which accounted in part for why he had detoured around life in general. But granting all of that, Ted Lazar stank.

Simon switched on the screen saver before Lazar could start reading his results aloud. "I've already told you to leave me alone," he said with as much threat as he could muster.

"Why? Afraid I'll make time with the BVM and you won't?"

Lazar had adopted Carter's government jargon, deciding that it was better than any satirical label he might dream up. He had also taken to calling the alien light the "Virgin of Roswell," but that had not caught on. The capture's behavior hadn't altered in the four days since the scientists arrived, and Stillano was angered that they had developed no viable hypotheses about where the light came from or the nature of the creature that inhabited it.

There were a variety of photos pinned up around the walls of Simon's cubicle. All were of the glass holding tank in the reinforced bunker. They were taken under various illuminations with a score of different films. In some of them the object was a black blotch. In some of them, the tank appeared empty. Simon felt worse than frustrated. Half the data they got from the object were simply impossible, and the other half so inconsistent as to be totally unreliable. One moment the energy field was magnetic, the next it wasn't. It was either visible on X rays and MRI or it wasn't. Its temperature—or rather, the reports of its temperature, since Simon no longer trusted the responses of any of his instruments—varied wildly from moment to moment, and sometimes the thing registered as having no temperature at all.

"All right," said Lazar, staring at the flying whales drifting across the computer screen. "If you're going to be this inane, I will actually have to start thinking about our little problem."

Simon scowled and waited. He doubted that anyone would come up with explanations better than his (once he arrived at them) but he couldn't accuse his partner of thinking so far. Let him try.

"The thing is, it's not a thing," Lazar said, flopping down on the lower bunk bed and staring up at the dirty mattress overhead. He hadn't shaved in four days, and the thick black stubble along his jaw gave him a piratical air. He was wearing the wild neon-pink shirt he had slept in. "By approaching it as a thing, the military got off on the wrong foot."

"What do you mean, it's not a thing?"

"Well, consider glass. A piece of glass looks solid, right? So we categorize it as a thing. But if you go to very old houses where the glass has been hanging in the windows for several hundred years, you see weep marks in it. The pane has been sagging all that time. Which means that glass is actually a liquid, only a liquid that moves very, very slowly. It takes a century for gravity to cause a window to sag by even a fraction of an inch."

"So what? You're telling me that a window is a fluid solid? Get to your point." Simon vaguely saw where Lazar was going, and the prospect of being one-upped annoyed him.

"Okay, the next example is a flying bullet. If a bullet is fired past your head, you can't actually see it. Therefore you have to take it on faith that a flying bullet is a thing. If your eyes could register movement in hundreds of miles per hour, you would begin to see the thing as a blur, but if you had incredibly fast senses, eyes that could see objects at millions of miles per hour, then what?"

"The bullet would appear to be standing still," Simon replied.

"Exactly. So take the example of the weeping glass and the example of the speeding bullet as two opposites. One is a very fast event and the other is a very slow one. But they illustrate the same principle: There is no difference between objects and events except in the eye of the beholder. QED."

"Really? What do you think you've proved?"

"That this captured light has to be slowed down. It may have some sort of form that is moving so fast, our eyes register it as just a blur. Get one of those cameras that can stop a speeding bullet or an exploding water balloon. You know what I mean—just photograph her at several thousand frames per second, then we might see what the capture really looks like. You're never going to solve what it actually is until you get a gander at her, no?"

Lazar started to make loud snoring sounds to underline that he could solve these problems in his sleep. Simon grudgingly admitted that he could no longer assume that his partner was simply a clown.

A super-high-speed stop-motion camera was transported to the base from Oak Ridge in Tennessee. Because the lenses were intended mainly for close-up work, it took a round-the-clock crew many hours to configure the mechanics right, but eventually the entire glass enclosure could be viewed. The removal of the shields went smoothly—the capture did not emit any sudden burst of power or send any bodies flying through the air. The remaining team members stood twenty meters away, operating the camera and strobe remotely.

"Okay, start your countdown," Stillano said into his controller's headset.

"Roger that." The countdown back from ten began. Simon fidgeted; Lazar stayed unusually calm, for him. When they got to three-two-one, he raised his hand suddenly, as if he had spotted a malfunction. Whatever his concerns, they came too late. The strobe fired, the rotating mirrors inside the camera whirred, taking thousands of frames per second, and then all was silence except for the buzz of the cooling fan that expended the burst of heat developed by the high-speed motor. Stillano whipped off his goggles.

"What the hell was that?" he demanded, glaring at Lazar.

"Nothing," Lazar said, but as he removed his eye gear, he wore a vacant expression.

The film was rushed off to be developed; there would be a four-hour delay before any results could be analyzed. The team scattered, leaving the machinery in place in case they had to go for

a second try. The last two left were Simon and
Lazar.

"I still don't think you're going to slow down
those pulsations enough to register visually,"
Simon said as Lazar turned to walk away. "But
if I may concede a point, we're closer to making
sense of the thing than before."

Lazar looked over his shoulder with total indifference. He didn't let loose a gibe, which actually made Simon a trifle nervous.

"I just complimented you," Simon said.

"It doesn't matter." Lazar sounded somber.

"No? Then I'll take it back, thank you very
much."

Lazar shook his head. "You don't get it. We're
on the wrong track, totally wrong."

"How do you know?" Simon asked, irked at
this new strain of arrogance.

Lazar turned away without answering, not because he had scaled up his arrogance but because
he had to. How could he tell them what had happened? He knew now beyond the shadow of a
doubt that the capture didn't like what they were
doing.

She had just told him so herself.

The Angel's Voice
You have been out of touch with God for
so long that you have developed stories and

myths about Him, like lost children remembering home. Some of these myths are beautiful, but others are destructive. Lost children can easily begin to imagine that they have been deserted. The longer they wait alone, with no father or mother to comfort them, the wilder their fears grow:

> *They fear that they did something terribly wrong to be so abandoned.*
> *They fear that their parents left them on purpose.*
> *They fear that some great punishment is all that they deserve.*

You have projected all these fears—and many more—on God. He is the father who judges you by staying away. Since all of these fears were created in your mind, we must tell you that they are untrue. Yet they are still powerful all over the world. You harbor many ancient stories about a wrathful God hurling thunder from the sky and plagues from the earth to hurt you, but the greatest pain you feel is from being left alone.

Absence is the cruelest punishment.

We angels serve to alleviate this pain. We are not absolute like God. We are not infinite and unbounded, beyond all limits of time and space. Our lives are spent in the subtle world that touches your solid, material world as lightly as a beam of light or a breath of air. Therefore we can contact you in subtle ways to let you know that you are not alone. This comfort does not reach everyone, by any means. How could it? The earth is shrouded in dark layers of disbelief. Men's minds are full of shrieking voices that cry havoc and terror all over the globe.

We never stop trying to bring the light to you, yet in this age when so many dark fears intervene between us, you must do your part. We never leave, yet you will only feel our presence if you summon us. God is summoned in deep silent meditation, but we are not so difficult to find. We respond to beauty and music; we listen for your laughter. Faith opens a channel for us, as does simple, heartfelt prayer. The innocent know us far more easily than the cynics and skeptics—this goes without saying—but in everyone there is a grain of innocence. If you can find that, we are very near.

But the most difficult time to look for us is when you are confused, chaotic, full of stress, fearful, and endangered. A turbulent mind cannot easily reach the angels. Instead of seeking our help only when you are in crisis, learn to communicate from your center of peace, your heart. We need an open channel. Our ability to help is not as limited as you might think, but neither is it all-powerful. You must meet us halfway, using your unique ability to sense the subtle world.

Angels are not brought to you by your sadness and fear. They are brought by your light.

"Gentlemen, we are running out of time," Stillano said at the next meeting.

"Technically speaking, I'm not sure that's possible. Time doesn't run, for one thing, and if it did, time would have to run out of itself. That's like saying that death is going to die, isn't it?" Simon leaned back in the lumpy office chair and leered at Stillano with the satisfaction of someone whose mind can veer from confusing truths to confusing nonsense at whim.

Lazar was hunched in the far corner of the commander's office, feigning boredom. "Perhaps time doesn't exist unless you think about it, so if you quit thinking that you are running out of time, you never will."

"Look at these," Stillano said abruptly, cutting

short the horseplay. He threw a batch of glossy photographs onto his desk.

"Already have," Simon said. They were the contact sheets for the high-speed photos taken of the capture.

"Good. Then what do they say?" the general asked.

"All right," said Simon. "My assessment is that the capture has no shape. The photos were not fast enough to stop all motion, but then, we didn't expect that. Camera technology is still limited, and a simple motion like a balloon being popped happens too fast to be stopped completely. In this case, the pulsations of light occur at many times the power of ten faster than that. I will concede that *something* shows up, however."

"Lay it on us," Lazar said ironically. "At your own speed, of course." Simon shot him a dirty look just to prove that their relationship hadn't warmed up.

"What shows up here is like a palimpsest. In case you are not familiar with that term," said Simon, "a palimpsest describes two images laid one over the other so both are visible; the word usually applies in archaeology to writing surfaces such as a parchment or stone tablet that has been used one or more times after earlier writing has been erased."

"Fascinating," said Lazar. "Simon, you see, was not actually born. He was found in some buried rubbish at a pyramid in Egypt."

"What does this have to do with our capture?" Stillano asked.

Simon lifted one of the contact sheets and pointed to a blurry image of the light, which seemed to have many overlapping shadows inside it, faint but distinct lines of shape that added together did not make any one shape.

"This thing is like a hologram, but not just a single one," he said. "Light can make definite three-dimensional shapes—that is what makes a hologram—but what if you stacked a group of holograms on top of each other? And what if they were moving and interacting all the time? The result would be a blur of light to the naked eye, yet if you used stop-motion, the nest of shapes would start to sort itself out."

"And if you had a fast enough camera, you would see just one hologram?" asked Stillano.

"Possibly," Simon said without encouragement. "Perhaps there is no one real shape. Perhaps the shifting multiple images are all there is."

Or there's one shape trying to be born, Lazar thought to himself.

Stillano stood up and faced the window, which looked out over a stretch of desert bordered a mile away by high-security fencing. "You're probably not trying very hard to help me," he said. "But in all that jargon, I think you're saying it actually is alive."

"Don't hold me to that," Simon cautioned. "Holograms aren't alive, and if we rely on normal logic, creatures can't be alive if their only substance is light. Otherwise we would have to say that the sun is alive."

"Maybe it is," Lazar offered. The other two men looked over at him. He had acquired the reputation of being the useful madman, and he liked it that way. "Our captive virgin, I think she's a she, and she likes Simon. That's why she allowed herself to be captured and brought over here. Just for him." Lazar's lanky hair looked particularly greasy that morning; he no doubt kept it as skanky as possible just to annoy the military, thought Simon.

"Make your point or get out," Stillano said impatiently.

"Okey-dokey. My point is that this light looks like a hologram, but it isn't one. The vibrations that we've slowed down to the point of making them intelligible are messages."

"It's trying to talk to us?" said Stillano, becoming alert for the first time after days of pointless work that came to nothing.

Lazar looked crafty. "Maybe it's painting pictures. These shapes may not be a language as we know it, they could be more like the images that race through our minds. Those make sense without being words, so these might make sense, too."

With unwonted force Simon pounded his fist on the desk. "Hold on. Before you kiss each other in congratulation, what do we actually have? A few shadowy squiggles on photographic emulsion, nothing more."

"So you think it's ridiculous? You're wrong," said Lazar, staring intently at Stillano to see the general's reaction. "Those first two soldiers that you found wandering around in Kosovo were in a state of religious hysteria, and shortly thereafter other technicians who came near the light exhibited psychological changes. Why isn't that happening now? The capture first tried to speak to those GIs, but they got fried. The vibration was too intense, so she lowered the vibes, but still they were too much for humans; they threw off our brains and scrambled the intended communication. What would you do under those circumstances?"

"Go home?" said Simon. "Or am I just projecting?"

Lazar ignored him. "You would lay back and reflect for a while on what went wrong. Then you would gradually test out new ways of getting your message across. You've already seen that this thing isn't giving off nearly the same intensity of light as it did at first—it's not melting walls anymore, and it's not driving anyone nuts."

"You're a brilliant son of a bitch, aren't you?" Stillano said with grudging admiration.

"He's a legend in his own mind," said Simon, who wanted to tune out this nonsensical speculation. After five days on the base, he wondered when he'd last slept and how reliable anyone's mind could be under these conditions. Lazar had taken to sitting in the bunker simply staring at the thing for hours on end. It was probably about as useful as navel-gazing and led to just as fantastic delusions.

"Simon's playing dog in the manger," Lazar said smoothly. "But he does manage at odd moments to transmit coherent thought in my direction, and during one of our brainstorming sessions he admitted that we should consider the possibility that our capture wants to communicate with us."

"Not quite accurate, old boy," Simon said sarcastically. "I proposed that the signals might not be completely random. Pulsars are high-energy stellar bodies whose emissions reach us in regular bursts; that makes them orderly but not alive."

Stillano threw up his hands. "Truce, gentlemen, truce. We're getting sidetracked."

Lazar was too fired up for a truce. "Listen, both of you—if the capture is trying to adjust itself to our brains, what is holding it up? Look at these photos. It's still working on frequencies that are too fast for us; it hasn't figured that out yet. So what should we do? We need to help it, and I have been."

Stillano looked startled. "How?"

"By spending time near it and thinking, or to be more precise, seeing images in my mind. I daydream. If she can figure out that I am trying to show her how we process images, maybe she will begin to imitate me, and then there might be communication."

"I see." The look on Stillano's face was curious, but more than that, Simon was certain that the military had its own agenda, and the general was trying to calculate, without giving it away, how the army's scenario jibed with the one just proposed by Lazar.

"All right," Stillano said. "You can continue as you have been."

"Illiterate Balkan peasants are keeping a vigil, why not our friend Lazar?" Simon remarked. A few minutes later he found himself walking down the gray hall back toward their workstation. "So you got that meeting to turn out the way you wanted," he said. Lazar nodded. "But you haven't exactly shared your motive with me.

I know you couldn't care two bits about helping these Army types. So what's in this for you?"

"You really want to know, chappie?" asked Lazar, lapsing back into his goofball persona.

"Yeah, I guess I do."

"Then ask yourself two things. Why would a smart guy like me waste time on a rickety hypothesis that a moron could disprove, present company excepted? But more importantly, and I hope you are listening, simple Simon, why do I keep referring to a cloudy ball of light as *she*?"

The Angel's Voice

Did we tell you the one thing that will keep us silent forever? Perhaps we should, so you will know to be on your guard.

It is doubt.

Those who banish doubt have opened the door to angels.

Ford Marvell had written so rapturously about Arielle Artaud in his diary that the real Michael had the feeling he already knew her. She was in her eighties, born in Paris, and had been an internationally renowned occultist for the last half century—if *infamous* wasn't a better word. Now she resided in a lavish Westchester mansion, where common mortals were allowed only for her frequent "angelic retreats." According to his diary, Marvell had attended seven of these long weekends in the past year. So visiting Mme. Artaud was the next step in solving the mystery.

On the long drive south, Michael thought more about angels. In particular he thought about Marvell's belief that they were near. Was that simply a banal thought, or had a dying man felt desperately compelled to write these words in the hope that another meaning would be understood from them? What did Michael know about angels? He knew that the word in Greek, *angelos,* means messenger. The message could be as familiar as the shepherds being told of baby Jesus' birth, or as little known (to Christians) as Gabriel delivering the Koran to the prophet Muhammad. In church doctrine angels were direct emanations of God, sexless beings created before Adam and Eve—in the Kabbalah they were considered the firstborn of God.

The dictionary says that angels, although superior to man in strength and wisdom, are actually the lowest creatures in the celestial hierarchy, which runs as follows: angels, archangels, principalities, powers, virtues, dominions, thrones, cherubim, and seraphim. These nine levels had evolved from mystical Judaism into medieval Christianity, and during that time the word *angel* had remained more or less intact as it was passed from Greek to Latin to Old French, then

Old English, Middle English, and eventually our present language.

Angels lack the capacity for sin. They are identified with, but not restricted to, the great Western monotheisms: Judaism, Christianity, and Islam. Beyond these meager facts, Michael really knew very little. Like most modern people, he lumped the study of angels in with medievalism, a bare notch higher in credibility than alchemy.

Michael found Madame Artaud's place easily. Neither a robber baron's castle nor an overgrown bungalow, the house called Hallows was an uncompromising square stone block built in the second half of the nineteenth century. It was set in the middle of what Michael estimated to be ten acres, heavily landscaped with lilac and wisteria, and it faced directly upon the Hudson. As befitted the residence of someone who presided over angelic retreat weekends, there was plenty of parking. At the moment no one else seemed to be there.

The weather had changed. What had been a bright spring day up in Columbia was dark and gray down in Westchester. The air held the candy scent of purple wisteria, cut through with the sharper, sweeter overlay of lilac. Michael started walking toward the house, already putting out his antennae for fraud.

The front door was six-paneled old oak, possessed of a brass door knocker in the shape of a cherub. Before he could use it, however, the door opened.

"Hello," Michael said. "I'm—"

"I know who you are. Now that we've established that, will you please go away?"

"Madame Artaud?" Michael stammered.

The old woman who stood in the doorway was almost childlike in stature. She had alert dark eyes and translucent skin. Her face had a grave agelessness to it, its shock of thick white hair swirled atop the head in a braided rope.

"Madame Artaud?" Michael repeated when she didn't respond the first time.

"You want to tell me about your problems, yes? Why do people always double their reasons for staying when you ask them to go?" The old lady turned back into the house but left the door pointedly open. Taking this as some sort of reverse come-on, Michael stepped inside. Arielle Artaud was sweeping toward a formal parlor beyond the dark foyer, her white hair bobbing like a lantern over her black dress.

"You are already an immense trouble to me, *mon cher*," she said cuttingly.

"I don't mean to be."

"Who does, except those lost souls who work for the tax bureau?" By this time the old lady had gestured to a low sateen love seat; she herself sat on an ottoman, her back proudly upright. Michael perched himself uneasily on the spindly furniture and leaned forward.

"You apparently know who I am. I expected as much," he said.

"Liar. Or should I say flatterer?" Despite her words, Madame seemed pleased; Michael had guessed that her weak point might be flattery, which has the peculiar ability to work even when your quarry knows it is being used. "This is a murder case, do you know that, too?" he asked.

"What idiot says that?" The old lady indulged in her first secret smile. "In my youth I was given a great gift, that of choosing to become a conduit between the world we know and that world which we cannot imagine. I am not a spiritualist. I have no patience with trivial notions of channeling the departed. Just because someone is dead doesn't mean they are worth talking to."

"You didn't answer my question, madame," Michael said after this practiced witticism wound down.

"Maybe you stated it too crudely," she retorted.

"It sounded pretty straightforward to me. A mysterious death brings me here. I can't apologize for asking you to be who you claim to be." The old lady now looked so annoyed that Michael half expected her to trade in her delicate

French accent for a Bronx bray, but that part at least seemed genuine.

"Will you take some refreshment, Mr. Aulden?" she asked almost in a whisper. It was a subtle return of service, since he distinctly remembered not telling her his name. Michael decided to let her have it her own way.

"Coffee, please," he said gloomily.

"A good choice. On a gray day such as this I do not feel that lemonade is suitable, and it is far too early for sherry." She rang a bellpull and turned back to him; either this was a prearranged signal or the whole house was psychic, because in half a minute a maid silently produced a porcelain cup of very good coffee. Michael sipped it and waited.

"I said you have been a great deal of trouble to me already," Arielle Artaud reminded him. "But I accept you as a warrior of the light, if that concerns you. I have no time for thrill-seekers. That is worse than a foolish waste of time. It is more dangerous than the people can easily comprehend. The innocent are easily fooled . . . and then destroyed."

"Which is what happened to Ford Marvell? Why didn't you stop him?" Michael asked, suddenly interested.

"You jump ahead of me, monsieur, you jump ahead," she protested.

"At least tell me what he was dabbling in that was so dangerous."

"Ah!" She let forth the single syllable as if it said volumes. Michael gritted his teeth. The problem with self-created dramas is that when you don't fall for them, they can be incredibly frustrating.

"I understand that you conduct angelic retreats here. Is that how Marvell began, before he was led astray?" Michael said carefully.

"Do not represent yourself in court," she said with a thin smile. "You are too obvious about leading the witness." Michael slumped back in his seat. She really was an impossible old control freak.

Madame Artaud said, "My particular gift is to see and speak with angels. Please don't attempt to frame a tactful reply. I am not interested in soliciting your beliefs. Let me offer you a quotation: 'Man is neither an angel nor a beast—the unfortunate thing is that he who would act like an angel winds up turning into a beast.' I have translated it for you from Pascal, the French philosopher.

"I do not try to turn myself into an angel, and I warn those who are tempted to that they will run afoul of their own inner beast. Marvell was not a good listener—few writers are. He didn't come to me to learn what I could teach."

"Only to pump something out of you?" Michael guessed. Arielle nodded. "If so, why didn't your psychic powers tell you to send him away the moment he appeared on your doorstep?"

She arched a thin plucked eyebrow. "My angels don't write advice columns."

"I see."

She was right to rebuke him, he realized—after all, Marvell had died of natural causes, whatever the police were misled into thinking. It was doubtful that sending him away would have changed much.

"There are those who are ready to believe," she went on. "Their angels make them known to me. Mr. Marvell's whole focus of existence was changing. He told me that he was filled with a desire to understand his purpose here on earth. At first, matters proceeded as I have seen them go many times. He passed from enthusiasm to doubt, then to confusion. It is a gradual process to gain full acceptance of the reality of the light; a mature understanding is not gained without confronting your own darkness."

"So it's possible to fail," remarked Michael.

"Of course—that is why we all need guides. Mr. Marvell didn't like the idea of guides, just as he didn't like the difficult terrain of the soul. He preferred being a tourist on his own. The results were foreseeable After a few months he grew troubled and despairing, as if he had opened a gateway of hope, only to have it slam shut in his face.

"Perhaps you do not understand this, monsieur, but it is impossible to despair once one has spoken with angels. They are the living embodiment of hope, and they love us immeasurably. When you are so loved, how can you possibly give in to the darkness? I do not know precisely what happened to Mr. Marvell. My guides said that this was not for me to see. I only know that he is dead now, and that his death may have import to those he has left behind."

Michael listened carefully and tried to concentrate on what Madame Artaud was saying. "Do you think that Marvell had genuine experience of angels?" he asked.

"This was a peculiar case. He had made a substantial fortune writing spiritual books, but he felt vaguely guilty, insecure, rootless in the face of a baffling world. Therefore an intervention occurred, of the sort I have seen take place many times."

"What kind of intervention?" asked Michael.

She smiled shrewdly. "Ah, do you think I give away all my secrets just because I am sitting in the parlor over coffee?" He had the feeling she wasn't being coy. Madame Artaud lived in a world inhabited by many levels of creatures that ordinary people would consider mystical or imaginary. Her only advantage over the skeptics was her ability to see these levels. Therefore she would have good reason to guard this advantage and to dole out access to her world very sparingly, one sugar cube at a time.

She said, "The angelic message is always the same: *Look, look, look!* We try to look with the eyes of the body, but that is not what we should use when we encounter angels. The messages pouring down on us are trying to open a different pair of eyes, the eyes of the spirit."

Michael was aware that the atmosphere around Madame Artaud had changed. She wasn't weaving a cheap spell anymore.

"Only in this present age is it at last possible that we will throw off the blinders and see these glorious creatures for what they truly are, unfettered by doctrine, creed, and superstition. But there are many misunderstandings to correct before that is possible.

"People believe, for example, that angels are instantly recognizable—insipid astral hippies with silly bird's wings stuck to their shoulders. They are not. Their shape depends on their function, and their function depends on the message assigned to them by God, however you choose to conceive of Him. There are many stories of people visited by angels who did not realize what had come to them until their sublime visitor had departed.

"People also mistake that angels are always good. This is true, but it is God's goodness, not man's. Angels accompany death, for instance. God has used them to wreak destruction upon the earth many times in the holy books. It was an angel who slew the firstborn of Egypt to secure the release of the Israelites from bondage, and an angel who drove Adam and Eve from Paradise. In other words, angels are always good, even if we cannot perceive that—with one exception. Most cultures also recognize dark or fallen angels as well, who are as powerful as the angels of light but who act for evil."

Michael ventured a theory. "Maybe Marvell got overwhelmed by that kind. Or maybe he was seeking them to begin with."

The old French lady shrugged. "Of such creatures I cannot speak. I have never seen them."

She stood up to indicate that the audience was over. Her parting words were ambiguous: "Perhaps Marvell despaired because he could not speak with angels, but I do not believe that this was the case. I believe that he did speak with them, and that somehow he fell from joy. Maybe you can uncover the reason."

"Let's hope so."

In two minutes the heavy door closed behind him. Michael stepped out into the landscape, noticing that it was beginning to be drenched with rain.

4
Angels Unawares

Upriver there was no cooling rain, and Susan had fallen asleep on her bed in a light sweat. It made her grateful to doze off with her cheek buried in a soft worn pillow. She was no archrationalist, but too much had assaulted her mind that day. She hoped that sleep would ease a little of the pang and slow down the grinding wheels of obsession. She had no idea when she fell asleep, or when her dream began.

Her name was Suze. She was seven years old, and she was running away from home. The reason was forgotten, but she was outraged beyond her ability to tolerate it.

Her father must have spanked her, and since he was a beloved father who had never raised a hand before, it shocked her as if she were an animal and no longer his daughter. She was running from the knowledge that he would never be a benign household god again in her eyes.

They lived near a tract of undeveloped land that was heavily wooded. She climbed out her window and headed for her green sanctuary, running with tears still damp on her cheeks. She had been warned repeatedly against going in there— every summer there were rumors of bears coming down from the hills—but nothing was more terrifying than the shock of betrayal. Anyway, her instincts made her run as much as anything, to wear out her rage. She pushed through brush and brambles, splashed through shallow streams, heading nowhere but away, too intent even to cry after a while.

As darkness began to fall, she was worn out enough to feel better, so she decided to turn back. It took almost an hour to realize that she was lost, and an hour after that she could not even see the woods surrounding her anymore. Running away had been a kind of salvation, but salvation had come too late to do her any good. She was wandering in pitch-darkness, and no one knew she was there. Her parents only knew she was gone from her room, that she'd disobeyed them once more, but it wouldn't matter because they'd never find her.

"I want to go home," Suze whispered, testing out the pleas of panic. Those kinds of pleas don't work unless there is someone to hear them. The woods that had seemed so tame by light took on a weird life, as if half-remembered monsters fed there. She could hear creeping things in the underbrush, and as she sat, shivering, a barn owl swooped down from a tree and pounced on something that squealed and struggled ten feet from her.

Whimpering uncontrollably, she crawled back into the thick brush she'd burrowed through earlier and curled herself up as small as she could. There was no difference between being alone and being unloved. It was child's logic and crystal clear: Because no one had come for her, no one would love her ever again.

Susan watched herself, the child she had been, going through birth. She was birthing a new feeling, the stranded desperation that adults imagine is theirs alone.

"Suzy? Suze?" a strange man's voice called.

Suddenly there was a bright light shining in her face. She hesitated a second before crawling out of her hiding place, too young to be afraid of anyone who knew her name. She kept her eyes on the light, and as soon as he saw her in the tangled brush, the stranger turned the light off so it wouldn't dazzle her.

The moon had risen, and she could see the stranger even without the light. He was no one she knew, but she walked toward him trustingly, and he reached down to pick her up. She nestled into his shoulder, her earlier grief forgotten.

When she woke up, she was in her own bed, dressed in her favorite Flintstones pajamas. It was a school day, and as she hurried to get ready in time to meet the bus, she waited for her mother to mention how she'd run away. If her father scolded her again, she vowed she would endure her punishment meekly.

But breakfast was the usual quiet ritual. Neither of her parents mentioned the incident. It was several days before Susan realized they never would, and some years passed before the strangeness and importance of the event really came home to her. She didn't have another fight as severe as that one with her father until she was in her late teens, and by then she was growing into her anger, old enough to use it like a weapon that she wanted to master, like a throwing knife. And one essential question never occurred to her.

For all these years, why had she never asked who the stranger was who saved her?

The Angel's Voice

Children want love and protection, and you continue to want those things from God. Angels are assigned to protect you. (Love is part of our nature, so we do not need that assignment.) We cannot protect you by materializing and fighting for you. We protect through our influence in your minds. When you are told to "listen to your better angels," it is your own thinking and feeling that you must turn to.

The angelic influence doesn't ask you to be good. Good is a choice based on your morality. We are beyond morality. We ask you to be aware, and the more aware you are, the easier it is for goodness to manifest. So in this way does love and truth manifest. These aren't qualities you can fight to win. Struggle makes life stiff and strained, and where there is strain, how can love exist? Love is delicate, and so is truth. If you strain to love someone whom you actually dislike, the wrong vibration is sent out. Because you are attuned to the subtle level (even when you rationally don't even believe in such a world), you can sense when love or truth or trust are present.

We protect you by sharpening your subtle senses. What you call your "gut feeling" is very crude, even though it can be reliable. A subtle feeling isn't crude. It allows you to make crucial decisions before any danger or crisis appears. True certainty about who you are is the best sign that you are attuned.

No one has to be religious to be aware. The more aware you are, the more quickly you will acknowledge our existence and the easier it will be for you to ask our help.

Guardian angels are often depicted with a sword, as if we fight like warriors on your behalf. The sword is a symbol, however; it stands for keen attention. When the sword of our mind is sharpened, you will know what to do and when to do it in any situation. What better protection can you possibly desire? Our deepest wish is to clear the dullness from your mind and sharpen the edge of your attention.

When Susan walked downstairs again, she had a premonition of trouble. She spotted flashing lights and went onto the front porch. The slanting light of early evening shoved through the high privet that screened the Auldens' property. Michael was on the steps, dressed in khakis and a camp shirt. His face wore the set expression for when he was very angry. A stir from back inside the house made her aware that men were moving around inside, nosing into dark corners.

"What's going on?" Her question came out with forced casualness. Michael turned around from talking to a man in plain clothes.

"Nothing much," he answered in the same

tone. "Peabody and Sherman are searching the house for murdered brides—and there's a Detective Disney here who wants to talk to us."

She regarded the middle-aged man in a rumpled suit who nodded stiffly to her. With a weary gesture he flashed a gold badge for an instant before it was withdrawn. "I'm Lieutenant Disney, Columbia County Sheriff's Department. Are you Susan Aulden?" So Michael wasn't being sarcastic.

"Yes," she said.

"Mind telling me where you were just now?"

"Why should I?"

"Can you account for your husband's whereabouts earlier today?" Disney continued in the same staccato fashion.

"Maybe, once you tell me what this is all about first," Susan shot back.

"Do you know a woman named Carol Hardin?" the detective persisted. Susan shook her head, but Michael hesitated for a second. "She's a patient of mine. She's a diabetic, on insulin. Has something happened to her?"

"You might say that," Disney responded, deadpan. "She was found dead two hours ago."

"In an insulin coma? Did she overdose on her medication?" Michael started running through probable causes of death. Long-term diabetics were exceptionally vulnerable to stroke and heart attacks. She could have forgotten to take her insulin and gone into acidosis, with fatal results.

Disney ignored Susan and concentrated on Michael. "Where were you today between noon and approximately two o'clock?"

"In jail, or just getting out. You didn't know that already?" Michael could tell where this was going, but he took the chance that the police were fishing. "Are you connecting me with Carol Hardin's death? As I said, she was just a patient."

"Do you care to make a statement about her, Doctor?"

"No. Aren't you required to assume that I'm innocent of any crime, particularly one you haven't informed me about, until I am tried and convicted?"

"You talk like a lawyer," Disney said sullenly. "Does the phrase 'the angel is near' mean anything to you?"

"No."

"Why don't you stop jerking my husband around asking stupid questions?" Susan said in a brittle voice. Michael had walked up the porch steps and put his hand on her arm. The muscles beneath his touch went rigid. "You're basically saying that Carol Hardin was killed, right?"

The detective gave Michael a warning. "Come down here away from your house or I'll be forced to cuff you." But Susan's mind had drifted from all of it. She could only feel one sensation, the grip of Michael's hand on her arm, and it was not his touch. Suddenly she knew that, as certainly as she knew anything.

At this point the two deputies came out of the house. Deputy Sherman stared at Michael. "I guess we've got everything we need," he told Disney. The deputy was holding a large plastic trash bag with C.C.S.D stenciled on the side in blurred yellow paint. The detective nodded and turned his attention back to Michael.

"Carol Hardin was killed just after lunch or in that vicinity. I'm afraid we're going to have to take you in for questioning, Doctor."

Susan would wonder afterward if her childhood dream or Rakhel's little visit was a practice round for that moment, because despite the new threat looming over Michael, she felt eerily detached. Standing on the top step peering down on the three law officers in the dying twilight, she couldn't shake the certainty that they were unreal. Many people report such feelings in a crisis. Passengers in plane crashes suffer delayed shock and all manner of post-traumatic symptoms, yet in the violence of the crash itself, they may report feelings of complete detachment, as if the event is happening to someone else.

But Susan was diving deeper into herself than that. It was as if she had retreated to an island untouched by the scene she was observing. It was an island in the sea of tranquillity, and calmness brushed her cheek like the coolness of a bird's wing; if she hadn't kept hearing the faint sound of a pulse in her ear, she might not have bothered to engage with anything outside herself.

From far away she heard Michael demand, "Do you have a warrant to search my house? And you better have another one if you intend to carry me in."

Disney produced two folded documents from his jacket. "You can read this if you want, but it's authentic, don't worry about that."

Michael shook his head. Viewing him from the back, Susan couldn't read his face, but she felt a wave of discouragement moving toward her; it was even more clear than if he had said the words, *It's hopeless.* Her husband continued to argue halfheartedly with the detective. In that last minute before they would haul him away Susan realized with utter clarity that everything was wrong.

Without a word she turned on her heels and went back into the house. She knew that no one would follow her. The police had thoroughly ransacked everything. She stepped over scattered papers, dumped drawers, a pile of clothing pulled out of the hall closet—none of this affected her, merely registering as images on the back of her eye. Inside she was still tranquil, except that added to the cool calmness was a small seed of another feeling. When people dream, the flow of images moves as if by itself; we are not in control, and very often the strongest emotions of fear and terror, which we want to escape with all our being, control us. But sometimes there is a small pinpoint of awareness that doesn't surrender to the dream, and as long as it exists, fixed like the glint of a diamond in the midst of the flowing dream images, we are in control. This pinpoint is the access to power, even though it is very faint and in normal life rarely touched on.

Susan was right there, touching it and not letting it fade away.

The pinpoint of power felt incredibly vital; it was the most alive thing about her, despite the fact that it held very still. She realized that at any moment control could be lost—with a burst of laughter, a whoop of sheer exhilaration, a sob of relief that after all this time—a time measured more in centuries than in years—she had found this infinitesimal thing once again. Because amid everything else she was now certain of, this was also a certainty.

Reaching the back of the house, she spotted the kitchen door and headed toward it, not walking mechanically like a robot but not pausing or breaking her step, either. Her goal was the old tin-roofed barn in the back, converted before they arrived into a garage. She had a slight fright when she imagined that the cat, dozing on the porch in the long slumber of old cats, would wake up and jump on her, but this slight pang of fear lasted only a second. What made it go away was her realization, very new yet very old, that this wasn't a trance; she wasn't in danger of waking up. What exactly it was, however, she couldn't say, not yet. The whole experience was too new.

Stepping outside, she only had a scant thirty feet to cover in order to reach the open door of the barn, where her old gray Jeep, veteran of many desert travels in the Mideast, stood in shadow. Unexpectedly the last thirty feet were incredibly hard to cross, because Susan chanced to look up. The canopy of the sky had turned a deeper blue streaked with orange and gray as the last of the sun tinted it. It wasn't the color that stopped her in her tracks but something incredible and unexpected. The sky was no longer flat; it soared away from her eyes, soft and deep, as if pulling her toward a vanishing point far, far away. Her body remained frozen in midstep, but her vision, as if pulled by an irresistible force, was sucked into the living beauty of the sky. The process didn't take time. Duration was sucked

out of her, too, as if seconds and minutes tele-
scoped noiselessly out into space.

Why the siren song of the sky didn't trap her
forever is a mystery. Involuntarily her eyes
glanced back at the ground beneath her feet, and
in that instant she was walking again. She made
it to the Jeep, climbed in, and started the engine.
Backing out, she steered around the house, following a narrow lane of driveway overhung with
a tall lilac hedge. She wouldn't be able to see
the front yard until the very end of this alley.
The faintest doubt tried to be born in her mind;
she felt like laughing and it skulked away.

Around the corner she saw that the remaining
stretch of driveway, perhaps a hundred feet to the
main road, was open. The sheriff's cars that had
blocked the way before were now pulled off on
the grass. She felt an inner thrill at this but tried
to control it. Michael was surrounded by the detective and the two deputies. They had turned
him around and were about to place cuffs on his
hands. His head was bowed.

She drove past the group without stopping. No
one looked at her or even noticed the Jeep. There
was a stillness inside her that the outer world
seemed to match. No breeze, just the faint falling
light and the cluster of men, nobody moving.
Was she the bandit queen rescuing her lover from
the villains? No, it didn't work that way. Without

wasted gestures, Susan stepped on the gas lightly, and she heard the crunch of gravel under the tires as the car moved down the drive. Lot's wife had looked back and turned into a pillar of salt. Susan decided not to peek into the rearview mirror. She turned onto the main road and resisted the urge to step on it. Five seconds, ten seconds, thirty seconds. No one followed.

Without leaving the Hudson Valley, the real Michael found a dilapidated log-cabin motel on the back roads, long ago stranded after the highway cut a route ten miles away. No one was on duty at the desk, but after he rang the bell a few times a raggedy woman pulled herself away from the TV in the back room and signed him in. The beds were as squishy as old fallen apples and sagged alarmingly, but it didn't matter. The pinpoint of sharp attention that had kept Michael glued in the present moment evaporated, almost with an audible whoosh. As a curtain fell over his awareness, his eyes were dazzled for a second by a flurry of white sparkles, and it was over. He was an ordinary man again, deserting his wife and home for some reason that was much too hard to think about.

He drew a moth-eaten coverlet over himself and fell asleep with his clothes on. Merciful sleep would have lasted at least eight hours; he woke up with a start after two, then walked outside. He still felt keyed up and wanted the cleansing smell of hemlock woods in his nose instead of the room's sickly aroma of mildew.

"Congratulations." The voice came from behind him as he happened onto a tanbark trail behind the cabin. Michael turned around.

"For what? Being stupid enough to step into a trap?"

He assumed that the voice belonged to Rakhel, so seeing her tiny form emerging from the hemlock shadows, without preface or explanation, didn't shock him. He hadn't seen her in almost two years, not since she had fought for him and beside him in Syria. It would be fruitless to ask where she had been. Her kind didn't deal in terms like where, when, how, or why. She was simply back again, in her odd persona that was a cross between Gandalf and Golda Meir.

"You're saying I did something good? If you ask me, I'm stumbling like a blind idiot," Michael said.

"No, you saw a chance not to be trapped, not to buy into Marvell's murder, and you escaped— that is tremendous."

"I didn't do anything. I split, and then the other me split."

"Don't make fun. The two of you were blended but always separate. Haven't you heard of your better self and your worse self? I'm talking to the better self."

"So to you it's that simple?"

Rakhel shrugged. "Not just to me. It *is* that simple. Believe me, if you had felt even the tiniest hidden guilt over this, you would never have gotten out." It wasn't the first time that Michael had heard such strange arguments—Rakhel thrived on overturning his usual way of thinking—but he must have looked blank. Rakhel said impatiently, "I congratulated you because you saw an opening to shape your reality, and you took it. That is what we call a test. It's like jumping through a hole in a net. The test is finding the hole, *nu*? Ordinary reality is very convincing. I've known people who believed in it long after they stopped believing in sawing a woman in half. Their belief hypnotizes them, but reality has holes in it. No one looks for them, or very few, and then what? The same old thing—everyone remains trapped."

"So Marvell's death wasn't just a setup?" asked Michael.

"No, you walked in with your eyes open. You are one of the rare ones. You have an itch to get out."

"Great. And did you have to go to this extreme to show me that?"

"Me? We haven't settled yet who or what is

responsible for these events, have we?" she said.

All at once Michael became aware that he was deeply afraid and paranoid; he wanted to erupt in a way that his insides wouldn't let him do. "I'm like a marble being pushed around in your cosmic game of Chinese checkers," he said with deceptive calmness.

"It must feel that way," Rakhel admitted. "Shall we set aside a few moments while I display some sympathy?"

"Don't bother."

"Your choice to start participating is voluntary, you know," Rakhel said.

"Meaning what?"

"You didn't see yourself as ready to be tested, and so you needed a push. That charming scene in Marvell's study worked. You jumped out of an impossible situation, and in so doing, you jumped out of yourself."

"That can't happen."

"You're going to argue? It did happen. I can tell you how later, when we have more time. Let's just say for now that the part of you that couldn't jump is walking around in the old situation. He's the one they arrested."

Without thinking about it, they were no longer standing nose to nose but had begun to walk into the dark hemlock woods. Michael felt a sudden pang when he thought of Susan.

Rakhel held her hand up. "Wait," she admonished.

"For what?"

"I can feel that you want to flare up at me. Try to postpone your anger if you can."

"Maybe you deserve it. Have you ever thought of that?" he asked.

"For what reason—because I came to show you the truth?" Rakhel declared. "You are not detached right now, you are reacting to events that you know are unreal."

His mind began to form images of his wife and *that man*. To hell with detachment.

"Unreality can hurt," Michael protested. "And when it hurts, people react—*I* react. I feel like exploding, and I'm this close to smashing whoever's in the way." Michael doubled his fist, but it was no good. His righteous anger was sounding hollow; he could not work up a head of steam as much as he wanted to. Rakhel watched him carefully, as if seeing another creature inside Michael's body or somewhere a few inches behind it.

"Thank you," she said mildly. "That's better. You are offended by unreality, and that is pointless. A day will come when being offended will no longer be such an automatic reaction. It is a waste of energy that you use to protect yourself."

"Why do I need protecting?"

"Because all people think they do. You all walk on the ground, feeling it solid beneath your feet, yet inside there is another image that haunts you: You are suspended in midair with nothing around you. You float without falling, but at any instant you may, for you feel nothing supporting you. So to smother that fear, you create a sense of support. You want someone to hold and love you, you want fantasies of money and power, or you even go to the trouble of piling up money and power. You crave status, and go to sleep at night dreaming of winding up on top of the heap. It is all so you will feel support from something outside yourself. That's also the reason you want to get angry with me. I am not taking away your support, but you think I am."

Michael felt slightly dazed; he felt as if Rakhel were drawing him into a world that forgot to put up border signs, so you never knew when exactly you had left terra firma behind. This was the country that had always intrigued him, so he couldn't say that he was being kidnapped. Yet he longed suddenly just to be normal again, and he couldn't lose Susan.

"Maybe I want to forget you and others like you," he said tightly.

"Ha! So now I'm a wicked fairy and you are a lost prince I am snatching back to fairyland?" Rakhel snorted. "You were not forced to either forget or remember me. Leaving you to yourself was the kindest way to deal with you." This last remark was said in almost a honeyed tone. Rakhel was making an effort at diplomacy; Michael didn't feel it suited her very well.

"So if the police decide it's me they want," he said, "you'll save me and I can go home again?"

"No one can save anybody, my dear, but that isn't what you mean, is it? You want to know how you can stop all this bizarre business. And you want to rescue your wife, no? Believe me, many have sacrificed their lives in similar situations, getting tied up trying to rescue someone they couldn't bear to leave behind."

"Stop it. You're hitting me with riddles while you aren't lifting a finger to help innocent people."

Rakhel shook her head. "That isn't what this is about."

"Then tell me what it is about," he demanded

"I've been trying to. Believe me, there hasn't been a moment when I haven't been trying to tell you everything." Rakhel stared far away into the woods. Its emptiness seemed to speak to her.

"Keep going," she said. "You have to have another peek into Rhineford Marvell's mind."

"I'm not returning to his house," Michael said. "I'm sure it's sealed off by now, or if not, what more can I expect to find?"

Rakhel shook her head. "No, don't go back there. The trail leads forward; for the moment no one knows why you are twisted up in Marvell's obsession, but his death landed on you, so that means you need something from it. Funny logic, no? But the only logic we have."

Michael stared at the ground glumly, suddenly feeling that a wave of exhaustion would topple him over. Rakhel left unnoticed, retreating maybe into the woods, maybe back to where she came from. If it was fairyland, the other fairies must be pretty damned scary.

Susan woke up in the motel with a thick head and a feeling of being sick. She got up, padded softly to the bathroom, and stood looking at the yellowed cracked sink. She splashed water on her face—it came ice-cold out of the tap. When she stood up, a flutter of nausea spread from her stomach and lodged in her throat. She muttered some swear words into the mirror.

What is happening to me?

Her wonderful sense of complete clarity had vanished overnight, leaving behind a strange toxic residue. Being deprived of ordinary reality struck a deep blow somewhere in her body, like seasickness. She didn't feel motivated anymore.

It was a critical moment. She could have drowned in unreality, simply letting herself fall apart. But when she walked to the window, Susan's heart skipped a beat. She saw a black Saab in the dirt parking lot. Hd it been there when she pulled into the old log-cabin motel after midnight? She couldn't remember. But that wasn't the point, was it? It had to be Michael. There was no other choice. Michael would be there because she had to have him; otherwise she would sink.

Susan threw on her jeans and thin cotton top, tying her sweater around her waist. As she walked outside, the air felt cool from the night before, but the summer sun had already made the black Saab hot when she ran her fingers along one door panel. She kept walking, heading for the main cabin that served as reception area and dining room. Her sense of conviction wavered at the door—with her hand on the knob, she felt for an instant that this was totally crazy.

But she went in anyway, turned left without answering the clerk's breezy "Good mornin', miss," and entered the dining room.

Michael looked up from his plate of eggs and bacon. At first his face was blank; he just faintly nodded to signal her to come over. Now her heart was in her throat, but Susan wouldn't falter, not this close. She sat down in a rickety ladder-back chair opposite him.

"Well," he said, and he permitted himself a

wide, then wider smile. "Welcome to wonderland."

The Angel's Voice

If doubt keeps us away, what brings us near is just as simple. You must not look for angels, only look at yourself. See yourself in the light. This will summon us. We have no other substance but the light of God, and neither do you. There is no difference between you and everything spiritual except a tiny shift in the light. The fact that your body seems solid is unimportant.

Imagine that you are sitting in a room with a ticking grandfather clock. You are reading a book, and suddenly you realize that you haven't heard the clock. Certainly the sound reached you. The vibrating air caused your eardrums to respond, and they in turn sent signals to your brain. Everything was in place mechanically, and yet you didn't hear the clock. This is because your mind was not engaged. And yet that alone isn't enough, either. Until your soul notices something, it doesn't exist. Mind, brain, body, the outside world—all these serve the soul. Light must be sent into the world for it to be real.

Angels help to move these messages and

bring them to your attention. We are like the unheard clock. You may walk this earth in certainty that we do not exist, but the gap is in yourself. You are not yet engaged with us. To be engaged, you must commit your mind to receiving the messages of the soul, and you must commit your heart to feeling them.

Every day we hint at the hidden meaning behind all events. A clock can be heard once you tune in to the physical, but we are heard only when you see beyond the physical. This is not an occult procedure. Instead, you begin with the other simple but invisible things that you know to exist: beauty, truth, love. Keep these before you and resist the dark shadows that hide them. Know that no one is a victim, that all people walk through a mirage of events that exist only to bring their attention back to the light. No one is left out of God's grace, for since every person is light and only light, how could anyone be left out? For all His power, God could not do this, and does not want to. The game is much more subtle, a game of hide-and-seek. You are hidden from your own light, and therefore God appears to be hiding Himself from you. Follow every clue, remain loyal to one

intention—bringing more and more light
into your awareness—and the result is inevitable. You will see us and the all-
embracing light that we serve.

Soon they were in her Jeep, turning onto the
main highway, when Michael told Susan everything. It was hard for her to listen. A sense of
the bizarre kept returning to her, like morning
sickness, at unexpected moments. She hadn't
eaten a thing at the motel and even felt nauseous
watching Michael slice his fork through his fried
eggs over easy.

"So there is another you that was left behind?"
she said. "How strange. Is there another me?"

"No, I don't think so," said Michael.

"But if you could separate like that, how do
you even know that you are real?"

"I can't explain it. Believe me, I feel like myself, only this peculiar thing has happened. It got
me out of a trap that I was supposed to fall into.
I just need to figure out why that trap was set
and by whom." Michael looked over at his wife
with sympathy. "Suze, it's tough, but you kind
of get used to it," he said.

"Promise?" said Susan. Michael left her alone
in her bewildered state as he consulted a map,
keeping his eyes on the road. She had to adjust
in her own way. Some instinct had told him to

stop at the rustic motel. He didn't know why he chose it, but that was not at issue.

"Rakhel showed up again last night," Michael said. "She thinks we have to go on."

"Was that the word she used, *we*? Meaning how many of us?" Susan asked.

"I think she just meant you and me. But she has a way of popping up," said Michael.

"So I've noticed. Kind of walks through walls. Spooky but charming. Or was she hiding in the backseat?"

Michael reached for Susan's hand, and he could feel that her fist was clenched. "Darling, you did an incredible thing," he said softly. "Rakhel said that we stepped away. She said we found a hole in the net of reality and jumped through."

He stopped, wondering if Susan felt at all the way he did. He had found it awkward, when they first met, to open up about how much he loved her. They'd spent a lot of time sparring and joking, avoiding the point, making light of their vulnerable feelings, finally getting to love by wearing everything else down. But this new thing, the spiritual hunger that he had kept under wraps even from himself, was much harder. You can assume that another person wants to be loved. If you have the courage, you can reveal that you have the same need, and then you are on your way to fulfilling it. But can anyone assume that another person wants to escape a trap that the whole world says isn't a trap?

Susan said, "If we fail at this, then what?"

"I don't know. I hardly know what the next minute is going to be like."

"Oh, Michael," she said, "why can't we just have each other? What did we do wrong?"

"Nothing. We've done something incredibly right. You really were incredible yesterday," he repeated, squeezing her hand.

"Then it must have worn off, because I feel like a mess today." She laughed, and for a moment almost cried. This release was a good sign. Her natural defense mode was to crawl inside herself.

"Marvell left us a few more leads, names I found in his Rolodex," said Michael. "I think we have to stop thinking about this as a murder mystery, because it's not."

"I know you're right, but at least that was something to cling to," Susan said, her voice losing its tightness. "I kept wanting to figure out how to get the judge to find you innocent, but that's absurd. It's like trying to defend yourself in a dream."

"Agreed. This may not be a murder mystery, but it's still a mystery. And maybe solving it is incredibly important. That's why we can't get out, at least not yet."

"We're in the maze," Susan said.

"That's exactly right. We're in the maze."

As Michael kept his eyes on the road, he had to suppress a sigh of relief. He had almost told Susan about his dream last night. He was hanging on to the hood of a car heading at breakneck speed over a cliff. It was frightening beyond anything he had ever felt before, and he scrabbled with his hands to hold on to the shiny surface. Over and over the car tumbled off the edge. He screamed for the driver to stop, but she didn't. It was Rakhel, who kept pretending that she didn't hear him, no matter how loud he screamed, and who couldn't stop laughing, no matter how many times they tumbled over to their deaths.

Despite being exiles from normal life, the Auldens still had the modern equivalent of total freedom: three gold cards and a Jeep. In a couple of hours they were crossing the 59th Street Bridge, then exited north for Harlem. Susan looked around. New York is an immigrant city, and when she gazed on it, the sidewalks showed her a world of peoples. She had worked with many of them in Africa and the Middle East or in south Asia a long time ago, when she first began to see herself as a helper of the poor. Once Michael turned onto Amsterdam Avenue, the mixture of faces darkened, but she still felt, probably falsely, that she had her bearings.

"Are you looking?" Michael asked. She nodded, and then pointed. The old brick building had no steeple, resembling a converted armory more than anything else with its squat gun-turret towers on the four corners of the roof. She checked the address on the Rolodex card he took out of his pocket. "This must be the place," she said.

No one ever supposes that a church has a back door. They went in front, mixing with a few of the congregation, all black and mostly women in flowered summer dresses and hats. The sign outside read MIRACLE MINISTRY OF THE BLESSED CHRIST, and the steps were of cracked cement newly patched in thick jagged lines. From the half-filled pews inside the big gloomy space with its vaulted ceiling, Michael assumed that the evening service would begin soon. He glanced at a row of wheelchairs and a large cardboard box of discarded crutches.

"Come on," he said, tugging at Susan's arm. Blank faces and indifferent stares followed them as they went up the side aisle. A swinging door to the left of the altar led to the vestry rooms. Michael pushed through, only to confront a large, very tall man in purple robes. "Reverend Gideon—we need to talk to him," he said.

"Everybody need to talk to him, but da option is closed just now," said the man, who must have been some kind of deacon, although he was built like a bodyguard. He had a faint Jamaican lilt to his voice.

"We've been sent; we're on a sort of mission," Michael argued. The man in the purple robes looked skeptical; he seemed to ponder whether to talk Michael into leaving or just bounce him on the spot. As he blocked their way, several of the black women in hats slid by, smiling and nodding. He nodded back, and spent several extra seconds to notice a woman leading a small boy by the hand. The boy was in a black suit and tie, his wide eyes very solemn. Michael was surprised when the boy spoke up, tugging at his mother to hang back.

"Why are you here?" said the boy.

"I'm takin' care of it," said the deacon. He took Michael by the sleeve and prepared to seize Susan with his other hand. The little boy raised a finger. Traffic seemed to halt in the passageway while he waited for his answer.

"We're here to see somebody," Susan said.

The little boy nodded. "There's only one somebody here," he said.

For some reason this made the large man laugh out loud. "Yessir, praise da Lord," he agreed enthusiastically. Without a word the little boy moved away, still holding his mother's hand. The large man rubbed his hands together and looked at Michael and Susan with sudden kindness. "You folks is invited to join our service, and then we'll see what we can do. Is dat okay?" Before they could answer, he swept away through the swinging doors and into the church.

The service was snatched from a documentary on gospel revivals. The deacon—they were right about that—worked up the crowd, which had filled the church in fifteen minutes. An old lady in a white veil thumped on a large wheezy organ, and even though everyone present had no doubt been through the same ritual a thousand times before, they seemed to revel in every familiar beat. As the deacon urged them on with shouts of, "Am I right? You know I is," and "Who's gonna save ya, tell me now!" the crowd cried, "Yes, yes, Jesus, my Jesus!"

Susan and Michael sat off to the left near the back. It was hot, and as the warm-up showed no signs of ending, Susan began to nod.

At some point her eyes blinked open; she was surprised to see the little boy from the hallway in the pulpit. He was still dressed in his solemn black suit. He was leaning into the microphone, speaking softly but in a high, piping tone.

"Doctor Jesus has a miracle for you!" With a theatrical gesture he pointed down at the pews with one tiny hand and raised a loaf of wrapped Wonder Bread up high with the other. Susan rubbed the sleep away from her eyes and looked again.

"What I got here is good for you," the boy said fervently. "What's it good for? Do you wanna know?"

"*Oh, yes,*" the crowd shouted back. "That's right!"

The boy leaned forward as if he had a gale at his back and intoned his next words with long, drawn-out syllables. "Dee—pression, ohh—pression, su—pression, and ree—pression. You don't have no need to suffer. Doctor Jesus has a miracle for you!"

"Is that who we're looking for?" Susan whispered. Michael nodded, his eyes fixed onstage.

The little boy tore the end of the wrapper off the Wonder Bread and tossed it on the floor. This must have been a signal, because the organ spouted a hymnal march, and people began to mill toward the pulpit. Several were in wheelchairs, more on crutches; obviously sick children, their faces drawn and worn, were carried in their mother's arms. The little boy took his microphone and walked to the front of the raised platform where the pulpit stood, stopping in a narrow white spotlight.

Compared to her first glimpse, Susan could see

the boy much better now. His skin was a deep tawny gold and his close-cropped hair the color of milk chocolate. As he shot his hands out to touch the sick, gold cuff links appeared at his wrists, and he had opened his collar wide, like someone preparing for hard work. As the people approached, he tore off a bit of bread, placed it in their mouths, and then put his hand directly, palm flat, on their foreheads.

This little gesture had an amazing effect. Those who could walk swooned and fell backward, needing to be caught in the arms of a relative or companion. Rows of them had gathered in advance, since everyone had seen the act before. Other victims in wheelchairs shuddered and slumped forward. There were faint or loud shrieks; tears flowed copiously, and many could not leave the stage without kissing the little boy's hand. He smiled and nodded, whispering to each one.

Susan had never seen this kind of performance in person. The child preacher seemed completely self-possessed, descending from the stage and moving among the members of his congregation with the practiced assurance of an adult. He had started singing a gospel, which was caught up on all sides until the air was full of shouts, warbles, song, and ecstatic yells.

"Shouldn't we get out of here?" Susan said loudly into Michael's ear.

"No, he's part of the maze. Let's see what happens," said Michael. She sat back, half mesmerized but half disgusted. This kind of show was too far off the screen for her. Her eyes saw cripples throw away their crutches, sobbing uncontrollably, and two others leaped out of their wheelchairs. It all registered as a dream inside the dream she was already being forced to live; she could only tune it out. But she had to admit that as the beaming boy, who never stopped singing, moved through the crowd of worshipers, a sense of serenity, of calm well-being, grew within the walls of the temple.

"That's all," the boy said simply at last. He walked away while the deacon resumed the microphone and began expertly moving the congregation slowly toward the door.

"You jus' be sure to keep those offerin's comin'! An' remember, the Miracle Ministry takes food stamps *and* cash!"

Afterward the emptied church was sweltering when a hidden switch clanged and the spotlight went off. In the dimness, waiting for the stragglers to leave, Michael and Susan made their way back through the swinging doors. No one blocked them this time. They knocked on the door at the end of the hall.

"Come in," the deacon's deep voice beckoned them, and as they entered the little vestry room, Susan realized that the three people inside—the deacon, the mother, and the little preacher—were a family. They were all dressed in street clothes, ready to leave.

"Reverend Gideon?" said Michael. The deacon pointed to the little boy.

"You could mean me, but I guess you is wantin' Little Gideon here," he said.

Susan realized she had been wrong about the woman being the boy's mother, because Little Gideon said, "Daddy, will you take Miss Leeann to the car? I need to speak with these people."

The deacon started to obey automatically. The woman, who wore a great deal of jewelry and showed the hem of a red dress beneath her long cloth coat, protested. "We can stay, sugar."

"God says you don't b'long here, Miss Leeann."

The woman in the red dress strode out of the room without disguising her huff, followed by the father. Michael wondered if Little Gideon was about to do something flashy, but he looked at them calmly with his wide sherry-brown eyes. If the adults around him were hucksters, it was hard to believe, seeing those eyes, that he was in on it.

"How do you do what you do?" Michael

asked. There seemed to be no point starting anywhere else.

"I don't. The angels do it," Little Gideon said.
"You ain't here from child services, are you?"

Michael shook his head.

"Do they make trouble for you?" asked Susan.

"They don't like my daddy," the boy said. "I
pray for 'em, but only sometimes."

"Can we ask you a question about angels?"
asked Michael. Little Gideon nodded. "Are they
always there when you need them?" The boy
nodded again. "And do they talk to you?"

"It depends. I pray before every meetin'. They
comes and shows me who to touch. Everybody
wants to be touched, but it ain't my choice. I
touch only the ones they show me."

"Okay," Michael said. He knelt down and
looked the boy in the eye. "How did you learn
about angels?"

"I've always known about the angels," the boy
said. "When I was little an' lived with my
gran'ma, she would always tell me that the angels were all around, watching everything we
did. And I'd see them, and talk to them, and
they'd answer me back. And when my Gran'ma
got real sick, I asked them for some medicine for
her, an' they put the light in me so I could make
her feel better. After she went to live in heaven,
they said I should use the light to help other peo-

ple." He sounded matter-of-fact; there was no hint of trying to convince them.

"So what would you do if someone came to you and told you that he wanted to talk to your angels, too?" Michael asked.

"You mean dat one man who was here? I done talked to him, and I tried to help him, 'cause I told him I couldn't make 'em talk to him."

"So someone did come to you like that?"

Little Gideon stared at the floor. "I don't think he is here anymore."

"You mean alive?" asked Michael.

The boy's lip trembled. "Doctor Jesus didn't have no miracle for him."

"This man who came to you . . . why did he pick you, do you know?" asked Susan.

"He said he was going to meet a angel, but then somethin' happened, I don't know what. I'm just a kid." Little Gideon looked wide-eyed at Susan; she wondered if he was telling the exact truth.

"You're a pretty special kid," she said. Little Gideon stood up, and there was yet another change in him.

"I think you best be goin' now, Miss Uptown," he said abruptly. "I have to talk to Mistah." Susan was startled. He was dismissing her as casually as Miss Leeann. She looked over at Michael, who nodded.

"I'll see you in the car," she said. After Susan left through the swinging doors, Little Gideon took off his black suit jacket. "Sit down," he ordered. His voice was as assured as when he was at the microphone onstage.

"Why?" asked Michael. He felt an urge to back away, as if from a dog that was wagging its tail but snarling at the same time.

"They jes' tole me that somethin' about to happen." The little boy's eyes had sharpened; he seemed to see Michael's apprehension very clearly. At that moment there was a knock at the door, and Michael almost jumped. The boy seemed very calm. "Come in," he said.

One of the congregation women in a flowered dress cautiously opened the door; she seemed very timid. "Rev'rend Gideon, I know this is way too late," she said haltingly.

The boy shook his head. "Tha's all right, I done seen your face. Bring her in." He waved as if already giving a blessing, and the woman in the flowered dress pushed "her"—an old woman in a wheelchair, through the door. She seemed very feeble but alert. Michael could see immediately that one leg was stunted, perhaps from polio, even though both legs were covered with a blanket.

From somewhere Little Gideon had produced a slice of Wonder Bread. He gestured to the crip-

pled woman. "I saved this for you," he said. Both
women mumbled a quiet, almost awed thank
you. They were so mesmerized by the little boy
that they hardly seemed to notice that Michael
was in the room.

"This is yo' motha', isn't it?" he asked the
woman in the flowered dress. "Jesus said to wait
for Yolanda—is that you?" The old woman
could hardly hold back her tears as she nodded.
"Bless Jesus," she mumbled.

"You can come right here, will you do that fo'
me?" Little Gideon pointed toward a table in the
middle of the room, a long trestle table that was
piled with vestments, cardboard cups, and old
McDonald's containers. He swept them off the
table and smiled. Hesitantly the two women
came nearer. "Get up there, all right? I know it's
not easy, but Jesus wants you to do that, and you
can, okay?"

Puzzled but obedient, the younger woman
helped her mother to rise. Michael saw with the
blanket gone that the left leg was shorter than the
right. Because of the old woman's long skirt, he
could not medically assess what was wrong.
Painfully she sat on the edge of the table and
then turned around; with her daughter's help she
laid herself out flat on her back. She was nervous
and didn't know where to place her arms, deciding to fold them over her chest, making Michael

think that she had been to a lot of open-casket funerals.

"Tha's right, you doin' fine," the boy said. He held the slice of bread over her. "Jesus has bless' this bread, and He wants you to take communion of it." He tore a small circle out of the middle of the slice and put it to her lips. The old lady took the piece and swallowed it. As before, when he held the crowd in his hands, Little Gideon began to sing, but this time softly, making up words as he went along.

"Da savior is here, yes, He is, He gone make yo' sufferin' go, the miracle is His."

With a swift, sure movement the boy touched the flat of his palm to the old lady's forehead. Her body twitched, and she gave out a loud gasp. Her legs shuddered after the spasm had passed through her, and as Michael watched, the shorter leg stretched out. Since her feet were pointed at him, he saw this motion without a doubt.

"Can you stan' up fo' me, good mama?" Little Gideon's voice was coaxing, and although she looked afraid, the old woman sat up, swung her legs over the edge of the table, and then stood. She looked strangely blank. The boy went over to the door and held out his arms. "Now, lis'n good, Jesus want you to run to me," he said. The old woman stood still, not daring to move. The daughter had covered her face and was quietly crying.

"Run! Now!" the boy shouted. As if galvanized by a shock, the old woman took a step, almost falling. She caught herself, grasping at the air, and then an invisible hand pushed her from behind—she ran toward the boy healer, covering the distance between them in four strides. When she saw what she had done, her hands flew to her mouth.

Praise God!

The words must have risen from the throats of both women and the little boy, but Michael seemed to hear them in his mind, not so much as words but as a peal of music. The scene seemed frozen in front of him, and it was only then that he realized he had been too tense to breathe—the wind rushed into his lungs with a whoosh, breaking the spell. His body wanted to jump up, but he held himself down in the chair, watching the weeping women, who were embracing and jumping up and down. They were too awed to hug Little Gideon, but the old woman kissed the top of his head in ecstasy. It was the first time in his life that Michael had witnessed true jubilation. The little boy's face glowed, but he said nothing more, just waiting for whatever happened. It was five minutes before the women left, bowing at the door as they backed out. Little Gideon kept his eyes on them until they were gone. Then he faced Michael.

"The angels did that. Did you see 'em?" Michael shook his head, and the little boy shrugged. "They said you could, and they ain't wrong." When Michael still had nothing to offer, Little Gideon reached for his coat. "I better go, my daddy's in the car," he said.

"Do you want me to walk you out?" Michael asked. Back in his black suit jacket, Little Gideon looked once more like the politest of Sunday school pupils.

"No, you betta' stay fo' a bit," the boy said thoughtfully. "They ain't ever wrong." Without warning he reached his hand up, and because Michael was only halfway out of his chair, the smooth cool palm reached his forehead. *Don't touch me,* he thought. *I don't need you.*

The little boy read his mind. "Don' matter. Doctor Jesus must have somethin' else in mind," he said. Michael felt himself cringe as he fell back into the chair.

"It's not like the angels gonna hurt ya," the boy said. Michael didn't hear anything else, nor did he register Little Gideon leaving the room, letting the door swing behind him. . . . Something much more important had begun. He could hear a buzzing in his ears, like a swarm of bees, and he felt a nauseous cramp in his stomach, which was suddenly strong enough to double him over.

Michael lurched to his feet, trying to call out, but he could hardly breathe. As if a strong hand had pushed at the back of his neck, he went to his knees. The buzzing became half articulate, then shaped itself into words.

"Help him."

And this time get it right.

He was in Marvell's study again, kneeling beside the writer's body. For some reason this wasn't a shock. The body was lying face up, as before, and when he could bring himself to glance around, Michael recognized the surroundings.

"Hold still," he said. "Can you hear me? Just hold still." He knew it was his voice saying these words, but he was hearing them as if from a distance. He could feel his hands pressing hard against Marvell's chest, pumping hard just over the breastbone.

Why was he trying to revive a dead man?

Suddenly there was a snap, the sound of pieces falling into place, and he had no other thoughts but saving his neighbor.

"Did you call 911?" he asked urgently, pushing harder on Marvell's chest, letting go, counting silently, and pushing again. The danger was that he might break a rib, but if he couldn't hear a heartbeat in a few seconds, he'd take that risk.

Beth stood in the doorway, distraught but trying to hold herself together. "Yes, I called. They said we're too far in the country for the hospital, so they're calling the county EMS."

"Good." Michael cupped Marvell's mouth in his hands and gave him a minute of mouth-to-mouth. When he put his ear to the man's chest, he heard the sound of a faint but regular *lub-dub*. *He'll make it*. Just at that moment the faint rhythm seemed to fade, but Michael felt a spurt of confidence, an unerring conviction that made him raise his fist high in the air. He brought it down with a loud thump and the crack of bone. The impact made Marvell's body jump slightly off the carpet. It worked—when Michael listened again, the heart was going louder and stronger.

"Oh, my God," Beth moaned, shocked by the savagery of the blow.

"No, it's okay," said Michael. "He's back. I think we're good until the ambulance arrives."

"I can't believe it," said Beth. Her voice conveyed shock and relief. "You're sure?"

Michael nodded but kept his attention on Marvell. "Can you hear me? Blink your eyes if you know I'm here." He spoke loudly as if to a deaf man or to someone far away. There was a faint stir, and he could see the slight twitch of muscle in Marvell's eyelids. "Just a couple of blinks, sir. I want to know that you're back with us."

Now a moan, and Marvell's eyes opened. He was alive, but it didn't look yet like anyone was home. Michael heard Beth give a ragged sob. He stood up and held her from rushing forward.

"Let's not touch him just now, okay?" he said gently.

"I'm here, darling. I brought a doctor," she said piningly. She resisted her impulse to jump to his side.

"You can do us more good if you go outside and flag the ambulance," said Michael urgently. "It's still pretty dark, and I noticed that your mailbox is hard to read." Beth hesitated without moving. "You need to go," Michael said, but still she didn't move.

"I need to stay here," the wife insisted. Michael took her by the shoulders and began directing her toward the door.

"You're on the verge of shock, and normally I'd get you to lie down, but we haven't got time for that," he said. Every moment counted, and he couldn't leave Marvell.

"You don't understand," said Beth. "I'm not on the verge of shock, not nearly as much as you." She was wiry and strong; with a quick twist she got out of his grasp. Michael stepped back. Beth's face had changed; her eyes were no longer the confused, darting eyes of a victimized woman in fear for her husband's life. But what were they?

"You've been here before," Beth said. "Listen carefully. It will be hard for you to remember, but listen carefully. This whole scene is about you. You control it. You are the center point around which events will turn. In coming back here, you've made a huge step, but you haven't got enough strength to hold on. Look at him."

She sounded very clear and strong, and Michael sensed that this was the real Beth. He looked down at Marvell, who was pale, a trickle of blood oozing from his mouth. The body bore no resemblance to the man he had just resuscitated. Michael was speechless.

"Can you understand what is happening?" Beth asked.

"No."

"Ah, but at some level you do. We all do. There is never just one event. Everything happens over and over, on level after level. The important thing—you must remember this—is which version we choose to make real. Do you understand? You are the only one who can choose which version is going to stick, and then all the others vanish into God's light."

Michael stared at her, and his heart started to pound.

Get it right this time.

Michael shook his head like a boxer who'd
taken a punch. He felt wildly off balance. Un-
consciously he took in the room. It was dim and
unremarkable. Books lined the walls, papers
were piled up on Marvell's desk. He must have
been sitting at his computer when he had his
heart attack, because the monitor was on. Only
one thing was odd—a tall yellow beeswax candle
of the kind used at high mass was burning next
to the computer.

"Don't look there. Doctor, Doctor!" Beth's
voice sounded very insistent. Why shouldn't he
look at a candle? It reminded him of something,
a faint glimmer of another room that was filled
with candles. That was it. The oddity was that
there were not enough candles. Enough?

Beth put her hands on either side of his face,
trying to swivel his head toward her. He was
feeling strange and blank. Beth shook him
lightly.

"All right, don't worry. This wasn't bad. It
was much better than last time. So that is really
not bad, is it?"

"Huh?"

Michael thought he could hear the buzzing
sound in his head again. He looked closely at
Beth, whose face was now very near his. She had
quite remarkable eyes, he thought. Not at all the

eyes of a panicked victim, not at all. She must be one of the pure souls.

Then the cramp in his stomach returned, twice as bad, and he had to bend over to keep from retching. He sat up in the chair in Little Gideon's vestry room, gasping. Marvell and Beth and the whole scene had vanished. Michael choked back a sob of frustration; he felt cold sweat under his shirt, as if he were oozing terror and failure.

This was nearly getting it right?

Suddenly he wanted to run from the place. He pushed through the swinging doors, his mind going toward Susan, hoping that she was all right. Whatever his time travel back to Marvell's death meant, it would have to wait.

The Angel's Voice

You will understand angels when you understand your own version of reality, and that depends upon vibrations. Everything in nature has a signature all its own, and each signature is made of a unique vibration. A rock is not a moonbeam. A tree is not a bolt of lightning. In your world the separation between matter and energy is strictly observed, but in the natural order, vibrations form a continuous stream, an arc, a rainbow of creation moving from the finest to the grossest things in existence.

Angels make any strict divisions seem absurd. We fluidly move across all lines, riding the rainbow. Sometimes we appear in dreams, sometimes we show up in broad daylight. We can emit a celestial glow or a scent of holiness—or nothing at all. Whether we are solid or merely look that way is pure conjecture, since few visionaries claim to have been so bold that they actually leaned forward to touch an angel.

If angels can appear as matter or energy at will, what about you? Perhaps you can step into our world, too. But for that to happen, you would have to see yourselves as creatures of light. Is this possible? The mystery of human evolution has barely been solved. In fact evolution itself has barely begun. No one can predict where the human spirit will go in the future. You are capable of sprouting wings, but you are just as capable of flirting with extinction. The light awaits you, but it doesn't command. If the light is your destiny, you must respond to its every hint, here and now. This means slowly giving up your allegiance to the illusions that keep you from the light.

To help you know yourself, God sends many messages, yet the most important by far is this one: Release yourself from fear.

Fear is powerful, but it is not of the light. Fear was born of separation, and to heal separation you must stop listening to fear. Angels devote most of their time trying to dissolve fear. Man's great leap forward depends on it.

5
Didi

Ted Lazar sat on the concrete floor of the bunker, a pillow against his back so he could lean against the wall, and a folded blanket underneath him. He looked at the hovering light, shielded again behind its glass walls. It hadn't changed since they'd taken the photographs. He had lost track of time but assumed that it was after midnight. The glow given off by the capture had become familiar to him. His eyes couldn't slow it down, and his mind couldn't decode its vibrations, but he had become used to its . . . moods.

That was really the only adequate word. The light seemed to be reviewing the human condition, using Lazar to feel sad and happy, ecstatic and forlorn, hopeful and despairing. These changes passed quickly like summer rain showers and sometimes overlapped. Lazar had the impression of looking into a tumble dryer as bits of shirts and shorts, pillowcases and underwear flashed by in a jumble of colors. Every piece of laundry was there, but it went by too fast to make sense of. The light was tumbling through human emotions like that. Lazar was fascinated.

"Way cool," he murmured. "Just don't stop, babe."

Lazar knew that the Army was ready to pounce if Lazar ever revealed how human the light was becoming. But there was no doubt about it. Lazar wasn't observing a phenomenon like a chunk of fallen meteorite, but a woman.

The game of secrets worked both ways, and he knew one of theirs. Stillano had been ordered to destroy the capture. Not immediately, because that would possibly miss out on its implications for defense. But if Lazar and Simon didn't produce workable results, the military had no choice but to snuff out the light; it couldn't be contained, and there was too much risk, if they shared the capture with the rest of the world, that someone else would beat them to the punch and create a super-weapon out of it.

"Could you slow your vibe down? You're driving me just a little bit crazy here," he said aloud. The capture didn't hear him, apparently, because the vibration entering his head remained intense and dazzling.

"Okay, change of topic. You know they're gunning for you, right? The military mind—and I use the term in its loosest sense—isn't amused when you freak it out. It's just a matter of time before they figure out how to fry you. Then lady go boom. Did you work that into your calculations?" After three days of projecting mental images at the light, trying to acquaint it with how the human brain worked, Lazar still had no idea if he was making any impression. He didn't even know for sure that she was listening.

"Maybe you're just not very bright," Lazar said. "Maybe you're a bimbo with great legs and a cheap come-on." As if to acknowledge this (or maybe laugh at it?), the light flickered ever so slightly. His heart skipped a beat—this was the first sign of comprehension he had ever noticed from the capture. He stood up.

"Dumb girls seem to like me," he said loudly. "Is that it? Have you been waiting to tell me that you like me? Are you shy?" Without hesitation the light flickered again. Lazar got excited.

"So, do you sleep around on the first date?" Long pause. He had pushed his luck; the light made no response. "Just checking to see if you had a sense of humor," he said. "That's cool, right?" No response. Lazar began pacing. What could he say that would keep her in contact? "I'm going to want to ask you a lot of questions," he declared, thinking out loud. "But we need to start simple. If I ask you something, I want you to blink once for yes and twice for no. Can you do that?"

He waited, but there were no flickers. "Is that unacceptable?" he asked. Again no flickers. "Shit. Uh, sorry," he said. "I get it. You would have to blink to answer that, and you haven't agreed to blink, right?" The light remained the same, an even blue-white glow.

"Hold on, let me think some more." Lazar put his intellect to work. He had never visualized himself as the first person to speak with alien life, much less to make bad jokes with it. Why had she picked this moment to communicate? Had she made some kind of breakthrough, muddling through his feeble, mushy mind (compared to hers), and finally hit upon the key?

The more he thought about it, the less likely that seemed. Her vibrational rate was higher than radio waves and capable of receiving an unknown number of frequencies at the same time. Which implied that her "thinking"—if she thought at all—was incredibly fast.

If she made Einstein look like a dim bulb, then her ability to get into Lazar's mind should be a matter of minutes, not days. So he had to assume that she had caught on to his thoughts a long time ago.

"I think I get it," he said "I'm the one who made the breakthrough. That's it, right?"

One flicker.

Slight as this change was, Lazar almost jumped straight up in the air. "It had to be me, didn't it? Who could come here to teach you anything? You might not even bother with *here* at all. I bet you can read everyone's mind on this whole base—all at once."

One flicker.

Of course. That was the only possibility that made sense. She vibrated at such super-high speed, it would be only natural to absorb a hundred minds at once.

"The reason you have to be careful with us is that you would blow our minds. That's your problem." Lazar suddenly wished that Simon didn't have a stick up his ass, because it would help to have another semi-bright mind around. No matter, forget that.

"Let me get his straight, okay? I am basically a one-fuse kind of thinker. I have to move from thought A to thought B and then to thought C, but when you look at me, you see them all at once. Maybe I remember one birthday when I was five, but you remember all my birthdays— all my memories, in fact. The good, the bad, and the unearthly. Whoa!"

This "whoa" wasn't a final punctuation to

show that he was impressed. Lazar had hit upon a new, amazing, and totally humbling insight.

"You already know me, don't you?" The light didn't flicker, but he could read what it said anyway. *I know you better than you know yourself.*

For the first time he wished he could protect her. The deepest human instinct, to be truly understood, was being fulfilled—at exactly the wrong moment.

"Great," Lazar muttered gloomily. "Now they're sure to nuke you." He slumped back onto the concrete floor, suddenly exhausted and almost tearful. It was pointless to think his conclusion was wrong. She knew him. She knew him completely. That was what she had been waiting for, for someone to catch on. Those two GIs hadn't caught on, but they must have gotten a glimpse, because the light put the fear of God into them, or something of God.

Lazar was tougher than them. When she had first noticed him, sending him flying across the bunker that day, it was probably just a love tap. Even so, it had taken him the better part of a week to figure out what she was up to. And now he knew.

"We gotta get you out of here," Lazar mumbled.

The light, when he looked up at it, simply hovered there. It didn't respond, and maybe it hadn't really flickered at him in the first place. No, it had. In awe Lazar realized that those faint flickers had triggered the whole tidal wave of mental activity engulfing him.

She was Einstein, Freud, Leonardo da Vinci, and Buddha rolled into one, times a thousand.

"I'm gonna save you," he whispered. "I may be crazy to think you hear me, but they are crazier to want to kill you. Help me, okay? This is important. We need a plan."

His own words surprised him. It was the first time in his life he had dared to express courage or feel the nearness of grace. It was a strange sensation. He jumped up. "Get your traveling clothes, baby. We're blowing this joint! I mean, if that's okay with you. And I can't stand talking to you without a name, so we're going to call you . . ." His mind went blank for a second. "Didi! How's that? I don't know where it came from, but I've been wrong to think I knew where anything came from. So, Didi, let's boogie— now!"

Lazar had gone giddy with excitement. He knew he was babbling, but as he twirled around like a drunken dervish, he missed the light's last flicker. She knew from the first moment what he was thinking, but his heart had been in doubt. That required time, and a breakthrough. Not to know her, to want to pry out her secrets, or even to protect her. This last flicker was to tell him that he was the first human to send her the slightest glimmer of love.

The Angel's Voice

Let's talk about the Enemy.

Human beings find it difficult to think about evil in the abstract, therefore they put a human face on it. Satan is your human face for cosmic evil. No one has met him, yet he is necessary to your way of thinking. In most cases evil is far from cosmic. It is rooted instead in selfishness, disobedience, and rebelliousness—these are impulses learned in childhood. You may dress these impulses up in adult guise and make them more dangerous through the violence of war and weapons, but to us they are not complex. A child who feels absolutely loved and wanted will not grow up to embrace such values. When the world no longer passes fear and hatred from one generation to the next, this sort of evil will be wiped out as completely as smallpox.

Much more deep-rooted is your sense that you are evil in your nature. This sort of evil is called demonic or sinful. You often trace it back to some kind of fall from grace; in many of your myths there is a legendary Paradise on earth that was lost because you could not control your baser self. Yet Eden is nowhere but in your mind, and if you overcome your sense of guilt, Eden is now. If you must insist that you are sinful because you are imperfect, then why not strive to discover what it means to be perfect, for God sees only perfection?

Perfection simply refers to wholeness. When you have an "evil" thought and generate violence out of it, or commit acts that lead to guilt and shame, your natural impulse is to push that act out of your memory. It becomes a fragment of yourself that you do not want others to see, that even you cannot look at. Such fragments never disappear, however. Thought is energy, and energy cannot be created or destroyed. The "evil" parts of yourself go into hiding, yet they continue to roam your unconscious at will. When the chance arises, if the pressure of old energy is strong enough, evil will erupt into the light of day. Sudden outbreaks of violence appear in the most peaceful settings; dark impulses that seem totally alien to you will come to reclaim their birthright. They were born in your mind, and their birthright is to have your attention.

If you give attention in the right way, then evil dissolves. The right way means accepting responsibility and bringing home your impulses, no matter how dark, to be at one with you. Atonement of sin basically means at-one-ment. God does not want you to suffer over your hidden shame and guilt. If you bring them fully to light, He will take their burden from you. This is another job for the angels, for if you ask us, we can transform any energy, removing its sting of shame and guilt, replacing it with light.

The only kind of evil we have not talked about, then, is comparatively small, and that is cosmic evil. Cosmic evil has nothing to do with violence or crime. It is merely the force of destruction. Life must renew itself, and in that process the old decays to give way to the new. You cannot have a single new thought without letting go of an old one. But if you attach fear to this natural force of destruction, you magnetize it to you. All energy works on the simple principle of like seeking like, and on the subtle plane the destructive energies of the human mind have collected into larger forms.

This is like cosmic dust that collects into stars and galaxies. The burning intensity of a star was born from cold dust that floated harmlessly around for billions of years. Cosmic evil—meaning the condensed force of destruction—also built up from tiny seeds. You add new seeds to this "satanic" evil with every negative thought, and no single person has the power to annihilate this huge darkness. The solution to cosmic evil is relatively simple, even so: You only have to stop magnetizing it to yourself. If you live in the light, evil has no interest in you. Again the angels are here to help, for our light is much stronger than yours, and if you magnetize us to yourself, then we add much more intensity of light to protect you.

If you take all these levels of evil, different as they are, you find one thing they have in common: All exist in your awareness. The only enemy you have is an inner enemy. Therefore, when you seek God within, you gain the awareness to defeat all evil. This is the proven way to defeat darkness.

"Get the hell down here, pronto!" Marty Carter yelled into the wall phone, even though yelling wouldn't get the message to anyone any faster. He looked at the thick glass walls that now looked dull and opaque. "And roust General Stillano out of bed. We have a major security leak. Get him now!"

Thirty seconds later he heard the first distant alarms going off somewhere around the base. In the darkness of the bunker he could see a shape approaching. Carter prided himself on having a cop's mind, and it occurred to him that the first person to arrive at a crime scene, especially by accident, is often the best suspect. Only this time, as the shape got closer, he saw that it belonged to the most insignificant person in their group, the aide Colonel Burke.

"Colonel," he said. "The cookie's out of the jar." Ordinarily Burke would have asked why it was so damn dark in the bunker, given that around-the-clock security surveillance had been installed. But darkness carried a more ominous meaning now.

"It can't just be gone," Burke said blankly.

"Is that the summation of your response?" Carter said bitingly. "Get someone down here who can think."

Burke kept staring. Where the hovering light should have been, center stage at the crosshairs of super-high-tech security beams and sound detectors, there was a blank. "How?" asked Burke.

"I doubt if anybody saw it leave in a convertible," Carter said. "Remember, it could have melted the walls. Let's check the security cameras. Meanwhile, we might have a chance to catch it again if we go on red alert on all security levels."

Burke recovered his wits and got on the horn to the general, who was on his way. Carter drifted toward the deserted cage, feeling disgusted. He couldn't help but think that the military had bungled it. Their lumbering mentality could never grasp when a situation had to be resolved in hours instead of weeks. They'd dawdled over the light too long, watching instead of doing, testing instead of forcing the phenomenon to react.

All that would change if Carter got a second chance.

When Stillano showed up, his face was a hard mask, but Carter was sure he was intensely afraid. This was a major bungle of the most significant find of the century, and Stillano's decision to keep out the scientific world, except for two isolated nerds—eccentric and hostile to each other—looked terrible in hindsight. The general would fry in front of a review committee.

"What do you mean? Who the hell gave them permission to do that?" Carter could hear Stillano shouting into a cell phone. He went over and tried to get his attention, but Stillano turned his back and kept talking.

"Was it more than an hour ago? Shit, and no one checked to see if the pass was authentic?"

Carter realized that this conversation must have to do with Simon and Lazar. He pulled at Stillano's shoulder. "Which car did they take? Give me the license plate," he said urgently. At the same time Carter pulled out his own cell phone and was dialing Virginia. The general, looking over his shoulder with a scowl, clearly didn't want to let go of his authority, but his judgment told him that there was no use digging his grave any deeper.

"It's one of those damn white things, they all look alike," Stillano grumbled. He barked an order, and in a few minutes Carter had the number of the white Buick sedan that had left the base. It had departed through Gate G in the south sector, which implied a southerly route. To Mexico? Within an hour the state highway patrols of New Mexico and Arizona as well as the local sheriff's department would be alerted. Carter had covered his own ass and also done the right thing procedurally. This didn't dispel his gloom, however. What did the police in New Mexico catch, taco bandits?

"Do you have any idea why they would skip?" he asked Stillano. The general shook his head.

Carter pointed to the empty glass cage. "They must have known about this."

Stillano agreed glumly. "It's too close for co-incidence, but who the hell knows what they've escaped with?"

"They figured out how to let the thing go and they kept the information from us," Burke inter-jected. "I call that a crime. I call it pretty close to treason."

"You think so?" said Carter sarcastically. "What charges are we going to bring them up on, stealing a Christmas tree?" He walked away quickly on his own mission. It might be that he himself was still under military authority, but their authority had flown the coop along with the capture, and if he was ever brought up for in-subordination or whatever the hell it would be, Carter was pretty sure that his own strategy for recapture would look a lot better than the one he was hiking away from.

Simon had been dozing at his terminal an hour before. He raised his head, unaware that he was drooping over the keyboard. He glanced at the clock and was amazed to discover how late it was. He felt unsafe, and it was more than the discomfort, understandable to any neatnik, of be-ing rumpled. His gray houndstooth jacket was draped over the back of his chair, and his vest was unbuttoned. His dirty blond hair looked as if he'd been running his fingers through it, which he had. He'd even worn the same shirt three days in a row. All the careful patterns and rituals of his life had been cast into disarray by the Army's overwhelming need to *know*. He decided that he should consider early retirement once he got away from them.

He glanced over at the workstation assigned to Lazar. The computer was repeating endless loops of Doom, but he couldn't hear any of the old Aerosmith records that were usually fouling the air. That meant that Lazar must be gone. This assumption was disproved when Simon felt the gun barrel against the back of his head.

Damn you, God, he thought.

"I need you, Watson, come here," he heard Lazar say.

"You're back. What's happening?" asked Simon. He felt the hard cold nose of the gun press a degree harder against his head.

"I said I need you, which means get up. We have to go." Lazar sounded calm and what passed for normal.

Simon considered that this might be his warped notion of a joke. But he got up cautiously and asked, "Can I turn around?"

"Yeah."

It wasn't a joke. Lazar was dressed in jeans and his favorite antiwar T-shirt from the sixties lettered (by Lazar himself), MAKE BABES, NOT

WAR—a small annoyance he enjoyed inflicting on the military drones. His eyes looked amused and detached, which was nothing new. What part had cracked? Simon wondered.

"What do we do now?" he asked.

"We leave." Lazar gestured with the snub nose of the pistol. Simon started walking toward the door. It had taken a while, but he realized that he was very afraid.

"I don't know if I can walk. I might throw up," he said, hoping he sounded reasonable.

"Not on me, please," said Lazar. "You'll ruin the tux." He let Simon open the door. The short corridor beyond their room was empty and unguarded. The outer door opened onto a piece of desert on the edge of the base. It too was empty, except for a white Buick with tinted windows sitting on the dirt road with its cracked asphalt laid down after World War II.

Simon stopped. "I believe it's customary in the cinema to say that now we are going for a ride. But I'm not." He felt a welling up of resentment that overcame his fear for the moment. A moment was all he got, because Lazar took the gun and poked it in his ear. Fear returned stronger than ever.

"Just get in. They know we hate each other's guts. But if they question you, either you'll squeal in some horrendously embarrassing suck-up, or else they'll rope you into a conspiracy and throw away the key."

Simon walked around to the passenger side and got in. In a few seconds Lazar was behind the wheel; they headed onto the main access road that circled the facility. The car turned south.

Lazar put the gun in his lap; he seemed to be in a very good mood. "I think it's also customary in the *cinema* for you to say that I'll never get away with it," he remarked. They rode in silence past a series of gates until they reached G. The car stopped.

"I need you to be very quiet for the next few minutes," Lazar said carefully. "If the MPs ask you any routine questions, give routine answers. Of course you can't do that very well unless you feel somewhat less afraid, right?" Simon nodded. "Okay, so let me reassure you that I'm not going to kill you. I'm not nuts. You are just a tactical necessity, got it?"

"What does that mean?" said Simon, feeling a degree less terrified.

"Here, drink this and hold on to the bottle." Lazar handed him some Evian, which Simon gulped gratefully. His throat was incredibly dry. "When I say that you are a necessity, I mean that I calculated my chances of getting out alone, without security doing a double-check, and I came to the conclusion that two can escape more cheaply than one."

Simon didn't reply, but the car had already started forward again. They approached a white guard shack that was double-fenced beyond with chain-link gates and laser alarms. Simon saw Lazar tuck the pistol under his leg. A hundred feet from the gate, Lazar started honking the horn. By the time they got up to the young MP, his whole mood had changed.

"I'm Dr. Lazar, why isn't the first gate open for us? Does this mean we're expected to wait? Jesus." He gruffly handed a sheaf of papers and his security ID to the guard, who began to look them over. "You already have a copy, and you were supposed to read them two hours ago," said Lazar.

The young MP shone his flashlight into the car, sweeping it quickly. The beam paused on Simon's face for a tenth of a second, if that.

"I didn't get any copy of this, sir," the guard said. He sounded apologetic.

"Christ, that probably means you haven't got the general's pass, either," said Lazar.

"The general, sir?"

"He's right behind me. We're supposed to get off base with as little stir as possible."

"I'll have to call about it, sir."

Lazar jabbed a finger at the sheaf of orders.

"As you can see, this is prioritized for General Stillano only. He's the only one you can call, and he's on his way. Try his car. Here's the number. Tear it up after you use it."

Nervously the MP took a scrap of paper from Lazar's hand and rushed back into the shack. They could see him conferring with another corporal, then one of them picked up a phone and dialed. Simon thought his heart would stop. He was amazed at the change in Lazar, who did an incredible job of imitating authority. A few seconds later the second MP approached. He swept the interior of the car again with his flashlight.

"Well?" asked Lazar.

"We got a message, sir. It said he'd be here at 23:00 hours."

"All right, then just let us through. We'll stop a mile down the road. I'm allowed to break silence then."

After a second's hesitation, the corporal saluted and waved at the shack. Simon saw the double gates start to swing open. The corporal backed away from the car.

"Haven't you forgotten something?" Lazar snapped. He pointed at Simon. "Check his ID against the one pasted on the order sheet." The corporal hurried around to the passenger side while Simon rolled down the window. He found his wallet and handed it over.

The guard handed it back and saluted. "Very good, sir, sorry about the delay."

"Hey, it's the Army, isn't it?" said Lazar, showing the first hint of a forgiving smile.

"Yes, sir." The guard sounded sheepish. Lazar made sure to drive quickly through the gates like a man in a hurry. Which, of course, he was, thought Simon.

"I don't suppose you want to tell me how you faked Stillano's voice on that message?"

"It's not much to brag about. He's been feeding us voice E-mails that can be stored to disk, right? So how tough can it be to edit and select what you need? I only had to digitize out the obvious splices."

"And the phone number to his car?"

"Faked. I gave them your number. Should make for some fun when they find out, eh?"

Simon cursed to himself. Lazar had him, well and truly, so much so that he didn't even bother to draw the gun back out and put it in sight. The desert was chilly—the temperature normally fluctuated by more than thirty degrees in each twenty-four hour period—and spookily bright under the moon. Simon shivered and began to feel exhausted. The car came to a halt when they were half a mile from the base.

"Ta," said Lazar, jumping out. He took the gun with him, and for a terrified instant Simon thought he was walking around the car to shoot him and dump his body. Instead he went to the trunk and opened it. There was a stir. Lazar returned and opened Simon's door.

"Listen, if you just let me go now . . ." Simon mumbled, his voice quaking. The image of his body lying in a ditch returned in a flash. It was only then that he saw the girl. She wore a light blue cotton slip dress without jewelry. The moonlight was too dim to make out her features well, though her hair was as pale as her dress.

"Come on, man, get out and let her in." Lazar gestured for Simon to step out. Silently, without looking at him, the girl slipped into the backseat, then Lazar nodded and Simon got back in, too.

"Be nice," Lazar warned. "This is Didi. She's not my girlfriend, and you don't have to say hello."

"You couldn't get a girlfriend," Simon retorted. For some reason this adolescent gibe amused Lazar greatly. In a few minutes they were heading down the road again, which stretched ahead of them as empty as midnight. No one spoke for several minutes before Lazar rolled his window down, took the pistol, and flung it off into the desert.

"Blew your mind, huh?" he said grinning.

"Stop the car, stop the goddamn car!" Simon shouted.

"Why? Because you saw me eighty-six the gun? Doesn't matter. You've breached security, so they are probably after you."

Simon was almost sputtering. "I'm going to nail you. No one will ever suspect me after they hear my story. You're completely crazy. You've gone Mad Hatter, and anyone with half a brain has no doubt been expecting it for a long time."

"Think so? What have you got going for you— a nice vocabulary? I can just hear you working up to a really juicy word like *dastardly* or *blackguard*. Something choice in the verbal department should put a noose around my neck for sure."

Lazar glanced in the rearview mirror at their passenger. The girl, who looked to be about twenty, was curled up in the backseat, silent, her eyes looking half down at the floor. She was either demure or very frightened. Simon didn't care about her or where she came from.

"I said stop this car!" He slammed his hand on the dashboard, which, being padded vinyl, emitted only a weak thud.

Lazar shook his head. "Use your brain. You may be on an adrenaline high right now, but I can beat the crap out of you any day. When was the last time you saw the inside of a gym, if ever? For all you know, I have a blackjack tucked in my pocket. You want to find yourself in the trunk of this car for a few hours or days on a side road that sees a lot more lizard traffic than cars? Second, I took the trouble of leaving a few clues pointing suspiciously to you. Like, for example, the forging of those orders, which happens to be on your hard drive. And then there's the gun registration faked in your name—cool stuff like that."

"You won't get away with this," warned Simon.

"What's that supposed to be, more *cinema*? You don't have the slightest idea what I'm trying to get away with."

Simon sat back, thinking. So far they were just on a joyride. It was against regulations, but the offending documents all pointed to him, and besides, Lazar had thrown away the gun that would prove kidnapping or armed assault. Simon really had little choice but to wait out whatever crazy plan was afoot. He sighed and stared out the window at the desert that he so disliked, moonlight or not.

"I can hear that little brain working," Lazar remarked coolly. "About time. If you're good, I might even give you your wallet back."

Simon didn't give him the satisfaction of reaching for his back pocket. Instead he unscrewed the Evian bottle and took a sip, deciding for the moment to say nothing at all to his absurd tormentor.

In a few moments Simon had fallen asleep from sheer nervous fatigue. Lazar had no one to taunt, and he had to face the fact that he was almost as afraid as his partner. He didn't want to think about Didi or the way she had appeared. It wasn't in any supernatural way. Lazar had been walking down the hall to his room when she was just there, around the corner in the drab corridor with metal fixtures and bare light bulbs overhead.

Neither of them spoke. Lazar instantly knew who she was and what this meant. The fact that he didn't have a seizure amazed him. But she looked like a pretty girl that he might have dated in his fantasies. There was no halo around her blond head and no *God has sent me* from her lips. She looked at him calmly, as if to say, *You wanted to help me escape? Here's your chance.*

The rest had followed as Lazar described. Only now, in the inky darkness of the desert, did he begin to feel uneasy. More than uneasy— creeped out. He almost ran off the road when Didi sat up and tapped him softly on the shoulder.

"Oh, my God, don't do that!" he cried, but already his eye had flicked to the left. Out there Lazar saw lights. She must have seen them, too.

A scattered twinkling of fires, and in their midst one larger glow.

"Stop," Didi said.

Lazar braked immediately. He turned around and looked at her. Didi kept her eyes fixed on the glimmering lights.

"You want to get out, right?" said Lazar.

"Us." Even as she said it, Didi was gesturing toward the driver's door. Lazar opened it and helped the slim girl out. In a few moments she was off in the direction of the glow, and Lazar knew to follow.

The terrain could have been treacherous at night, streaked with arroyos or sudden drops in elevation, but their footing held secure. The top layer of soil, which had never been disturbed by human intrusion, crunched lightly as their shoes broke through its light crusting of mineral deposits. The fires seemed very far away from the car, but Lazar and the girl drew near very quickly.

Where are we going? he wanted to whisper.

Reading his mind, she pointed off to the left.

Okay, Lazar thought, *we can talk while I think.* He hoped she wasn't looking into the embarrassing parts of his mind. She must have read this, too, because her head turned in his direction, and Lazar didn't have to see in the dark to know that Didi was smiling.

What's off to the left? he asked. No reply came into his mind. *Is this going to be one-way telepathy?* No answer came to that question, either.

Then something did come through, because Didi actually spoke again. "People, not so many. Family."

"So you're going to talk some of the time?" Lazar whispered.

"Learning," said Didi. It hadn't occurred to Lazar that she would have to learn anything. He filed the question for later reference.

Lazar realized that they were creeping up on an encampment of Navajos who had wandered from the reservation. There were no hogans or adobe dwellings in sight. The camp was a matter of scattered fires and a larger one in the middle where a dozen pickup trucks gathered in a circle. They were almost close enough now to see figures, and there were sounds. Chanting, actually—in the low, warbling notes of the Indian women, and then a more keening, guttural sound from the men.

Suddenly the angel held up her hand, asking Lazar to be completely still. (It would be a couple of days later, when he was eating a tostada at a roadside stand, before Lazar realized that this was the first moment he actually allowed himself to think the word *angel*.) Didi seemed to be listening closely to the chanting, and Lazar assumed she could understand it. A ceremonial dance was under way, with rattles and slow, stomping dancers; he sensed this more than saw it. Lazar let the alien but mysterious rhythms touch him.

"Come."

With a small gesture Didi pointed him off to the left. This time the ground grew steeper. Rocks began to hit against Lazar's thin, old Nikes. Something loomed over them, a bulk blacker than the sky. It was a butte or mesa, and without asking him if he could hold out, the girl started to climb.

"I don't know about this," Lazar muttered. It took all his clenched attention not to stumble, and when the going got steeper, he was glad that he couldn't see down below. Scree and pebbles flew out from beneath his feet constantly. At one point he thought the word *avalanche,* and saw himself getting cracked on the skull with a flying chunk of sandstone that would send him hurtling into space. Immediately he could hear Didi laughing inside his mind.

You think I'm funny? This is the strangest damn date I've ever been on, he thought, not caring if she read that or not.

Finally the trail led hand-over-hand, and Lazar could have been seriously freaked, but after half an hour they were at the summit. God only knew how Lazar made it, because once the moon fell, seeing anything was impossible.

Good training, he heard in his mind.

They walked to the edge of the mesa, and now, down below, the band of campers could be easily made out. Twenty Navajos in ceremonial dress were seated around a fire. The chanting had come to an end. The fire's orange glimmer made the desert rock seem to glow from within. Lazar knew zip about the sacred, but there was no mistaking a sacred moment.

What have I gotten myself into?

In one of those panicked insights that combat soldiers have when they hear the whiz of a mortar shell just before it kills them, Lazar felt the presence of death. It was in the air, and it was what Didi had come for. For a split second he had the crazy notion that she was going to throw him off the cliff like some ancient Toltec sacrifice. Then he saw the baby.

Not ten feet away, the baby was poised on the edge of the mesa. It had black hair and eyes, and in the fire glow its naked body looked shiny, as if newly made. Did smiled at the baby, and it stood on tiptoe. With a gurgle it started to twirl. The whole thing made no sense. The baby couldn't have been more than a year old—it looked like a tiny Navajo doll come to life—and babies that age don't stand up, much less twirl.

Lazar was trying to make the scene fit his version of acceptable reality. The next instant, though, the baby was spinning on one toe, like a miniature dervish, and from its throat came sounds of total joy. Its tiny body turned weightless, and slowly it began to rise from the ground, not to hover but to keep rising, still twirling in ecstasy.

Wow. I'm jealous.

Didi raised both her hands, palm upward. It was this that seemed to lift the baby, who tilted its head back.

Holy God, I'm going to see a pack of them, Lazar thought. He was sure that more angels were being summoned, that they might even be there already. It was an incredibly awkward moment, because Lazar had only the crudest idea what he should do. Bow, venerate, speak in tongues, cross himself? He had never done a single one of these things (he wasn't even Catholic), but in the air was such a charge of energy that his mind kept trying to grasp for a holy response.

Don't mind me. I'll try not to think. He meant it, feeling it was better to be as small and invisible as possible.

After a moment the baby was gone, though Didi continued to look upward a little longer.

"Was he dying?" Lazar asked out loud.

Didi shook her head. In his mind Lazar heard,

He passed this morning. He wanted to hang around his mother. They were both very sad. When he saw me, he was ready to go, and this made him happy.

Lazar said, "Boy, if that's happy, I must be really depressed 'cause I've never been anywhere close to that happy in my life." It was a thought worth thinking about, but he didn't get to explore it, because the campfires down below were starting to go out. The circle of families broke into fragments, each heading back to their truck. Angelic visions or not, Lazar had his hands full getting back off the mesa without breaking his neck.

I don't care if you're not helping me here, he thought, *but at least keep me from obsessing on that damn word avalanche.*

He could hear Didi laughing in the dark.

When he stumbled out of the church in Harlem, Michael nearly panicked, because Susan wasn't in the Jeep. He looked around. Some tough black youths stared long and hard at him from the opposite corner of the street; farther down he saw a squeegee man working his scam as a string of cars pulled up to the light. None of it touched him. This street, these people, these things might as well have been on another planet.

When Susan did appear, rounding the corner from the back of the church, she was practically running. "Get in, Marvell left us another clue," she said.

"How? We don't have his Rolodex." Michael jumped into the passenger side and let her drive. She almost did a wheelie in the street and headed fast down Amsterdam Avenue.

"I checked at a phone booth to see if anyone had left messages for you." Susan said. "Jack Temple left a couple, but here's the key one: Marvell was briefly in a mental hospital. He admitted himself."

"When was this?"

"Just before he died. He spent maybe a week there, then checked himself out. It could have been as recently as last week. And he must not have wanted anybody to know, because he chose a private hospital just outside the city." Susan was driving intently, running red lights when they were close, weaving around slow taxis and double-parked delivery vans.

"What's the place called?" asked Michael.

"Mount Aerie Hospital. Ever heard of it?"

"Vaguely, maybe."

"I think there's also an expensive rehab clinic there, for drying-out wet celebrities." She sounded happy and confident. Whenever the trail took them down more normal paths—toward something Susan could solve or at least understand—her energy level rose dramatically. Mi-

chael postponed telling her what had happened
with Little Gideon. Going back into the past was
strange enough, but why was it another *version*
of the past?

Mount Aerie turned out to be in Westchester,
a low series of bungalows that could have been
a resort community. No gates, no high fences.
They pulled into a small parking lot tucked under
a grove of old elms. "Perfect place for us," Susan
said, getting out of the car.

"A lot more than half the world would agree
with you," said Michael. Past the heavy wooden
front doors of the main bungalow they found the
first indications of what Mount Aerie was about:
a glassed-in reception desk with two nurses behind it and a guard off to one side.

"Can I help you?" the desk nurse said into her
microphone.

Susan didn't miss a beat. "I'm here to check
myself in."

"Excuse me?" The nurse leaned closer into the
glass, peering at them. Michael didn't know what
Susan was doing, but he went with it.

"She means me. I'm here to admit my wife,"
he said. The nurse paused for a second, then
lifted her call sheets fixed to a clipboard.

"Admissions has closed for the day," she said,
rifling through the sheets. "What's the name?"

"Aulden," Michael said quickly. There was a

long pause while the nurse furrowed her brow. He tried not to look in the direction of the security guard. "Don't worry, it will be all right," he said to Susan in a comforting voice. They held their breath. Whatever strange power they had gained to influence reality, bending it to their wishes, here was the test.

"Oh, yes. Susan Aulden?" the nurse asked. Susan nodded. A burst of excitement coursed through her body. She tried to suppress it, then wondered if maybe a crazy woman would seem crazier if she looked excited.

A buzzer sounded; they were let through into a small examination room that resembled a drawing room. There weren't any strong locks on the doors. The only physician on call was a resident, who treated Michael with deference once he knew he was a doctor.

"Your wife has been admitted before, correct?" the resident asked, looking at a chart that had been produced from the files. Michael decided to guess at the diagnosis.

"Right, she's suffered from recurrent depressions, and there may have been an acute schizophrenic break in her early twenties. No reliable records about that."

"Hmm." The resident scrawled a few notes in the chart, flipped to another page, and looked at Susan sympathetically. "And what's happened recently? More suicidal thoughts? That's why you were here last January, yes?"

Susan nodded. "I don't feel safe right now staying at home," she said. It was amazing how natural this charade was all beginning to feel, as if they could improvise anything and it suddenly came true. Or did everyone already believe it to be true beforehand?

"There's a note here from the attending that you might be late," the resident said. "Dr. Bruson wanted you to come in for observation over the weekend." Susan nodded again; it dawned on her than in a few minutes she was going to be totally alone. She glanced anxiously over at Michael.

"I can visit her tonight and then come back in the morning?" Michael asked.

"Of course." The resident smiled at Susan. "There's no reason to be anxious. We're going to take good care of you." From his forced assurance, she knew that she must have looked fairly terrible to him. She smiled back gratefully.

They assigned her the third cottage back, a small rustic structure hidden in the woods that turned out to be like a tiny country inn inside. Her eyes surveyed the twig furniture, Yankee blankets, and hooked rugs, then lingered on the two twin beds.

"Don't worry," the nurse said. "You have it to

yourself for a few hours. Your roommate is at dinner." Susan bit her lip; she hadn't counted on whatever a "roommate" meant in mental hospitals for the well-heeled. But since there was no padlock on the door, she assumed that this must be the minimum security section. Did Marvell stay in such a cottage, or had he been locked up in the more secure areas that they had passed on their way through the grounds?

"I'd like to stay with my wife until the other patient comes in," said Michael. The nurse smiled and departed, leaving a pile of clean towels and a hospital gown on the bed.

"So, we got in," said Susan after the door closed. "Now we have to figure out why."

Michael sat on the empty twin bed opposite hers. "My hunch is that Marvell was getting very stressed toward the end. He thought he was on to the find of a lifetime. Look at his last note: *The angel is near.* He was expecting an encounter. But then he lost it, started to crack—so he wound up here."

"Maybe. But he could have come here to meet somebody. He could have been directed, the same as us."

"Okay. In which case you may be able to spot who that contact is."

Susan nodded. She started slipping out of her jeans and into the blue gown left on the bed.

Michael tied the gown on behind her, neither of them talking anymore, then he kissed the small of her back.

"Maybe I could be your roommate," he said, suddenly realizing that they had not been together alone for too many days. She turned around and kissed him, letting her lips linger on his.

"I don't know where we are," she said. "And the scary thing is that I'm getting used to it."

"That's my girl." They lay down on the bed together, holding each other lightly. It wasn't a sexy place, and they didn't feel sexy, but the eeriness of their situation faded. For the moment they took refuge in physical closeness; the warmth of touch salved hidden wounds and shocks.

"You're not going to be scared staying here?" whispered Michael.

"We'll see. I quit betting on me some time ago." Susan didn't want to think anymore, and she turned off the light, lying there and stroking his face. Time dissolved slowly; they found themselves relaxing into a floating kind of half forgetting. If this was what it meant to walk away, they were no longer afraid of it. Freedom wasn't their home yet, but it wasn't no-man's-land anymore.

*   *   *

"You can stop looking for state troopers," Lazar said to Simon, keeping his eyes on the road ahead of him. The car sped along the asphalt road as if Lazar had never even heard of the concept of speed limits. "There's not going to be any." It was almost dawn, and Simon had been awake for an hour. He sat up, his back aching, and kept his eyes off both Lazar and the girl behind him.

"How do you know? Do you have police privileges to kidnap at will?" Simon said, using no effort to hide his contempt.

"Because New Mexico is a rural state, and I'm avoiding all the main roads. They can't afford to put troopers out here," said Lazar. "Besides, you and I need to talk. We're in a veddy tight spot, wouldn't you agree, old boy?" By now Simon should have been impervious to Lazar's childish Briticisms, but they only seemed to grow more grating.

"We wouldn't be in any spot if you'd let me go," Simon pointed out.

"Can it for a second. You're a total pain, but better the devil you know than the one you don't, right?" Lazar glanced in the rearview mirror. Didi had not slept, apparently had not even changed position during the night once they returned to the car. She sat silently in complete calm. When he noticed her, she smiled. "I'm taking you along merely as a witness. That's all you are here for," Lazar continued.

"You can tell that to my lawyers."

"I will, if I have to. But you haven't caught on in the slightest. This young woman in the back is our capture."

"Jesus, you kidnapped her, too?" said Simon.

"Simon, I said our capture. The one the military brought to the base as a chunk of laser light."

"What?" Simon's head whipped around, and he stared hard at Didi. She didn't look back, her gaze trailing across the desert as it lit up in the pale gold dawn.

Lazar kept his eyes straight ahead. "This is what she turned into. She needed a shape, and she chose this one. I helped her." He smiled secretly to himself. His last statement was only a slight exaggeration. He had sent many images into the light. Didi closely matched someone from his life, not a sister or old girlfriend, but a desirable young woman he had seen only for a brief instant, out of the corner of his eye, crossing the campus at college. She had slipped away, but he had never forgotten her face, and he gave her the fantasy name of Didi.

"Are you gonna react or what?" Lazar said, glancing over at Simon, whose jaw had fallen. "Look at the speedometer before you try to jump out," said Lazar. "Anything over thirty is usually fatal."

"Please, please consider what you are doing," Simon said, letting a note of pleading enter his voice. "You are very sick."

Lazar laughed, "I'm doing you a favor letting you in on this, you know. You just don't realize it yet. I'm doing you a favor because you get to be at ground zero for a unique experience. You think anything like this has ever been observed before? Stillano was going to snuff her, I'm sure of it. So it was my duty to save her."

Simon tried to block the insanity out. As luck would have it, he spotted a county sheriff's car a quarter of a mile ahead. He started concentrating on ways to get himself noticed when they caught up.

"Christ, you don't give up," said Lazar. "I'm going to hang behind that cop until we reach a gas station. Stop wasting your energy. You need to think."

Simon whipped around in his seat and faced Didi. "Who are you? Do you realize how crazy this man is?"

She looked at him, not smiling, and seemed to take him in for the first time. The sun was high enough that the light caught her hair, making it glow in a bright aureole around her head. She swept a few strands from her face.

"The wire service has made it official, President Kennedy died at approximately one-thirty Dallas time," she said softly. *"Everything goes better with Coke. It's not nice to fool Mother Nature."*

"Great, so you've pulled her into your hallucinarium with you?" said Simon with exasperation.

"She's testing out language," said Lazar. "She absorbed a lot of random phrases from my brain, and she has to sort them out."

Simon slumped back with nothing to say.

"That's just a sample," added Lazar cheerfully. He turned his head toward the backseat. "Are you sure you are all right?" he asked.

"Fly me, I'm Sandy. And the eyes in his head keep the world spinning 'round," Didi said carefully.

"I kinda wish she had copped onto a brain that wasn't as filled with junk as mine," Lazar remarked. "You think there are any left?"

"I think you'll both be very happy in adjoining rubber rooms," Simon grumbled. True to his word, Lazar hung behind the sheriff's car, and now was turning off into a dingy gas station, stirring up a cloud of dust as he pulled off the road. He stopped at the unleaded pump. The cashier inside waved but didn't come out.

"Okay, if anybody needs to go, this is the

place," Lazar announced. "I have to pay inside. And Simon, baby, I'll be sure to keep my body between you and the attendant, so don't rush for him, okay?"

When Lazar had stepped out of the car, Simon turned around again. "Listen, did this guy drug you, did he give you something?"

The angel was calm and motionless. "Dearest Simon, you have been much in our thoughts," she said carefully. She seemed to know that this was a coherent sentence, because her face brightened.

"Good. Great." In a fit of frustration and disgust, Simon jumped out of the car and headed for the restrooms. He had the notion that perhaps he could lock himself in, but the door was wide open into the hall, the old rusted hasp lock torn half off. The interior stank, and Simon held his breath without looking down at the facility. It was going to be an entire cursed day in the car unless he thought of something. But what? As he exited, Simon gave the restroom door an angry kick. He heard it clunk against something on the hall wall. His heart skipped a beat, and he looked cautiously behind the door. It had hit a pay telephone that couldn't be seen before, and when Simon lifted the receiver, God was on his side. He heard a dial tone.

Now his heart was racing. In two minutes or

less Lazar would come after him. He couldn't
allow himself to be caught. But if he tried 911,
how could he be sure it would connect to anyone
out here? Lazar had made sure there was no
change in his pockets. In a split second Simon
made his decision. He'd have to use the classified
number that he was never supposed to use and
take the blame if hell came down on him for it.
Did he have any other choice?

Lazar was standing by the car when he came
around the corner thirty seconds later. "Leaky
faucet? Or were you making new friends?" Lazar
asked, but Simon thought he saw a suspicious
glint in his eye.

"Go check for yourself." Simon climbed back
into the car. He didn't know if he was being defiant or foolish. If Lazar did go to check and saw
that pay phone, he would react drastically. Of
that there was no doubt. Instead he got back in
and started the engine.

When they were back on the road for ten
minutes, Lazar said, "You haven't responded to
what I told you. Tell me what you think, as a
scientist."

"When I said you were insane?" said Simon.
"That was my opinion as a scientist. The rest,
about the capture and this girl, deserves no comment."

"You think so? What was your theory about

the capture? It had to be animal, vegetable, or a very clever mineral. You can't credit it with awareness? Imagine a conscious hologram that can assume any of its myriad shapes. That's what she is."

"Babble on, MacDuff," Simon muttered.

"So that's all you have to say?" remarked Lazar. "Too bad, 'cause that means we are going to be together a while longer. While you learn."

They rode for most of the next hour in silence. Lazar didn't know how well Didi was learning to use English, but in case she needed more than brain waves, he turned on the radio. The all-news channel carried no reports about them. Lazar wasn't surprised, given the ferocious security surrounding the capture. The angel murmured softly to herself as the radio droned on. Suddenly she tapped Lazar on the shoulder.

"Yes?" he said. "Are you hungry? Do we need to stop?"

"No, my friend," the girl said in a clear, certain voice. "It has taken some time for me, but I know where we need to go. We can proceed by automobile, in the usual manner. The trip will be worthwhile."

"Wow, you almost got it down," said Lazar. "You still sound like you're talking through a Soviet translator, but that's cool. Tell me where to go." Simon kept a stone face as the girl whispered instructions into Lazar's ear. His call had gone through, but he hadn't counted on a change of route. It would be just his luck if the Army helicopters missed the car when they finally showed up.

"*Gloria in excelsis Deo,*" said the girl in the backseat. Lazar gunned the engine and headed north.

The taco stand from hell smelled of old lard, goat's meat, and green chilies. It was actually a wonderful combination if you forgot your standards and took in the whole setting—the vast New Mexico sky that domed endless reaches of piñon pine and red dust.

Lazar breathed deeply. "God, doesn't it remind you of April in Dorset?" he said, but Simon was ignoring him. Famished as he was, his attention was focused on picking suspicious bits from his burrito grande.

The stand was out in the open, covered with a ramada and a stretch of canvas to keep out the sun. Two Mexican ladies in black and an old gentleman talked to each other in low voices off to the side.

Didi, at least, was loving it. Lazar wondered if she would eat, and she did, a taco spilling out of one hand and a Coke in the other.

"How very A-murr-ican you look, little lady,"

Lazar drawled. He couldn't help trying to entertain her, perhaps out of sheer nervousness, but the gleam in her eye fascinated him, since it never went away. Didi made him feel funny and interesting all the time, a total illusion that was becoming addictive.

"It was made well here," Did said, sweeping her eye over the desert. "Clean and open. It speaks of peace."

"Right." Lazar still detected a lot of translator-ese in Didi's talk, but it charmed him. They finished eating, and her attention was drawn to the makeshift souvenir shop off to one side. The old pine rafters of the ramada were hung with blue turquoise beads, black Navajo shirts, jeans, and assorted gimcrack that might catch the eye of a speeding tourist-mobile on the way to Albuquerque.

"Come over here," Didi said. She was pulling some clothes off the rack and examining them.

"Find something you like?" asked Lazar.

"No, it's for you. You need to be different." Without waiting for a reaction, she held out a pair of prefaded jeans, a black T-shirt, and a poncho in garish red and orange.

"Anything but the poncho," Lazar said agreeably. He got into the car and changed, then returned to pay the two ladies, who started carefully making out a receipt by hand. But Didi wasn't ready to go. She waved at him with a pair of scissors in her hand.

"Where'd you get those?" he said. Two minutes later he was crouched by the side of the road as greasy hanks of hair flew in the wind.

"I'd only do this for God, you know that?" Lazar said. She snipped for a nervous-making length of time, and when Lazar ran over to check himself out in the car's side mirror, he had a true, irreversible buzz cut. The first glimpse of it made him almost panic, and then he felt Didi's soft warm breath near his ear.

I'm turning her on, he thought in alarm.

He yelped as a sharp sting made him jump. His hand ran up to his ear and came away with a fleck of blood. Didi had pierced the left ear, and now she was carefully placing in it a small silver ring.

"That hurts a lot," Lazar whined.

"Baby," she said. But she touched his earlobe gently with her index finger, and the pain was gone.

Now that the makeover was complete, Lazar stared at his reflection. He had turned into the image of a cool dude, age seventeen, from his most hellish years in suburban high school, when coolness was a dream he would never attain.

"How did you know?" he asked. "No, forget that question, because you know it all, everything

I've ever thought. The real question is, why?"

"It's just something for the trip," Didi said, smiling mysteriously. Wherever she had manifested the scissors, they were now gone. Lazar didn't ask about the earring or how she had pierced his ear. Back in the car, he waited for Simon's barb, but his partner said nothing, except that half an hour later Lazar was sure he heard a single word being muttered. It sounded like, *"bitchin'."*

The Angel's Voice

When the angels receive prayers, we often hear this one: "Please, God, tell me why I am here. What is the purpose of my life?" The answer is always the same, and it applies to your life as well as the least or the greatest life ever conceived.

The purpose of life is life itself.

Does this seem like a circular answer, one you cannot really use? It is not circular, because life contains a mystery. The mystery is that of all things, only life does not have to look outside itself for meaning. Many of you believe that God approves of one way of life and disapproves of another. This is not so, for life itself contains ultimate meaning. It is pure gold. God loves life. He created it to be lovable, and because

He put so much of Himself into it, life doesn't have to ask God for permission to exist or to be worthwhile. Life is enough, all by itself. Your highest purpose is not to do, to feel, to accomplish, to strive, to struggle, or to succeed but to live.

How can we understand and use this truth? Think of becoming a mother. In itself motherhood contains joy, but there is much more to it. "Mother" is a universal energy. The universe had a birth, and so does a mosquito; a sequoia has a mother, so does a demon. Mothering is close to God's creative impulse. The energy of "mother" represents life's ability to generate more of itself without any help from the outside. The aspect of God which is felt by all loving mothers is immortal and sufficient unto itself.

The same is true of every aspect of life. What gives love its meaning? Love itself. What gives compassion its meaning? Compassion itself. We angels praise God because we see Him so clearly, and we realize that we are part of Him. So there is a closed circle. When we praise God we praise our own life, our own creation, our own selves. Yet God doesn't ask for this praise. He doesn't buy it or hold a threat over us if we stop praising Him. He made us free—we are drops in the cosmic ocean of life, as are you.

Does life become more meaningful if you use it to improve yourself?

Yes and no. You cannot improve upon life in its universal aspect, which is God. Yet because you live in separation, as an "I" with its own will, you can move far from the source, which means far from yourself. In that case you can improve life by coming out of separation. This isn't your job; God doesn't take anything away from you if you decide to postpone knowing yourself. Such postponements are always temporary. Why? Because life itself is the only true, eternal source of joy. You have no reason to permanently deprive yourself of joy. You seek it in money, status, possessions, achievements, sex, and all pleasures. Yet all this seeking is really rooted in one hunger, the hunger of life for more life. Thus the whole creation moves in the direction of God.

If you never heard the word *God,* if no one had taught you the most basic thing about religion, still your soul journey would take you closer and closer to God. You want to find your source. Some people realize this, others do not. Confusion is allowed, just as the mischief of a child is allowed by a loving mother.

Because life is infinitely worthy, so are you, whatever path you choose to take.

Half an hour after Michael left the cottage at Mount Aerie, Susan fell asleep. The door never opened; she didn't hear any roommate come in. When she woke up the next morning, however, she felt someone watching her. Susan sat up to face a large, intimidating woman sitting on the opposite bed, already dressed.

"I came in so as not to wake you," the woman said. She was fortyish, with close-cropped hair and a square jaw. Her pale gray eyes were fixed on Susan, who felt that she was confronting a prison guard or a matron in an insane asylum. It took her a moment to remember where she was. She sat up and grabbed for the bedside clock that would have been on the nightstand if she were at home.

"It's seven-thirty. I'm going now, have to work," the roommate said. She was wearing old jeans and a denim shirt. Susan made herself wake up quickly.

"Wait, let me tell you my name, at least," she said.

"Okay, but save your diagnosis for later. I

don't need to hear it." The roommate stuck out
a large hand and introduced herself as Claude.
"My parents were French. It's a woman's name,
too," she said.

"Can I get breakfast now?" Susan asked.

Claude nodded. "Wander down the main path.
There's a larger building, you'll find it." Claude
got up and exited, leaving the door open. A cool
breeze came in, bringing smells of pine resin and
a distant kitchen. As she went through her morning routine, Susan realized that she didn't know
why she was at Mount Aerie, given that only
Marvell's purpose for coming here could tell her.
Michael would be back at nine-thirty; she wondered if she would have anything to report.

The dining hall, like the rest of the place,
suited a resort more than a hospital. Clusters of
patients were eating alone or in groups. Susan
walked toward the serving line and noticed that
six or seven nurses and orderlies stood nearby.
None of them were eating. The orderlies looked
strong, and they kept their eyes roaming the
room. She took a plate of pancakes from a cheer-
ful serving lady, and a cup of black coffee. The
utensils weren't plastic, which she thought
showed a lot of confidence.

She took a seat alone in one corner and started
to eat, not really tasting anything. Normal as the
scene looked, the image broke down in its de-

tails. One old lady sitting alone weaved slowly in her seat and mumbled to herself. Another younger woman had hair that looked like it had been stirred with a fork.

If Marvell had needed a retreat, this was certainly a good place. No doubt he had the cash, Susan thought. But she wouldn't get anywhere unless she could put herself in his place. Few people would be so detached from creeping madness that they could get into a car and drive three hours to commit themselves. It was more likely that he had come here for some other purpose. Maybe he had been here before—or maybe his wife had—and he was returning to the scene of something that had happened here.

Something with angels? The ingredients simply made no sense. Just then a commotion broke out at the opposite end of the dining room. A youngish man with a hawk face and wild eyes became agitated and started pouring hot coffee over his head. Two orderlies rushed over to subdue him. Susan found that she needed to get out of there, and as she passed the old woman who was mumbling to herself, she heard the words, "I want to fly jets, sir. I want to fly jets."

She shook off her sense of eeriness by walking the grounds. Masses of old azaleas and boxwood were interspersed with dark pine groves. Susan was idly wandering, trying to find a patch of sunlight, when she felt a tug at her sleeve.

"What are you going to do about the six assassins?" She looked; it was the old lady who had been mumbling to herself. "I know about you," the old lady hissed. "You are responsible." Her fingers, bony but strong, dug into Susan's forearm.

"Listen, you'll have to let go," Susan said, prying at the fingers.

"The agency told me all about you," whispered the old lady.

"I'm sure they did. They never keep secrets." Susan realized too late that playing along with psychosis doesn't work. The old lady's eyes were shot with sudden deep fear. Her mouth trembled, and Susan saw at once that she barely knew where she was. Her own fear turned to helpless concern.

"I don't know what to do for you. I'm sorry, but tell me what to do," she asked. The old lady's jaw fell and she stared blankly. At that moment someone walked out of the dark woods. It was Claude, who took the old lady in her arms and lifted her like a baby.

"Let's go now, Mrs. Blakeley, we're going to get you back," she said. The old lady draped her arms around Claude's neck like a small child. Susan rubbed her arms where the madwoman's nails had dug in.

"Thank you," she said. Claude nodded matter-of-factly and turned to go.

"Just remember where you are," she said.

"Can you teach me where I am?" asked Susan. "I need to find out." She didn't know why these words came out, but Claude gave her a sharp appraising look, as if she were judging a prize toy terrier in a show, then left quickly. In a moment Susan was alone again on the path.

The incident stuck with her on the way back to her cottage. It would be an hour still before Michael showed up. Ten minutes after she lay down on her bed, Claude appeared. She blocked the doorway in her work clothes and dirty gloves—apparently she was a gardener—and said, "You don't belong here."

"Why?" Susan sat up.

"You know why."

"I'm glad you know better than my doctor," said Susan, finding it hard to meet Claude's glaring eyes.

The other woman snorted. "You should leave the games to the pros, honey. That's my advice," Claude said.

"Who are the pros—you?" Susan stood up, not to be defiant, but because games weren't her style. She needed to know real facts, even if they were facts about a very strange situation.

Claude continued to stare her down before

faintly softening. "Okay, if you insist, come on with you." Claude nodded over her shoulder, beckoning Susan to follow her. They were outside the cottage and on one of the woodsy paths before she spoke again.

"Normally I wouldn't pay any attention to you. Lots of others have showed up. I work here as a semi-patient, semi-staff. It saves money."

"And it gives you a good cover," Susan guessed aloud.

Claude laughed, and this time it was with faint admiration. "If you will," she said. "I mean, I saw you were faking it just by looking at you asleep. *That's not a crazy one*, I told myself. But then how did you manage to wind up with me, in my cottage? You had to be more than a random intruder."

"What did you conclude?" asked Susan.

"I didn't conclude. I sat up all night, and I couldn't figure out how you fit in. Mind telling me?" asked Claude.

"You first. How do you fit in?"

"All right, fair enough." Claude stopped in the middle of a large gloomy azalea clearing. "I'm a kind of helper. I came here because these people are in trouble, and they need someone like me. Of course, I don't make myself conspicuous. You would know why, I think."

Susan didn't need to ponder. "You walked away, just like me."

"Yes. There's quite a lot of us, but if I'm the only other one you've met, you're probably surprised." Claude squatted on the ground, dropping her gloves. She was off guard, and she seemed ready to hear what Susan would say.

"I *am* surprised," Susan said, lowering herself onto the soft mat of pine needles that blanketed the glade. She felt as if she were meeting leprechauns in some primeval Celtic wood. "But if we are the same, that must be why I found you."

"No doubt. Once you walk away, nothing is planned except by fate. If you believe in that sort of thing." Claude lay back, getting more relaxed. A pale dot of sunlight had worked its way through the canopy and landed exactly on her face. She smiled as if she had summoned it. "You don't know how lucky you are. Not one person in a million figures out how to walk away, though in their hearts almost everyone wants to."

I didn't want to, Susan thought, but she instantly knew that this might be a lie. She had seen enough suffering that thoughts of escape weren't foreign to her, only she hadn't taken them seriously, meaning she hadn't dared believe someone was listening. "My story is really strange," she said. "Like you say, nothing about it was planned. But how do you help the people here?"

"You saw a small example. I'll show you more if you stay around." Claude rolled over on her side to face Susan. "I don't get the feeling that you will stay around, though."

"I'm here because of a man who died. His name was Marvell." Claude's eyebrows shot up. Susan was happy to see that she had the ability to surprise her, if only for a second.

"You're a good snoop," said Claude. "He was here nosing around. You say he's dead? I barely ran into him. He seemed fairly crazy as people go who don't know they are crazy. But he didn't come here to commit himself. He was trying to find someone."

"I kind of figured that. Who? A patient?"

"Yes and no. More like a ghost. Come, I'll show you." Claude got up, and with an abruptness that Susan was getting used to, she headed off down one of the many side paths that branched off nearby. Susan followed her to one of the more remote cabins. Before leading her inside, Claude looked around to make sure they were not noticed.

The interior of the cottage was dark, and it took a moment for Susan to see that someone was sleeping in the room. Moving closer, she saw that it was a teenage girl. But she wasn't sleeping, she was strapped down with broad leather restraints, her hands tied to bed rails with white cloth ties.

"My God," Susan whispered.

The girl was awake. She turned her head and looked with blank eyes at the two intruders.

"Mary, it's me. Do you know me?" Claude asked, bending over the bed and stroking the girl's damp, tangled hair. In response there came a stream of garbled syllables, uttered rapidly in one breath before the girl gasped, inhaled sharply, and began to spew out gibberish again.

"Is she speaking in tongues?" asked Susan.

"If you mean is God talking through her, the answer is no," Claude replied. "It's not that nice. In fact, it's not nice at all." The girl started twisting against her restraints, still babbling. Her face was not contorted, though; she didn't look like a tormented psychotic.

"It's a strange case," Claude went on. "Her name is Mary McBride. You might have read about her, about three years ago, in the papers. 'The girl possessed by an angel.' That was the general gist."

"Possessed?" Susan walked closer to the bed, but Mary McBride took no notice of her.

"Yes, it became a cause. The parents took her to the priests asking for an exorcism. At that stage she was hearing heavenly voices and spontaneously seeing visions. She kept saying that she wanted to be with the angels."

"I thought possession was always evil or demonic," said Susan.

"Why should it be? If you happen to open up in the right way, you can invite in anything." Claude walked around the room closing the curtains; she flicked on a floor lamp so they could still see.

"You're telling me this girl has an angel inside her?" Susan said incredulously.

Claude shook her head. "Oh, no, she's not that lucky. There was a big fight over the exorcism, and then the media found out. The parents couldn't take it, so they sneaked her off here. Hold on." Gesturing for silence, Claude approached the bed and placed her hands on either side of Mary McBride's temples. Immediately the girl stopped writhing, and her tense body went slack under the sheets. "That's good, that's good," Claude whispered.

"This is how you help people?" said Susan.

"Sometimes, but in this case I'm just soothing her. I said that this was a strange case. This girl is only possessed in a certain way—she wants to be. She thinks she is in contact with heavenly creatures, but she isn't. They are just good impostors."

"They?"

"Astral drifters, lost souls, greedy entities who don't know where else to go, so they prey on people like Mary. They should be moving on, but they keep hanging around us like barflies who won't leave after closing time."

Susan had gotten used to Claude's deadpan delivery of incredible statements, but she felt confused. "How could such a thing happen?" she said.

Claude shook her head. "Lots of people go mad for God, my child. Maybe you haven't met them, but there are lots of ways to get lost between here and hereafter, believe me. This is who Marvell came to see. He'd read about her in the tabloids, I suspect."

"Because he hoped it really was an angel?" asked Susan.

"Right. That was some kind of obsession with him. But it wasn't just to talk to this poor girl. Look up there." Claude pointed to a small framed picture over the bed. Susan approached, and in the dim light she saw a chalk drawing of a slim young woman in a pale blue dress.

"Mary drew that," said Claude. "She thinks it is her angel. Marvell saw it printed somewhere, I guess. Like I said, there was a lot of publicity."

But Susan was hardly listening. It struck her that this drawing didn't simply intrigue Marvell or draw him like a moth to a flame. This was the angel in his note. "The angel is near," Susan murmured.

"Not near enough. This is just a hoax." Claude looked over at Susan. "You said you wanted to know how I help them. Sit down and watch. I don't want you to startle her."

Susan obeyed and shrank to an old stuffed armchair in the corner. When the room was completely still, Claude quickly went to work. She undid the leather bands and the cloth wrist restraints. Then she lifted Mary McBride up in bed, almost as a mother would lift an infant to breastfeed it. She placed the girl's head against her heart; there was a loud, deep sigh that was almost like a moan. The girl shuddered once and pulled away.

"Mary?" whispered Claude as if calling someone from a distance.

The girl raised her hand to her mouth. Susan thought she was stifling a scream, but when the hand dropped, Mary was smiling. "I'm so glad to see you," she said.

"Me too," said Claude. "Your mother just stepped out. She'll be back in a moment."

Mary nodded and looked around, noticing Susan. "Who is that?"

"A friend. When they brought you here this morning, they wanted to make sure you weren't alone. So I'm here, and so is my friend. Her

name is Susan." This explanation seemed to sat-
isfy the girl; she smiled gently and nodded her
head in Susan's direction. By whatever power
Claude had used to wake her up, she clearly believed that she had arrived at Mount Aerie that
morning instead of three years ago.

"I was having such a beautiful time," Mary
said dreamily. "They were showing me heaven.
I must tell Father Patrick. There were great cas-
tles and gates. Have you ever been there?"

Claude shook her head. "No. Do you really
think you went there?"

Mary McBride looked confused. "You don't
believe me?"

"I didn't say that. Do you believe it?"

Susan could see the girl slightly cringe. "You
shouldn't ask me that. They wouldn't like you to
talk that way."

"Why not? If you are so certain, my doubts
wouldn't matter, would they?" Claude was fixing
a sharp gaze on the girl. "I think you know the
angels didn't take you to heaven, don't you?"

A strong agitation filled Mary McBride's face.
"The lady showed me. I saw her."

Claude shook her head. "I don't think so.
Think carefully. You saw the lady, yes, but
someone else took you to heaven. Am I right?"

The girl shook her head violently. "No, that's
wrong, very wrong."

Claude was not put off. "You must listen to me, Mary. I have visited you a couple of times already, and I will come back. I'm not here to hurt you. As convinced as your mind is, there is still a small speck inside you that isn't convinced. You've been fighting against that small, tiny doubt. You think it is your enemy. I'm here to tell you that it isn't. It is your only friend, and until you see that, no one is going to let you go home. Do you understand?"

By the time this long address came to an end, the girl was trembling wildly, and Claude had to hold her to keep her from thrashing. "They're trying to take you back, aren't they?" Claude asked, holding her gaze on the girl.

"I want to be with the lady," Mary McBride cried. Tears were rolling down her cheeks, and she had squeezed her eyes shut tight.

"I'm not going to stop you. You can go where you want, but I'll be back. Try to remember that, will you?" Claude lowered the girl back onto the bed and stood up. Mary McBride's body lay very still, almost comatose. "She'll go very deep now," Claude said with regret.

Susan got up and approached the bed. "You can't keep her here?"

"Only for a moment, sometimes a little more than that. I can't make her impostors go away permanently, because as I told you, she wants to believe them."

"Why?"

"Who knows? Her fantasies may go back a very long time, maybe before this lifetime. She's infatuated." Claude methodically began to reattach the various straps and restraints.

"How pitiful," Susan murmured. *A prisoner of heaven,* she thought morosely.

"No, not pitiful. She's getting what she wants, like all the rest of us. The pity is when we want what is bad for us," said Claude. She pointed again at the picture over the bed. "So that is your clue, if what you need is a clue."

Susan looked at the slim lady in blue. "What can I learn from a hallucination?" she asked.

"Don't mix up the message and the messenger," Claude said with warning in her voice. "Marvell became tremendously excited when he saw that. He rushed away almost in ecstasy, I would say."

"He had gotten closer to his own obsession?"

"Maybe." Claude opened the curtains again, turned off the lamp, and rearranged things as they had been before. "I don't pass judgment. It's a thin line between the fools and the holy fools, between those who go mad for God and those who simply go mad." Claude put her hand on Susan's shoulder as they left the cottage. "The important question, I would think, is which camp you fall into when all this is over."

The Angel's Voice

Seekers are like magnets. We do not heed their prayers so much as their yearning. To seek is to yearn for the light, and any request for more light attracts the angels. Anyone can call us in this way, but too few do. Many prayers are cries for help, and although God hears these, humans are self-sufficient. If you gain enough light, you can solve any problem. For light is more than either energy or a feeling of bliss. Light is intelligence; it is power. God and His entire realm are made of light, and from this primal source everything in the cosmos was created.

When you value the light, it serves you. You can change relationships by injecting light into them. You can resolve conflicts by sending light to those who oppose you. The answers to all profound questions are sent via the light, for as light fills the mind, it heals those feelings of isolation and meaninglessness that plague everyone who is in separation.

Many struggle needlessly on their own to solve the most difficult dilemmas in their lives. Tormented thought cannot bring answers, nor can emotional suffering, anxiety, and worry. Long ago human beings should have learned this. Yet rather than call upon the light for clarity, you prefer to wander in the darkness of your own making. This lack of awareness is the great tragedy of the world at this moment. It dooms you to repeat the same false solutions over and over, to the point that you carry them out mechanically without even believing in them. Few clear deeds can occur when there is no light, when consciousness is sunk in selfishness, fear, and isolation. The family of man is a disbanded family until you find the true tie that binds, which is your shared consciousness of being with God.

The greatest blessing that God can bestow is the gift of light. He charges his angels to deliver this gift. We do so intermittently, visiting and then leaving. But what would it be like if we came and remained among you?

I am the angel who was sent to answer that question. Call me the angel of the blessing.

6
Marvels, and More

"I married an alien," Simon mumbled.

"What did you say?" Lazar stared over at his partner. Another few hours in the car had passed; they were on the outskirts of Albuquerque, where the greener terrain along the bottomland showed that the Rio Grande Valley was near.

"I was imagining your headline in the tabloids," Simon explained. "Next to the three-headed calf and the rabbit crossed with a chicken so that it can lay its own Easter eggs."

They were talking over the music on the radio, which Didi still enjoyed listening to. Her speech no longer came out in stilted snatches, but she rarely spoke. Suddenly Lazar braked in the middle of the highway.

"Go ahead, jump out," he said. "There are a lot of trucks on this road. One is bound to pick you up or run over you." He leaned across and opened Simon's door. "If you are so thick that you can't see the incredible importance of what's happening here, who needs you?"

Simon didn't accept the invitation. "The only objection I have to your story is its sheer unbelievability. But that seems to have been a feature of the whole ridiculous business from the start."

"And?"

"And since my charge was to explain this phenomenon as rationally as possible," Simon went on, "I can safely be said to be doing my job here. I am not conspiring with you. I am observing."

Lazar remained impatient. "If that's your way of dry-cleaning your conscience, goody for you. In your wildest dreams, do you really believe she was better off in the Army's hands?" When Simon didn't answer, Lazar closed the door and started off down the road again. Sparring with Simon had grown tiresome. It was only a matter of time before he snitched to the first authorities who would pay any attention to him. And Lazar really didn't need a conspirator or an observer anymore. He hadn't seen the hovering light change itself into a girl in a blue dress, but he felt incredibly close to Didi. She was like a cloud of fantasy pieced together from his unconscious.

"You can stay for now," Lazar conceded to Simon. "But we're settling up tonight."

"Meaning what?"

"Meaning we agree on a story you can go public with, and if you break the rules we set down, I come for you in your sleep with unpleasant sharp instruments. *Capisce?*"

If he was being completely honest, Lazar had used Simon as a crutch. Being alone with the angel had seemed too scary back at the base. Anyway, the Army brass and the CIA were up the creek, too. No law or regulation covered kidnapping an alien. Only that wasn't the right word for Didi anymore. She was the first absolutely unique thing Lazar had ever encountered. Which was why he would let her control everything— where they went, what they did—as much as possible.

"Almost there," he said, looking into the rearview mirror. "Do you still think I look cool? I mean now that my ear's not bleeding? It's weird reliving my high school dreams. Now I'm kinda wishing I hadn't put kerosene rags under the gym before the prom." Didi smiled. She had wanted to get to the nearest city. Albuquerque involved exposing the car on main roads before Lazar had the chance to switch license plates at a motel or gas station, but he stopped being paranoid over that. A few cop cars had passed them, yet so far none had paid the slightest attention. Either the highway patrol didn't check their license number, which seemed unlikely, or else the angel could make them heedless. Who could tell?

Traffic became dense as I-25 routed them into the city. Didi showed no interest in the packed cavalcade of cars and trucks, or in the drivers honking their horns and gazing fixedly ahead. Lazar turned off to the old town, where there would be tourists on foot. It was what she wanted to see.

As soon as the car was parked, they walked to the outskirts of an open plaza that resembled Old Mexico crossbred with a strip mall.

"It's beautiful," Didi said with genuine admiration. She had gained a burst of energy, seeming to bound onto the plaza on gazelle legs. Now she stood as if hypnotized by the passing scene.

Observing Didi was puzzling. In Lazar's eyes, there were only ordinary people passing by; in Simon's eyes they were less than that, lumpy T-shirt people with brats and no higher degrees. A mixture of Hispanics and poor street people filled out the tourist kind, and some Navajo women were selling cheap silver jewelry, squatting impassively under a shaded *portal*. But the girl clearly felt amazed to be seeing all of them.

"Different from your planet?" asked Simon, who was bored before they arrived.

"What is it? Why does this blow you away?" asked Lazar.

He thought tears were welling up in Didi's eyes. "I have to find a way to tell you. Give me a moment. May I try something?" she asked Lazar.

"If you want my permission, sure. But you don't need it," he said.

"You stay here, then, just in case," she replied. Not expecting this, Lazar hesitated, but he nodded and hung back, keeping Simon by his side. Didi started to walk into the crowd. There was a steady traffic of tourists going in and out of trinket shops, another yuppified group refilling the tank with lattes at a coffee shop, kids leaning on the war monument in the center of the plaza, and the bright darting of skaters in and out of everything else. The only thing that made Didi stand out was that she looked straight into the eyes of every person she passed. She pcrambulated around the square very casually. This took no more than five minutes. She returned to where she had started and looked expectantly at the two men.

"Are you asking me something?"asked Simon.

"I think she is," Lazar said. "Did you notice anything just then?"

"No, did you?"

Lazar seemed a little shaken. "When she was walking around, things happened."

"I didn't see anything," said Simon.

"You had to look close. You hear the church bell ringing from that old adobe church on the corner? It started exactly when she stepped in front of the door. The rosebush about twenty feet ahead had three open flowers on it, but after she passed, it had five. That couple near the war monument? They were having a pretty loud fight a few minutes ago. Now they're kissing."

"You noticed all that?" asked Simon. Lazar confirmed it with a nod. "Then you are very susceptible to suggestion, my friend." But Lazar wasn't paying him any attention. He was intensely interested in Didi, who had turned her back and was studying the crowd.

"That was way impressive," Lazar told her. "You did all that stuff, but nobody noticed. Should they?"

Didi looked over her shoulder. "It depends. Stay here." She began her second circle around the plaza, and this time Simon made sure to follow her with a hawk eye. As before, she walked casually, but he spied none of the changes Lazar had claimed to see. Within a few minutes she was back with them.

"A dud that time," said Simon.

"Think so? You don't notice it?" Lazar asked. "What was it this time?"

"Quietness. The general noise level has fallen by at least half around here. I haven't heard a horn honk since she left. And the skaters—none of them has bumped into anyone on the sidewalk. Amazing."

Simon had to admit that the air seemed calmer in their vicinity. But that could be something Lazar put into his head, and ascribing it to the girl was more than far-fetched. "I'll show you how to catch on," Lazar said, cutting off his partner's objections. "She's increasing her intensity each time. She's not learning anymore. She's testing our limits now."

For the first time the angel acknowledged their speculations. "Yes," she said. "I need to be sure." And again she began to circle the plaza. Simon didn't need to watch closely this time. As she passed people, the girl brushed them lightly with her hand, usually low down on their clothing, never directly on their skin. She selected perhaps one out of three passersby, yet each one reacted the same. They burst out laughing, or at the very least into a broad smile. If she had touched everyone, the crowd would have been a manic chaos, but she was careful. Not enough people were joyous to raise a commotion, just enough so that no observer could doubt that she was the cause.

"Pretty intense, eh, dude?" said Lazar.

"Don't call me dude until you remove that absurd earring," Simon replied, but his retort lacked its usual acid edge. He said nothing when the girl came back and indicated that she wanted to return to the car.

"Was that a success?" Lazar asked curiously.

"Yes."

"So you can make people happy just by touching them?"

"Uh-huh."

"Is that what you're going to do from now on, go around making people happy?"

"No. It's not part of the plan." Lazar had never heard anything like the word *plan* from her, but Didi seemed finished with her experiments for the moment. She had nothing more to say in the car, and Lazar needed to sleep and eat. Their movements had been dictated by her for two days. Now normal human functions were catching up. Since he didn't care whether Simon bolted or not, life could become slightly more normal.

They found a motel back near the interstate. There was a moment of awkwardness about how many rooms to take, but it was sorted out that Simon and Lazar would each get a room and the girl would remain in the car. This was her wish, and since she did not seem to need any sleep, Lazar didn't object. He wanted time alone to think things over. Having seen what Didi could do with a touch, and knowing that the light had been able to send two GIs into religious hysteria, Lazar couldn't consider himself immune. She was keeping him calm. And probably Simon as well, since his flippant derision was just as abnormal a reaction. The normal response wasn't easy to predict, but Lazar assumed that it would fall somewhere between paralyzed numbness and screaming gibberish.

He couldn't sleep thinking about it.

Three A.M. dewfall had already blurred the windows of the car when Lazar tapped on them. Didi stirred inside and rolled down the window in the back.

"What is the plan?" asked Lazar, standing out in the open air in his T-shirt and boxers. "I couldn't sleep, and you said you had a plan."

"I meant the divine plan," she said calmly. Her blue dress was not wrinkled or worn; it seemed as fresh as her untangled hair and open, friendly features.

"What if I don't choose to be part of it? Do I get to opt out, or are you just dragging me along until you futz around with my mind again?"

"You don't get to opt out. You're saying that to protect yourself," said Didi. "Aren't you cold?"

"No. What would I be protecting myself from?"

"Being left out. If you're afraid that you've

been left out of the plan, then your defense is to opt out first. Then at least you feel you had a choice, you were in control." It was the most words she had strung together since they'd met.

"I see." Lazar really did see, and he knew that this was again her effect. "I imagine you can make me feel any way you want, frightened or amnesiac or whatever." Lazar blurted this out at high speed, nervous but defiant.

Didi reacted to none of that. "You are with me. There is no danger to you. Helping you with your fear was necessary at first, but no one controls you."

Lazar said, "Can I tell you what's really wrong with God?"

"I already know."

"I've thought about it a lot, you know."

"Abandonment. Everyone thinks the same thing." Didi sounded very sure of herself, not arrogant or presumptuous. "They are all afraid that God either doesn't exist, or if He does, He abandoned them. It's a no-win situation."

"All right, but it *is* the situation."

"Get in," Didi said. "I'll show you something."

Lazar crept into the front seat and Didi leaned forward. "Imagine something you've wanted very deeply and couldn't have. Don't calculate, and don't think up something new at this moment. Just remember a desire."

Lazar closed his eyes. She tapped him on the shoulder and when he opened them, there was a stack of hundred-dollar chips on the dashboard. He picked up the top one—it said CAESAR'S PALACE on it. "These are real?"

"Yes. Did those fulfill a desire of yours, a real desire?" asked Didi.

"Sure, but—"

"All right, those little things appeared because of your intention. I helped make them show up at this very moment, but you began the process and you received its fruits. That is the divine plan, as simply put as possible." Didi gave him a nod, and Lazar swept the chips into his lap.

"In no way does this feel like a divine plan," he said.

"Why not? Because you usually experience so many steps between intention and fulfillment? All of that is drama, it's not the plan."

"And God sees no reason to deprive us of drama?" asked Lazar.

"Not one minute."

"But if you can materialize these, then He could sweep away all the bad stuff with a brush of His hand, right?"

"It's not about magic tricks. The universe is a machine. God has ordered and calculated every molecule. Two atoms at the far ends of a galaxy spin together because God's mind wills it to be so. He then willed one single anomaly. He set into the machine a creature who did not have to obey his will. That is you. Even angels are not given such a privilege. Yet in dark times you feel abandoned, and you cry out to be saved. God always listens to these prayers, but His rescue isn't what you imagine. He would never simply take over, for to do so would be to strip away the only true privilege you have in Creation.

"The end of dark times comes when you understand your own will, which is a piece of God's. Will is part of the plan; it is God's artfulness in giving you everything but allowing you to achieve it yourself. The invisible ordering of life is mechanical, but the working out contains love. It's a mystery, that a machine could run so precisely and yet exist as an instrument of grace."

"And where do you fit in?"

"I'm just part of the plan," said Didi.

These notions were having a deep effect on Lazar, who had heard them more than once as intellectual explanations, but from Didi they made him feel a pang in his chest. "What is this pain?" he asked.

"Conflict. You are relieved to hear what I'm saying, but you're afraid it isn't true. Fear and love fight in everyone's heart, which is why the drama goes on."

"If you're part of the plan, then what is this trip? Just a lark or a visit to the zoo?" Lazar saw Didi's face fall and felt sorry for that last remark.

"You have no idea how valuable each of you is. My descent is a way to demonstrate that, as God wills it," she said.

"Who are you going to demonstrate it to?" asked Lazar.

"That depends." After saying so much, Didi fell silent, and Lazar had the impression that she was not being enigmatic—she was just putting a period on their conversation. But a darker thought had just occurred to him.

"What about Simon? Is he part of the plan, too, or—" Lazar cut himself short.

"No one controls Simon, either," said Didi.

As if on cue, Lazar heard Simon's voice outside the car.

"It's impossible to sleep around here. You've upset everything with this mad dash to nowhere, and I'm not going along anymore until you tell me who you are. Please consider this a warning you must take seriously."

"God, he's like my evil twin," moaned Lazar.

"Don't lose that thought," said Didi, who seemed to have infinite patience. She rolled down her window and confronted Simon. He had emerged from his room fully dressed.

"Think before you answer," Simon said severely. He looked past Lazar toward the girl. If he was surprised to see Lazar in his underwear holding a pile of casino chips in his lap, he didn't show it, no doubt because his mind was fixed on getting out his practiced speech.

Didi said, "You already know who I am. If you deny this knowledge, you must need to be in denial. I would not disturb you. If you wish to drop your denial, you will. All in time." The girl rolled the window back up; she was no longer visible in the dark interior of the car.

"That was no answer," shouted Simon, banging his fist on the car roof.

Lazar suddenly felt cold and foolish sitting half naked in the parking lot. As he jumped out of the car, this turned to pure anger. "Christ, Simon, look at you. You throw up one blockade after another. You don't believe this is our capture? Okay, so call Stillano and that jerk Carter. Ask them if they lost their baby. Are you willing to do that?"

"I already did."

"Cool. Bully for you. Then ask yourself why they aren't here to save your hide."

Without waiting for Simon's retort, Lazar stormed back into his room. He was too agitated to fall asleep, but he must have, because the next thing he was aware of was the sound of heavy trucks in the parking lot and a bright light shining into his eyes. Without a doubt the troops had finally come over the hill.

Michael sat on the edge of Susan's bed at Mount Aerie. He had arrived at nine-thirty with a few supplies: toiletries, washcloth, first-aid kit, bottled water, and a white shirt blouse so that she would have something to change into. Rummaging through the stuff, Susan had smiled at the first-aid kit. "Afraid of snakebite?"

"It's my security blanket. Indulge me," Michael said. He listened to the shower as she got herself ready. "You don't think we need to find out anything else here?" he asked.

The water stopped and she opened the bathroom door while drying herself off. "No, Marvell thought that this young girl, Mary McBride, was in touch with angels. That's what he wanted to be, but something had gotten fouled up, I guess. His connection snapped, or else he did. Either way, I think he fell into the role of failed messiah."

Michael was thoughtful. "I'd give him a little more credit. He was savvy and pretty well put together, so far as I can gather. Maybe he was getting messages and that freaked him out, but I don't get any messianic tendencies."

"You're the doctor," Susan said. "You've got the first-aid kit to prove it." She smiled, slipping into her jeans and the new shirt Michael had unfolded on the bed.

"I'm one version of a doctor. What do you think the other one is doing now?"

"Not the slightest. Didn't your friend Rakhel divulge that secret?"

"No. I just hope my double doesn't go around screwing with my patients."

Susan crinkled her nose. With the cottage door open, they could smell the woodsy odors that filled the night, but now these were mixed with disinfectant, alcohol, and perhaps the sharp tang of electroshock.

"You can't worry about *that man*," she said. "We haven't the slightest idea of what the rules are anymore. Maybe he's a full-fledged doctor, maybe he's a hallucination that will fade away. Or he could be your doppelgänger come to life. God knows."

"I need to find out. Marvell didn't leave us any more clues. His obsession stops here." Michael was well aware that Little Gideon had triggered a new phase of their strange journey. The fact that Michael had gone back to Marvell's study and seen him alive, if only for a moment, added a third version of events. It all had to be sorted out somehow, and going back home was the only way to do that.

The ride upstate took three hours, which brought them to their driveway at around one. It felt strange to turn in, and Michael half expected to see himself come onto the porch with a shot-gun. The garage in back was empty, however, which meant that the Saab, abandoned several days before at the rustic motel, didn't have two lives. Susan parked the Jeep and turned to him. "You're sure this is what you want to do? You're still out on bail, you know, and maybe you're wanted on charges around Carol Hardin."

"I know. But I don't think we were meant to be driven away permanently. Don't you want to know which version of Marvell's death is going to be the real one?"

"There could be a version that is even worse for you," Susan warned.

The warning crept up Michael's spine with a shiver. He had no guarantee that he could handle the next turning of the quest. Having escaped once, was he a fool to walk back into the trap of his own accord?

The back door was open, as Susan had left it. The house was dark and felt empty. Michael went in first, cautiously, then waved Susan in after him. Despite the summer heat, the kitchen felt like a cool cave.

"Do you think he's gone?" Susan asked.

"Don't talk yet. Let me check around."

It came as a relief to see Rakhel waiting for him in the dim dining room. She was sitting on the edge of the long oak table, her legs swinging like a schoolgirl sitting on a wall waiting for boys to come by.

"You're back," she remarked.

"Yes, and you're not surprised," said Michael.

Rakhel shook her head with a hint of disapproval. "You think I don't follow you?"

"All right, so you must know that I saw Marvell again. He wasn't nearly as dead this time."

"Yes. It is strange but so. You are getting used to things, which is good." Rakhel regarded him carefully. "Why are you so nervous?"

"It's my double—is he still around? This may not be my house anymore," said Michael.

"He's not around. They arrested him for the second murder, and this time he didn't get out." Rakhel sounded very calm announcing this news. It made Michael feel more than strange, however.

"Just a moment, we all need to discuss this." He went back into the kitchen and fetched Susan, who had waited by the back door. She nodded at Rakhel rather than greeting her; there was still a lingering suspicion of the old woman who seemed to appear just when something else was ready to pop out of joint.

Rakhel ignored the tenseness in the room. "Are you able to be detached yet?" she asked.

Michael laughed. "Detachment is supposed to be a sign of sanity, right? Sanity looks fairly useless in my situation. I thought you said it helped to go mad."

Rakhel shrugged. "Or to wake up, which was my point. I won't bother to congratulate you again," she said. "It appears to irritate you. But you made a successful journey. Some people get confused, and they wind up dead or in Philadelphia."

"Do you read old joke books or something?" Susan asked.

"I was around when they wrote those books, my dear. I am only trying to say that you have made some good choices. This double of yours is not a double. He is another version of your inner world. Normally people experience one version at a time. In this case two were allowed to exist. You can let him go, and then you will be free of any obligations."

"But if he's me, then I'm locked up and about to be tried," Michael pointed out.

"True. That part is illusion. It will end when you feel that you are not responsible for Marvell's fate."

"I can't believe I'm buying this logic," Michael said. "It's scary."

Rakhel sighed. "You're not really scared. I think you've both adjusted fairly well. You've been sleeping okay, right? No nausea or dizzy spells?" They shook their heads. "See, it's not so difficult."

"So what this boils down to is that Michael chose to be accused of Marvell's murder?" Susan asked.

"Oh, yes. Naturally the opportunity was ripe. Everyone chooses their situation. People remain under the illusion that this isn't so. They believe that events just happen, like rain falling out of the sky."

"Rain does fall out of the sky," Michael pointed out. He felt the feebleness of what he was saying, and he remembered Beth's words. *You've almost got it right.*

"I think we should choose to get out of this whole mess," Susan said. "Right now. There hasn't been a minute when I didn't feel incredibly threatened."

Rakahel said, "If it weren't threatening, you wouldn't have paid attention. That's a kind of rule, my dear. You might want to remember it. But if it makes you any happier, you don't have to use this double. We can get rid of him and put you in jail instead." Rakhel smiled at the thought.

"So the choice is mine?" Michael said.

"Right."

"Okay, so what are the alternatives?"

"Keep going. Dodge the bullets, improvise, create as you go along. That's the only real way to live. The rest is just going through the motions, and that isn't enough," said Rakhel.

She went on, "It was important to let you improvise, not just as training but as a taste of reality. Until you can survive the situations that you create, you'll never arrive."

"Even though there is nowhere to arrive at, right?" asked Michael.

"Right. The journey just goes on. But let me tell you, it does get more interesting. Assuming that you *are* interested."

Michael looked over at Susan. If nothing else, her sense of adventure made her want to go forward. But he also knew that there were other reasons to keep on. The last few days had affected her. She hadn't caught up to everything yet, but he felt her closeness to him as never before. If he had walked away, she had walked with him.

"All right," said Rakhel, who looked pleased. "There's someone you need to meet. I don't have a name or a face, but it's definite. If you show up at the right place, the meeting will happen."

"That's it? No other clues?" asked Michael.

"No."

"And where do we need to go?"

"That's not important. What's important is whether you want to."

"And how do we figure that out, since we don't know who this is?" asked Susan.

"You don't figure it out. You know and you go, that's it."

"The way Marvell did?" Michael said, aware that he was shooting in the dark.

"Marvell only guessed. If he had known, he wouldn't have died," said Rakhel. "In any version of what you call reality."

"Okay, so what you're saying is that we need to be ready to meet our fate or something like that?" said Michael.

"Aha, now you are getting warm. Fate is a funny gamble. You don't risk all or nothing. You risk all *and* nothing." Rakhel looked so pleased with herself that Michael wasn't even tempted to ask her to explain. She stood up and brushed her skirt as if tidying up crumbs that had fallen into it. It was a small, unconscious gesture, but it flashed on Michael that he really had no idea how Rakhel lived when she wasn't with them.

"You can come along, you know," he said.

"Don't worry, I always do," said Rakhel. "But first things first. Stay here for the night, no longer. It wouldn't be good to stick around. This house has the potential to turn into a black hole."

She examined the four corners of the room suspiciously but seemed satisfied that no one was in imminent danger, then she left. Michael and Susan needed the comfort of their home for the time being. Whatever Rakhel meant by a black hole, they never found out.

The Angel's Voice

Christian angels are new on the block, even though they were borrowed from much more ancient Judaic ones. The angels of India are far older. They are called *devas,* and they don't have wings, but like Gabriel, Raphael, and Michael (whose names all end in "el" because that is Hebrew for *God*), devas fight for God. Their enemies are the *asuras,* or demons.

It is said that the whole of creation was churned into existence by the devas pulling on one end of a long rope and the asuras pulling on the other. This world is butter churned from cosmic milk. The angels and demons are still tugging at each other and will continue as long as time exists. It takes light and shade, good and evil, for life to keep going. Because of that, India found itself feeling fairly casual about the demons; they would never completely lose in the long run, and the angels would never completely win. The two forces had to coexist. It occurred to the ancient Indians that human nature must do the same.

It's depressing to think that the devas will never win, but that's if you believe in relativity. The ancient Indians didn't. They believed in absolutes. Beyond the angels was absolute pure awareness or Being. To be or not to be wasn't a question for them. Being was like an invisible diamond that no one could ever hope to see, but its facets are love, truth, will, strength, compassion, and beauty. You have seen the light glimmering from the jewel of God when these values are held deep inside you.

As the absolute Being merged into creation, it took on a tremendous variety of forms. The form of an elephant is not the form of a silk slipper. Yet both are made from the same absolute ingredients. If you melt them down, you will arrive at God's light. If you melt down a human soul, you arrive at God's light.

And if you melt down an asura or demon, you arrive at God's light.

This is the cosmic joke. The devas are in on it. They fight the battle joyously because they realize that evil and darkness are ultimately nothing but light wrapped inside a very, very good disguise. The asuras aren't in on the secret, which makes the war very sincere on their side—or maybe they do know the secret and keep fighting so hard because they cannot stand the idea of their preordained defeat.

Lazar pulled on his pants and walked outside the motel. From the sound of the heavy engines, he expected to see military Jeeps or trucks, and he even had more lurid images in his head—a tank rolling over the car, the girl squashed inside. But there was only Carter, the CIA poster boy, stepping out of a black van with a second one pulled up beside it.

"We were prepared to come in after you," said Carter in his smooth, flat-accented voice. The first van's headlights were shining into the room where Lazar had been trying to sleep. Carter was wearing his gray suit, unwrinkled as usual.

"Don't worry, I was already waiting," Lazar lied, although he'd assumed that Simon's call would get someone on their trail. He squinted at the sky. "No helicopters? I thought you'd go Waco on us."

"You have delusions of grandeur. Where is Potter?" Carter asked. Two other men in plain clothes stepped out of the back of the second van.

"Next room," Lazar said, nodding in that general direction. Carter gestured, and the two men went to knock on Simon's door.

"You left in a hurry," Carter said. "Why?"

"Spring fever. I wasn't a prisoner, was I?"

"You were behind a security shield. Amounts to the same thing," Carter replied. "You ran just about when the capture disappeared. You knew about that, didn't you? Otherwise it would be quite a coincidence."

"You tell me." Lazar had come to the conclusion that Carter probably wasn't there to arrest him, so he decided not to offer any helpful information. No one could suspect anything about the girl, unless she had been caught on security cameras.

Simon crept out of his room, with two men on either side.

"Are these the guys you called?" asked Lazar.

Simon evaded the question. "You came for me?" he asked Carter.

"Not exactly," Carter said. "We picked up a transmission you made from a pay phone north of Las Cruces. The Army sent some scout 'copters along your route. I decided to wait, and after a while a few credit card receipts came in. It wasn't hard to track you."

"I see," said Simon. He stared owlishly at Carter, then at the white car where Didi sat behind tinted glass.

"Your message made it sound like you were a hostage, and I could call in the police on that assumption," Carter went on. "Is that still your story?"

Lazar tried not to hold his breath. If there was going to be a moment of truth, this was it. Simon looked at the white car again. "Just a moment," he said. He walked over to it and peered in the back window. "No, I'm not a hostage," he called over his shoulder. "Lazar gave me a chance to get out of the car. I stayed of my own free will. I stayed as a scientist."

At a signal from Carter, the two men drew weapons from their shoulder holsters and trotted over to the car. They rapped on the roof, and Didi stepped out. She didn't seem surprised. The same couldn't be said for the government men.

"Put your hands up," one of them ordered. She obeyed without glancing at him.

Is this part of the plan? Lazar thought.

Carter scowled. "Bring her over here," he said. But Didi was already coming toward him, Simon and the two armed men trailing behind. "Which of you does she belong to?" asked Carter.

"Put your cop mind on hold. It's much more interesting than that," Lazar said.

"This is why we left," explained Simon, who

remained nervous and uncertain of himself.

"Go on," said Carter tightly.

"She's the capture. Lazar decided to abscond with her, although I don't know why."

"What the hell are you talking about?" said Carter angrily.

"There was some kind of transformation using extremely coherent light, like a hologram of an unknown type. I think she's basically an optical illusion."

Carter interrupted him. "Stop. I'm not an idiot. What you're trying feebly to cover up is that you took off over a girl. What is this, geek love?"

"You're not listening," Simon persisted, looking more desperate. "The Army wanted an answer to what they had on their hands. This is it."

"Christ."

The two G-men smirked, putting their weapons away; they started to get back into the second van. Carter considered the girl for a moment. "Are you being kept against your will, miss?"

Didi shook her head. "I'm here because I want to be. You are the ones who are not safe, not if you keep living this way."

"That's it," said Carter. "We'll take the bunch of you in. I don't care if you wind up in jail or in the hospital. I have enough security violations to keep you under surveillance until that girl isn't worth chasing after."

For one of the few times in his life Lazar's mind went blank. A veil of white rage blinded him, and he swung out, hitting Simon hard in the pit of his stomach. Simon didn't cry out, but only emitted a whooshing sound from his lungs and a faint "Oof." The sense of betrayal was so strong in Lazar that he wanted to drag Simon up by the scruff of his neck and punch him again, but he didn't have the chance. The situation became far too strange. Carter yelled and began to reach for Lazar, while the two armed men rushed in to cover Simon—if you could call it rushing. For the three of them were moving slowly, reduced to quarter speed in a movie whose projector was grinding down slower and slower.

Lazar opened his mouth, expecting to hear himself sound garbled and muzzy, but his voice was completely natural. "Fight back, you coward!" he shouted. Simon paid no attention, staring at the three G-men, who continued to move like robots on discharged batteries. Didi put her hand on Lazar's arm.

"How do you want this to be?" she asked.

"What?"

"We must not be taken back with them. Simon has brought them here because he is afraid. Are you?"

"No." Lazar found that his head was amazingly clear, even though he could still feel the rush of adrenaline in his body.

"You accept that I am from God?" the angel asked. Lazar nodded.

Both of them had ignored Simon, who staggered to his feet.

"I can't go on like this. Tell me why you're here," Simon whispered hoarsely.

"To make things better," the girl said.

Simon felt like screaming. "No, that's not good enough," he croaked.

At that instant, and for the only time while they were together, Lazar felt compassion for Simon, because they were alike. Simon's covenant with creation had always been a very simple one. Creation held mysteries, which he was permitted to unravel. He might die before he achieved the ultimate answers, but as long as he lived, he had the assurance that all mysteries *could* be unraveled, that the workings of nothing anywhere in the universe were reserved to intuition or divine fiat. Now creation had chosen to break its promise, presenting him with a phenomenon—a nightmarish phenomenon—that logic and reason could not solve.

"You think of me as an alien," the girl said gently, "because that fits your expectations. But I will change those. Gradually and over time."

"I'm not giving you the chance," said Simon defiantly.

Lazar might have tried to argue with him or he might have embraced him as a brother. In the split second of his indecision, the angel took him away. He couldn't see how this was done. She might have quickly placed her hand over his eyes or pushed him off balance from behind—Lazar didn't know what. But the next instant they were alone standing out in the open desert. There was no more Simon, no more motel, no more Carter and his sidekicks. For some idiotic, mechanical reason, Lazar looked at his watch before he even took another breath or cried out in amazement. It was four-thirty in the morning, about twenty minutes earlier than the motel clock when Carter had first showed up.

"They're gone," Lazar said. He still kept his talent for anticlimax. He couldn't actually see Didi in the dark but felt her next to him.

"Yes, we're on our own now. It could have happened earlier, but I wanted Simon to have his chance."

Overhead the stars were bright and perfect. The Milky Way, invisible in overlit cities, spread across the sky, turning a river of blackness into pure silver. "Every star has a story," the angel's voice said musingly. There was no hint that she had been through any tension or unpleasantness.

"Really?" Lazar said. A shiver went up his spine, and he had the eerie feeling that she knew every story the stars told. He did a quick examination of himself. Nothing physical had been damaged. He didn't feel any lingering race in his pulse from his adrenaline high, nor was he drained in the aftermath of fierce anger. Instead he felt very alert and alive and extraordinarily happy.

Lazar laughed. "I'm kind of disappointed, really. I thought you were going to turn them into toads or something." Now that his eyes were adjusting, Lazar saw that they were about a hundred yards off the highway. Not even long-haul truckers were out this late at night. A heaving dark shadow on the horizon must be Sandia Peak, he thought, so they were still on the outskirts of Albuquerque.

"Here, let's get to the road. I guess we're hitching," he said. "I'll help you." He found Didi's hand in the dark, but she pulled it away.

"No. Sit down," she said. Lazar obeyed, wondering what speck of insanity had made him treat her like a normal girl. The sandy earth was still radiating warmth from the hot day. It felt soft and clean under him.

"I've got to tell you, this is still way weird for me," he said.

"I know. You are in need of calmness." Surprisingly, Didi drew him close, until her body was lying enfolded in his. She put his hand over her breast, lightly, and though this panicked him for an instant, there was a primal calm in what she did, and he desired it.

After a moment Lazar said, "I know we call you angels, but what are you to yourself? Is there a name you use?"

"Not really. When I see myself, I'm only a window," Didi said. "If you wish, you can look through me."

"A window is nothing, it's a symbol. Are you saying that you are nothing?" asked Lazar.

"I didn't mean I was nothing. I simply told you the truth. I am transparent. That is how I am to God, and therefore to myself."

"I like your answer. But a part of me is very nervous around you. I try to figure you out all the time."

"That was why you needed Simon," Didi remarked.

"Because he was my mental ally, my rationality buddy?"

"Yes. It was hard for you to let him go—when you lashed out at him, you were hitting your own reflection."

"But now that he's gone, I'll have to figure out if I have the guts to see you, or through you, whatever."

"No, you won't have to figure that out. I will adapt to you. I will only be what you are able to see. This is how we always do it." Perhaps it was the sympathy in Didi's voice or a deliberate act of reassurance that made Lazar feel suddenly relieved. A deep sigh escaped him. "Could you feel that?" he said. "It's like a hundred pounds fell off my back. I still thought—forgive me for saying this—that you might fry me."

"That would never happen. I am from God."

It was the second time that night she had used this phrase, and Lazar almost felt like crying. *Don't stir me up too fast,* he thought. That anything could be from God gave birth to a seed of hope that had withered on parched ground for longer than he could remember. There was a pain in his heart where the seed began to sprout again.

"You're going to be a hit when the media gets wind of you," he said, at a loss for anything more cogent. His inner feelings were too strange and raw for him to cope very well. Maybe he should just quit talking. She must have agreed, because she never gave an opinion about the media. Something like a cool breath passed over Lazar's forehead, and the next instant he was asleep.

The Angel's Voice

Although it seems to be a given, reality is only a potential. The most creative thing that you do every day is to make potentials real. Invisible wisps of possibility take shape and are born into the world. Angels help with that. We are the machinery that every thought, desire, dream, or vision must go through before it can manifest.

What you manifest in your life is your choice. We help, but we do not dictate. Everyone has a different interpretation of events, everyone has a unique perspective on life. In a very literal sense, what you are experiencing right now, down to the smallest detail, is a solidified form of your perspective. A current of life energy flows from the source in God. It arrives at the level where you exist, and using your mind, you turn it one of two ways.

In one direction life energy produces all the good things in your life. In the other direction life energy produces all the negative things in your life. This invisible river of life energy, flowing down its two channels, creates everything. Why do you not notice that this is going on?

Because your five senses record only the tiniest slice of the universe. Out of an infinitely bubbling quantum soup, each person selects those aspects that fit his interpretation of life, which means that you are always moving from one prior conception to the next. You see what you have conditioned yourself to see, you think what you have conditioned yourself to think.

Once selected, this string of prescreened "reality bites" creates its own flow of cause and effect. This is what is known as karma: a packet of events, combined with energy, that you use to move from A to B. Every time you create or exchange karma, you exchange possibilities—you pass along old "event lines," which can be major dramas or very minor incidents that you wish to experience, and as these play out, you gather up new ones. All interactions with the outside world first involve the mind, which is processing every bit of data and fitting it into your overall pattern of old conditioning and received beliefs. The mind has little aptitude for dealing with information that comes outside its habit patterns. That ability belongs to the soul.

You see, although your mind is capable of changing any event line, any script, any drama, it is trapped by its past decisions—this is the binding karma that you must work through before you can achieve real, deep transformation. The soul, if it had its way, would direct all your life energy into good. It would select events that lead you as quickly as possible to freedom from all conditioning. This is the ultimate goal that religions call redemption. But the soul cannot have its way immediately. Redemption is a process.

Just as you choose companions for your journey through life, you also have companions for your soul journey. We are among them. An angel can be a companion in many ways—we help you create the form of energy you want to manifest, we encourage you as you evolve, we stabilize your energy when it reaches certain critical points. But we are not kindred souls—only other humans can be that kind of companion. If angels were to walk the earth and not simply visit it, humans would have to live on the soul level. You would have to do this consciously, as you now live consciously on the material level.

Such a change would accelerate your soul journey immensely, and it would affect billions of people. Why, then, do we not foster this great mass change? Who says we aren't trying?

Michael found Susan downstairs just after dawn. Their old house did not welcome them anymore, and after a bout of fitful sleep, she had found herself wandering the dark rooms downstairs.

"It's strange," she said. "I don't mind leaving here, but I get the feeling that no other house is going to replace it."

"Does that make you regret?" asked Michael.

"I don't know. It's not something I ever expected to face." Absentmindedly Michael turned on the TV. What he saw made him suddenly grow excited.

"Susan, come here—look at this." Michael crouched in front of the set. Onscreen was an aerial photo that at first looked like no picture at all but a burned-out white glare. On closer inspection, however, the details of a ruined building could be made out in the middle of a bombed village.

"In southern Kosovo this morning," a voiceover announced. "U.S. military officials are denouncing the leak of classified photos released from the remote village of Arhangeli. Apparently taken from reconnaissance planes, the night photos purport to be of a mysterious light source that earlier had been denied."

Susan said, "Does this mean anything to you?"

"I'm not sure, but I think it's what Marvell was searching for," Michael replied.

The next image showed restless crowds gathered in daylight around the church that was the building in the photos. "Religious demonstrations had been occurring in the village for more than a week," the announcer went on, "despite steady refusals from NATO officials that any supernatural event had taken place. A spokesman for the local Orthodox church cautioned that no confirmation of a miracle has been issued, and that the government is invited to explain this startling new evidence."

When the news switched to the next segment, Michael turned it off. "Marvell was waiting for something that in his mind had never occurred before, a supernatural event. I think that's it. That was his angel coming to earth."

"Incredible. What happened to it?" said Susan.

"We'll never get an answer as long as the military are playing their denial games, but any massive intrusion like that gets noticed and checked out by the Army," Michael guessed. "We've practically been staring the possibility in the face, yet I never really considered that Marvell was on to anything real."

"You think that this one photo makes his fantasies real?" Susan said.

"No, not entirely, but where do we find ourselves right now? It's an all-bets-are-off situation, and this fits."

The first slanting light of the morning was filtering through the lace curtains at the back of the house.

"What difference does all of this really make?" Susan asked. "Is it leading us anywhere?"

"It's leading to the last person to know about Marvell's obsession besides us," Michael said.

"Beth?"

"That's right."

"She's the one who lured you into the trap. Doesn't that bother you?" said Susan.

"It's all I can do to remind myself that it wasn't a trap. It was an opening, a strange door that I wanted to be pushed through."

"So you want Beth to cooperate with us now, and she's simply going to agree after putting you in jail?" Susan was well aware that she kept being cast into the role of skeptic. Yet it wasn't skepticism that was fueling her questions, or even worry. She couldn't shake the feeling that she was outside a movie that others wanted her to step into when no one had asked what she herself wanted. "You know she might turn you in again."

"No, that's the least likely outcome. The police already have me in jail, so far as society is concerned," said Michael.

"That's tricky, though. Even if Beth hasn't bought into that version of things—which is asking a lot—you are putting her somewhere in the maze, but where?"

"I can't tell until I talk to her. I don't see any other way." The excitement Michael had felt seeing the TV report hadn't entirely faded. He had been talking calmly, trying to summon some sort of logic, but his body language was restless. In his mind he was already confronting Beth Marvell, and he knew the first question he would ask.

"All right, I guess there's nothing to be gained by holding back," Susan admitted. Their goal now wasn't to solve Marvell's death, to track down an angel, or to test whether Beth would fly into hysterics the minute she laid eyes on them. All they were after was the next turning in the maze, the one that would show them out instead of ever more deeply in.

When they pulled the Jeep into the Marvells' driveway, Susan expected the hulking house to have a mythic presence. Instead the dwelling looked almost flat against the sky, waiting for clouds and a higher sun to give it contour. There was not much time for mystique anyway, since her glance immediately went to the car sitting in front. Someone apparently was in residence again. Michael pulled up behind it.

"It's theirs," he said. "I remember it from my first visit." Against his will, Michael's voice sounded constricted.

The question of whether to knock was answered by the open front door. Walking up the steps onto the broad Victorian porch, Susan hung back, as if this were a bad omen. It implied that they were expected, and no one in that house had ever been friendly to them. Michael knocked anyway and stepped into the cool foyer with its intricate Oriental carpet and massive potted ferns. It did not feel like a house of the dead.

"Beth?" he called. No one answered, but there were sounds like conversation from deeper in the back. Michael led Susan down the familiar hallway that led to Marvell's study. When they got to the door, it was closed. The sounds were coming from the other side, but it wasn't conversation—a radio or television was playing.

Michael looked significantly at Susan, but before either could say anything, they heard loud laughter from inside the study. Michael stiffened. It was a man's laugh, followed by the muffled sound of clapping. Marvell had to be in that room, and although he didn't know what he would do or say, Michael wanted to meet him. He had his hand on the door knob when a woman's voice interrupted him.

"Wait."

Walking quietly in house slippers, Beth Marvell approached from the end of the hall opposite them. She was dressed in a white shift that could have been bed clothing, but she didn't seem at all surprised or alarmed. "Don't go in until we've talked," she said. Perhaps because it was her house and they were intruders, Michael fought off the impulse to throw the door open, but it wasn't easy.

"I need to talk to him," he said.

Beth shook her head. "Come away, please. Both of you."

Susan didn't wait to be introduced. "If that man in there is your husband, we need to do a lot more than talk."

"Please," Beth repeated, gesturing toward another room. Her voice carried an insistence that was not easily resisted. She was asking for an unspoken agreement that seemed to include these two strangers but left out the man behind the door. A moment later Susan and Michael were facing Beth across an large sofa in a side drawing room, outfitted like the rest of the house in lush, somewhat fake Victoriana. Her first words surprised them.

"Poor man, he so wants it to be true. You can hear how delighted he is," she said.

"He's watching the news from Kosovo?" Michael asked.

"Yes. He has it on tape and keeps playing it over and over."

"That only makes sense," said Susan. "If his

diaries say anything, they say that he was obsessed with an angel coming to earth. Not just coming but being captured." She decided that it would be pointless to pretend that they hadn't looked into Marvell's personal effects.

"You're right, he was obsessed," said Beth. "The problem is, sometimes we can't stand to get what we most wish for."

"It might even kill us?" Michael suggested. "So you are basically on the scene to protect him? But even if you are a pure soul or some kind of helper, I'm still confused."

"I'm not just his protector. He attracted me because he was a visionary. I needed to be with someone as unusual as I am," Beth said with disarming simplicity. "Not that it's been easy to figure out who I am and where I fit in."

"So for a long time you've realized that your life contains very strange events that other people wouldn't even accept as possible?" Michael said. At that moment he remembered the question he wanted to put to her, the first question he had promised himself to ask. "What did you mean when you said that I got it *almost* right?"

"I meant that you almost saved my husband."

"I can't figure that out. In some way his death is tied in to how I act or react, but why?"

"He couldn't survive what he wanted. His heart is not good, but there's more to it. You can't hunt angels down like prey. There has to be a rightness, a deserving."

"And he didn't deserve?" asked Susan.

"Oh, he deserved. But the world didn't. Or to be more specific, the world might or might not deserve what my husband envisioned."

"Which was what, permanent salvation? A great and holy messenger who would change everything from bad to good?" asked Michael.

"You're simplifying, but you're not far off. Rhineford desperately wanted some kind of public display, but he had not counted on the consequences. He had taken on himself to summon this great visit, yet he didn't realize that good would not be the final result. There might be chaos, or even devastation."

This statement took Michael aback more than anything else in the whole affair. "You're suggesting that the visit of an angel could harm us?"

"I'm suggesting that our reaction could. Can the world stand to touch heaven, or are we too violent and torn apart? Prophets are often killed, are they not, Michael?" It was the first time Beth had used his first name. A minor gesture, but it seemed to draw them all into a conspiracy.

"Yes, they are killed," Michael said somberly.

"My husband wouldn't let me into his obsession. I could have kept him back from the edge. I could have softened his intensity, but he insisted on driving himself to the brink of insanity," said Beth.

Susan stopped her. "Marvell had to die?"

"Events are woven into a tangled web. If the world couldn't stand to have this momentous event, then my husband wouldn't want to be here any longer."

Michael looked startled. "My God, I never caught on. When you called me, he had committed suicide," he said.

"Exactly. I told you he was on the edge of insanity. An injection of potassium chloride would induce a heart attack. Very difficult to spot on autopsy. He didn't want me to be left without the insurance payment."

"I'd like to point out something here," Susan interjected. "We're talking about him in the past tense, as if he were a body. Isn't he here right now, alive?"

Beth stood up and became alert. She cocked her head in the direction of the hallway. "I have managed to keep him in a suspended state."

"Explain that," said Michael. "There's already a coroner's report on the cause of death."

"I don't mean I've suspended his body," Beth said. "I've suspended his fate. Do I have to explain every detail?"

Michael almost answered that she did, but his mind was working quickly. "You called me in," he said, "to start another story going, a story that might save him."

"Yes. I was as desperate on the phone as I sounded. I love my husband. He is a great man, or that is how I see him. And I am not without selfish motives—I need him. "

Of course she does, Michael thought. *They are the two people in this world who would understand each other.*

Susan objected, "If I get this right, Marvell is both dead and not dead."

Beth retained her dignified air of formality. "Yes, and for that I must apologize. By now you realize that I did not set a trap. But events were allowed to play out in a most unusual way."

"I'll say," Susan remarked. At that moment they all heard a door open.

"Where are you?" a man's voice called. "You have to come see this most amazing, damnedest thing. Beth?"

Marvell was emerging from his study. Without a word his wife rushed into the hallway. One could hear the two start to talk, but the words couldn't be made out.

"Let's go," said Michael. He assumed that it would be disastrous for him to encounter Marvell. Beth had set things in motion without being able to finish them. She was only improvising now.

Michael pulled Susan toward the door. Peering out into the hall, he saw no one. He suspected that Beth would have the sense to distract her husband. It would only take a minute for the visitors to slip out the back, and Michael already knew the way.

Five minutes later, when they were in the car and well away from the Marvell house, Susan spoke. "I have a lot of sympathy for her, but . . ."

"But what?" Michael headed the car on the road away from their old home, in the general direction of the city.

"She made you a dupe," said Susan.

"Not quite. She needed an ally, and either by chance or by intuition she latched on to me," said Michael.

"Expecting what?"

"They are a queer sort, the Marvells, but so am I. I fit into her puzzle, which wouldn't be true of a lot of people."

"Okay, let's agree to that. Assume that Beth or Rakhel or somebody up there could figure this out. As you so eloquently put it, now what?"

"Beth has her hands full keeping Marvell suspended. I imagine it wouldn't be so great if he left the house, for instance, or if the wrong people saw him alive."

"I don't see how that lets her off the hook for what she's done to you."

"It doesn't. But something else does."

For the first time Michael had pierced through the veil, and he began to feel jubilant. The burden of his quest was about to be transformed. "Beth pulled us into a truly crazy reality," he said. "But if you boil it down, what's the result? Only one thing. We have to find ourselves an angel. There's no other way out."

Albuquerque didn't hold them much longer. Lazar woke up from sleeping on the warm desert sand. He didn't know how long he had slept, but he did register that the sun hadn't come up, so it must have been only an hour or two. Didi was sitting some distance away.

"I guess you're awake," he said. "I mean, you must always be awake." She looked at him, and Lazar wondered if she felt stuck with him. "I'm a pretty queer type, and maybe you should find someone more . . ." His voice trailed off.

"Holy?" she said, finishing his sentence. She sounded amused. "We don't make those kinds of distinctions. We leave that to you."

"Okay," Lazar said. He stood up, and there was a distinct roar over the horizon, not from long-haul trucks but from overhead. There was a good chance that Stillano had not been far behind Carter.

"Listen, we really have to go now," Lazar

said. "I know who you are in reality. But this body I'm looking at and this person . . . can they be killed?"

Didi nodded quietly. Sheer terror rose in Lazar's heart despite her calmness.

"Don't look so frightened," she said. "Nothing will touch me, no matter what happens."

Lazar felt paralyzed. The overhead roar was getting closer, and he thought he saw a glow over the peaks that could be searchlights. Everything else went out of his head. He had wanted to ask her about death and evil, uncontrollable violence and the rape of the planet, all the things that proved there was no divine plan. Didi tuned in and said, "You were designed to live nothing but God's plan. All of you. If that is true, there's no need to ask for instructions. You have to be free."

"No matter what?" said Lazar. "Even if it hurts?" He thought about the modern forms of torture, so completely clean and mutilating to their victims.

"Even if it hurts too much," said Didi.

Lazar wanted to grab her and run out of there, but he kept calm. "Hear that sound? Simon is bound to cause more trouble. I'm surprised we haven't seen attack choppers diving over our heads already."

"I wouldn't worry about that." Now he was

sure Didi was laughing at him. It didn't help.

"You didn't just bop down to keep me company, did you?" he asked restlessly.

"No."

"Then you must be here to accomplish something, and if Stillano gets hold of you, that won't happen—or at least he's going to make it much harder. Damn it, tell me what to do! I know they can't hurt you, but they can. I feel it." His panicky words didn't arouse Didi. The air became instantly still and without noise, then without warning the angel took over. She didn't take Lazar's hand or click her heels together. Lazar thought he heard a whoosh, but it could have just been an owl flying over. A minute later they wound up on a green moor flooded with sunlit mist. It was a setting for Arthurian exploits or the grandest of doomed romances.

Where is this? Lazar wanted to say, but before he could open his mouth, the scene changed instantly to a mountaintop serrated by glaciers into breathtaking jaggedness. Lazar was standing on the very edge, the world falling away on every side. He managed to talk this time—his mind wasn't so blown that it couldn't spot an odd detail.

"How come we aren't cold?" he asked.

"Look for your sign," said the angel. Didi was still beside him in form, but her voice had supernatural command. Lazar looked down at the ice sheets flowing for miles down the mountain slope. He wondered why he wasn't throwing up from vertigo.

What sign?

In fast motion the places became more fantastic—from dream worlds of horned and spangled beasts that could only live in myth to a dark planet spinning around three suns in a woven, intricate dance.

The angel was laughing at his amazement. "Do you see it yet?" she said. She didn't wait for him to answer. They were off again. Lazar tried to remember all the places, but it was impossible because every time he fixed his eye on a single detail—an exotic sapphire wildflower reflecting the open sky—it would reflect back his eye instead. She had taken him into a mirror world, and everything was too perfect to remember, so intense in color and beauty that it was all he could do to breathe.

The angel kept her promise and adapted to him. When the power rose too high, it would ebb away just enough so that he survived the next transition. She seemed to have a list of marvels, or maybe she was letting him script it. A voluptuous Eve appeared on an island, gesturing to him from an impossibly clear lagoon. He swam with her, and the angel went away for a night while he lay in the sand wrapped in Eve's arms. Another time the sky was full of musical clouds that seeped into one another like harmonic haze, so sweet that any other music was just scrapes and squeaks.

Is this like making a bargain with the devil? Lazar thought in one fleeting instant.

"There's a difference," the angel said, reading his thought. "We don't send a bill."

It could have demolished him to plunge into a mirror of every fantasy he had ever had, crystallized into keen slices of joy, knife blades of ecstasy. It could have humiliated him to confront the tawdriness of some of his desires. Yet it didn't. At some point Lazar knew that she was reviving dreams that had been sleeping in his mind before he could remember, fantasies from a time before he became himself.

Then for the first time in his life he grasped part of the plan and knew it was true.

"We can have whatever we want," he said. "Nobody's denying us."

The angel seemed pleased. "It's the only reason for the plan," she said. "God has no ulterior motives. Since he already knows everything, sees everything, has everything, there would be no need for a plan except to serve you."

"God serves us?"

"Absolutely."

"Then why don't we get the fantastic stuff you've been showing me?" asked Lazar. "Doesn't God want us to believe in him?"

"No. That would be a need, and he doesn't need anything," said the girl.

"Let's say I buy that. Doesn't God want His plan to work? Otherwise, why bother with it in the first place?"

"I can't tell you in a way that you would believe. Perhaps you want a second sign?" she said. They were walking in a deep emerald rain forest where butterflies with foot-wide scarlet wings hung from the trees. It was incredibly beautiful, and Lazar knew that he had become addicted to his marvels. He said, "I only get the next sign when I want it, right?"

"God doesn't force knowledge on anybody."

Lazar hadn't considered until then that maybe all clues about life are dropped by God. That was an intriguing possibility. But he still didn't know what he wanted. So the angel waited. Time passed. The rain forest captivated Lazar more than anywhere else. They wandered under its waterfalls and rested in its grottoes for many days—their journey had no nights—until Lazar felt the first hint that he had had enough. His mind cogitated on a question that would break the spell. "How real is all this?" he asked.

The girl said, "These are images."

"You mean they're fake—all of them?" He tried to resist the sensation of having his heart fall.

"No. You wanted pleasure, and pleasure mostly comes down to images. The five senses make images, and you go after the pleasurable ones. Image and sensation are what you wanted. I thought we should start there."

Lazar looked up at the canopy where hyacinth macaws soared by the hundreds. They seemed to be cut out of children's colored paper. "I don't want just images," he murmured. "Is the next thing going to be an image?"

"No."

He paused. Maybe he shouldn't throw away paradise until he got really sick of it, not just faintly dissatisfied. Or did the first restless impulse mean that paradise was already over?

The angel read his mind. "No, it only means that *this* paradise is over. There might be better ones, you know." Lazar remembered that she knew him completely, and therefore if she held anything back, it was only out of consideration for him.

"I don't want just images," he repeated. This must have been the same as saying that he was ready for the next step. The fantastic emerald forest disappeared, and they found themselves in the middle of a dirty city, standing with a hundred other pedestrians on a packed street corner at rush hour. How the angel did this, Lazar couldn't tell. Her mere impulse—or maybe his—just took them. The light on the corner changed, and the dry flood of impatient human bodies started moving. Lazar and the angel moved with it, being pushed and shoved. A man in a cheap gray suit knocked against Lazar, hitting him sharply on the knee with his briefcase.

Lazar felt like punching him. The man, who was in a blind rush, scowled and trotted on. He grabbed a taxi and was out of sight in a second.

"You think he whacked me on purpose?" Lazar asked.

"What do you think?"

"I wouldn't put it past him." Lazar wished he could grab the moment back and punch the guy the way he had wanted to. It wasn't the kind of impulse that you have in paradise. He wasn't pleased at their sudden descent. "I thought you said this wasn't going to be an image. This looks like a pretty grungy image," he grumbled.

"Keep looking."

"At what? I've seen this a thousand times already," said Lazar, doing all he could not to be trampled by the next wave of bodies crossing the street.

"Keep looking."

A bulky woman dodged around him, carrying

two shopping bags like defensive armor.

He wasn't the kind who liked being goaded into an answer. But his ironic mood felt useless, so he stopped walking, causing a curse from someone behind him. He turned around and faced into the crowd. It parted to move around him, paying no more notice than it would to any other isolated or crazy impediment. Faces were blank, eyes were averted. No one could be sure whether Lazar was going to cause trouble. So they paid him the supreme insult that was also the supreme mark of respect on the street—he was treated like a potential danger.

"This is pretty ugly when you really look at it," he said quietly.

"That's not the point," said the angel. "You'll get it if you try."

Lazar hated being wrong. It was one of the reasons he rarely spoke seriously to anyone. The crowd, seemingly endless, kept pouring out of buildings and subway entrances. Unexpectedly, Lazar felt like crying. He didn't move, and the angel stood beside him, watching.

He saw why God couldn't intervene.

"They've all given up. On the plan, I mean. They don't know that they amount to anything, so they have to keep moving, just moving." He didn't have to look at her for confirmation. Suddenly Lazar felt much worse. None of the ravishing pictures or the valleys in paradise could make up for a devastating sense of loss. "Did I give up, too?" he asked.

"You're like all the ones I hear—you gave up on the plan without meaning to."

"What did we think we were doing?"

"You were doing the best you could. Giving up seemed logical because you wanted something that you thought you'd never be good enough to deserve—God's love. You made up your mind to live on substitutes, and you do a lot to pretend that they are the real thing." The angel looked around with deepest sympathy. "Everyone knows in their hearts that they gave up, but then they decided to forget."

"So they could survive?" asked Lazar.

"That's what they think." She let him remain on the edge of his desolate feelings for a while longer. He wanted to say something petulant like, *I don't want to be hurt like this.* Instead he heard himself say, "You are only showing me what I need to see, right?"

"Do you trust me yet?" she asked.

"I think so."

"Then that is your answer."

One thing was sinking in. The angel didn't coddle; she offered a kindness—if you could call it that—beyond coddling. "It's not hopeless," she finally said. "The plan's going to work."

"How? Don't tell me, let me guess. Your answer is going to be a question: Do I want to see the next sign?"

"Do you?"

"I'm getting more wobbly about that. Is the next part more like Tahiti or more like getting hit by a bus?"

"It depends on what you will allow. If it were up to me, you would see all this"—her arm swept in a wide circle—"through my eyes. Then it would be very different." She seemed to be promising compassion that was just out of reach. The plan was her whole life.

"Let's go," he mumbled, none too sure of himself. "Anything's better than rush hour."

Unlike on Michael's first visit, the parking lot at Madame Artaud's was full when he and Susan drove in. One of the famous weekend retreats was in session. They got out of the car, heading toward the manor house. The path wasn't clear this time but lined with booths and tables, giving the appearance of an angelic garage sale. Plaster statues of cherubs were on display in every size from dashboard (with suction cup) to knee-high, seraphim up to chest high. The tinkle of angel chimes was silvery in the air.

"Seems like the right place," said Susan ironically. A hand-printed sign next to one booth proclaimed, IF YOU WERE BORN WITHOUT WINGS, DO NOTHING TO STOP THEM FROM GROWING.

"This is the only place I could think to go," said Michael. But the kitsch kingdom spread out over the paths and lawn didn't encourage him. He wanted to make it to the front door and into the house. If he could confront Arielle with his case, she might reveal some occult knowledge, or at least a hint, that would enable them to save Marvell. But the front door, he could see now, was blocked by a registration desk and several officious-looking types handing out name tags. .

"When you look at all this junk," said Susan, "you can hardly believe in anything. Is there such a thing as atheism by overkill?"

"Come on," said Michael, heading around to the back. Avoiding the registration line, they followed small knots of people who were going into a large white tent on the lawn near the river. A man's voice was coming through a loudspeaker:

"In 1996 astronomers at Palomar Observatory spotted an unknown light in the sky. Positioned on the edge of the Milky Way, this mysterious light could not be identified by any known method. It did not match any star or galaxy. Three years have passed and still no answers have been forthcoming. We of Angelic Outreach know what this light is. I think you do, too. Are you with us?" An enthusiastic but genteel roar went up from the tent.

"That's strange," said Susan. "Is that what got Marvell started?"

"Who knows?" Michael had stopped in his tracks, not following the others into the tent. He wondered where the back door to the house was and if anyone had thought to man it against intruders.

From behind them someone said, "That guy's in fantasyland—angels don't hang out in deep space."

When they looked around, Michael and Susan saw a lanky man in his thirties with three day's beard and cropped black hair. His clothes looked slept in.

"You know about that thing he's talking about?" asked Michael.

The man shrugged. "It will turn out to be some weird kind of quasar. You're the doctor who's in jail, right?"

Michael was stunned. He had no idea that any press reports had gone out about him. "You saw my picture, did you?"

The lanky man shook his head. "Nope. Inside information. Come on." With no more formality, he headed for the house. Since they didn't have any better course at the moment, Michael took Susan's arm and followed.

"I need some kind of explanation," Michael remarked over the man's shoulder.

"You should be way past explanation by now," the man replied. "You just needed for me to catch your attention. My name's Lazar, by the way." They had rounded a screen of large yew trees, and beyond it was the back door to the manor house—an old servants' entrance, guarded by a young fair-haired woman in a pale blue dress.

"I don't think we're getting in that way," Susan said, beginning to hang back.

"Oh, yes, we are," Lazar said. He seemed to know the girl. They stood together waiting for Michael and Susan to catch up.

"He was being cynical about that light," the girl said when they were all together. "A quasar could be an angel. There's no rule against it." Seeing the look on Michael's face, she laughed. "Perhaps you didn't really want an explanation."

"I need an explanation of how this gentleman recognized me," said Michael warily.

"I told him." The girl had a poise that was preternaturally mature and graceful. Her answer was no help, but Michael didn't feel like challenging her. She was looking at the tent with an intense but unreadable gaze. After a moment she turned it on him.

"If you were born without wings, do nothing

to stop them from growing," she said. Apparently she had read the same sign out front.

"Do you think I've stopped mine?" asked Michael.

"Less than most people," she said. Turning around, she opened the back door and led them into the house. The rear portion was even darker than the front parts that Michael had briefly seen on his first visit. But the girl seemed to know the place, weaving through side rooms and cramped passageways. The house was a regular warren, and after a few minutes it was impossible to know where they were. She found a narrow stairway—another relic from the days when many servants negotiated their invisible work—and climbed it. Michael's vague feelings began to coalesce; the girl was someone he had either met or seen in a photograph very recently.

"Here," she said. They were on the second floor, standing in front of a carved bedroom door. Michael knew at once that Arielle Artaud was in the room behind it.

"Do you know the old lady?" he asked.

"Yes." She opened the door and stood back to let the others in. It was as if she owned the house. Filing into the room, they saw a tiny figure in a white shift standing by the window. When she turned, Michael saw a shadow of Madame Artaud, much shrunk and older than the week before.

"I'm back," he said, stepping away from the small group. The girl had shut the door and was hanging almost out of sight.

Madame Artaud looked at him without interest. "You shouldn't have bothered," she said. Looking back outside at the river and the tent, she muttered to herself, "Ridiculous."

"Are you going down there? I'd like to talk to you first," said Michael. He looked over at Susan, who still seemed glum and detached; she was letting him handle this any way he wanted to.

"Go down?" said Madame Artaud bitterly. "I want to tell them all to get out. They are ridiculous, and they have made me ridiculous." Her voice quavered slightly, but then it rose with her old dramatic flair. "I have seen more than any of them, but I have seen nothing."

She pulled away from the window and sat down on the edge of a huge four-poster bed that was overhung with a red silk canopy.

"What have you seen?" asked the girl, still hanging back behind the group. Arielle Artaud sighed.

"It was very long ago. I was eight or so, unworldly as a goose. My father had olives and grapes in the south of France, in the Midi, and that patch of land was all I knew. One day he took me in his big cart down to the harvest, a cart pulled by two big dray horses. He told me to stay out of the way. The cart was put under the shade of a tree and I must have fallen asleep. Then something woke me up. Somehow the harness had broken or the wagon's tongue got loose. I was rolling downhill. It was slow at first, but then the cart sped up.

"The slope was rocky and steep, and it ended in a dropoff. I must have started to scream, because I saw my father and two olive pickers running toward me, waving their hands and shouting. The sun was very high and bright. Time moved very slowly. They could never have reached me, the cart was gaining such speed. Then all at once it stopped, I mean instantly. I was almost thrown out, but I turned around. There was this slender young man, and he had stopped the cart with his bare hands. He was holding the back and smiling. He asked me if I was all right.

"I nodded. Over my shoulder I turned and saw that my father and his workers had stopped dead. Their faces were pale as chalk. The man who had saved me was now walking away. I wasn't frightened anymore, and I wondered why my father didn't run up to thank him.

"It took a moment before my father rushed

up and embraced me. I asked him if he knew the one who had stopped the cart, and he shook his head. 'Arielle, this is a three-hundred-kilo wagon. Do you know what that means?' I didn't, and he let it go. Of course no one could have halted such a heavy wagon on a downhill slope. It was the only important thing that ever happened to me."

No one in the room said anything. Susan had a hard time catching her voice before speaking up. "Who do you think it was?"

"That is not the question. I know who it was," said the old lady. "But he never reappeared. Since then I have worked on faith, and on what I hoped were voices. Yet today the voices have only one thing to tell me. They don't tell me to hope or pray or believe. They just say that this is the anniversary of my father's death."

In his mind's eye Michael had a certain picture of a heavily-built farmer with callused hands, but dressed in an Army uniform instead of his usual rough wool garments. He was lying on the ground, not moving, and half of his face had been destroyed by a mortar shell. The pain of his death was nothing compared to the pain inflicted on those he left behind.

"It was a four-hundred-kilo cart, not three hundred," said the young girl, who stepped forward so Madame Artaud could see her. She said this in a casual voice, but the old lady started with obvious fright.

"You," she said hollowly. The shock was far more than a few words could have caused. The girl walked over to the bed and placed a hand on Madame Artaud's shoulder.

"Take one last look at me," she said.

"Does this mean I am dying?" asked the old lady.

"No. Why do you think so?" said the girl.

"You know why. You know who I see."

This exchange took only a few seconds, but Michael's mind was racing, trying to summon up from half-remembered images a fact that he should know. Then he hit it. The girl had been in the old photos on Madame Artaud's mantel downstairs. She had been in so many—some in Paris, some on the docks at Cherbourg or on the promenade decks of steamships crossing the Atlantic—that there was no mistaking. She was the young Madame Artaud.

"How can this be?" asked the old lady. Her initial shock had passed, and now she was in a state of awe. There were tears in Susan's eyes, and the lanky man Lazar had gone pale.

"God wants you to know that you have kept your faith rightly," said the girl. "This is only an image, but by letting this image live on, you will know that you live on."

Madame Artaud took the girl's hand and kissed it. Michael didn't feel stunned. He had seen too much for that. He felt as if the room were invisibly expanding. It had no walls anymore but extended beyond his senses, stretching to meet a horizon that would always be just out of reach, even though God was certainly beyond, keeping watch. Afterward, when reality returned to something like its normal state, this feeling would remain with him as a kind of initiation.

"I want to talk to you," Madame Artaud said faintly to the girl. "About so many things."

"There's no need. This image is not going to meet you again. It is only a small thing that you asked for," Didi said. "It was important for you to know that nothing is too small to be answered." These words had a soothing effect on the old lady, but also an exhausting one. She fell back slowly onto her bed, and they could tell after a moment that she was asleep.

The small group was back in the hall and halfway down the stairs before anyone spoke again. "She does this," the lanky man remarked. "I tag along."

"Is that your disclaimer?" asked Michael. He was surprised at how loose he sounded, given what they had just seen. Maybe it was a good sign that he could return to normal so quickly.

Lazar said, "I didn't want you to think that I

understand any of these tricks myself. You see me walking around, but basically I'm in the intensive care unit for stupefied mortals."

"I get you. After all, I'm in county jail," said Michael.

The reminder brought him up short. He knew he didn't need to consult Madame Artaud anymore, but what was the young girl going to do for him? She was leading the group quickly, taking the downstairs at a bound. She reached the back door ahead of them and headed out onto the lawn.

Susan caught Michael by the arm. "We must be near the end of the maze," she murmured.

"I hope," said Michael.

Didi had crossed enough lawn to reach the opening of the big tent, where she stopped and waited. It seemed like she was making a calculation.

"Are you going in?" Lazar asked.

"I want to. There are three in there who desperately ask to see me," the angel said.

"But?"

She sighed. "It is not in the plan." She seemed regretful. Her arms had come out from her side slightly, as if she were ready to unfurl a show of wings. They fell loosely back again; she had made up her mind. At that instant a strong gust of wind came up. It was powerful enough to catch everyone's attention as it rattled the canvas. Heads turned, faces looked up. Three people swiveled far enough around to catch sight of the girl standing at the door. Their jaws fell, and simultaneously they jumped out of their seats. They would have run toward her, but a second gust, more powerful than the first, tore up the moorings on one side of the tent. A dozen yards of tenting fell inward, causing a swell of confusion.

"Let's go," Lazar said. Didi was already moving toward the parking lot. In three minutes they were all in the Jeep, heading toward the highway.

"What do you think?" Lazar asked.

"Of what? Everything or just the parts that got us on the interstate with an angel in the backseat?" said Michael. He was tremendously excited again, and too impatient for explanations. Like Susan, he had a sense of an ending. Madame Artaud had had her ending already—she wouldn't cross paths with her younger self again, only carrying the memory as a certainty that would take her courageously through death and beyond.

"I don't care what you think about any of that," said Lazar. "I mean the chopper."

Michael looked out the window. A helicopter with Army markings was rattling loudly over-

head. It looked like a small reconnaissance vehicle, not one armed for combat.

"Does that have anything to do with us?"
asked Susan.

"It's tailing us," said Lazar.

"Why?"

"There's this guy named Simon." Lazar knew
he couldn't prevent the clash between the angel
and her pursuers now. He assumed that this was
the next part of the plan. No other explanation
washed out in the end.

"What do we do now?" asked Michael, his
sense of exhilaration replaced with a stab of anxiety.

Didi spoke up. "Keep going. We need to reach
Marvell."

Michael nodded, unsurprised when that name
escaped her lips. He stepped on the gas. Whether
the chopper and its crew understood what he was
doing, they didn't interfere but backed off and
kept following the car doggedly at three thousand
feet, waiting for the moment of contact.

When they pulled up into Marvell's driveway,
three military vehicles had gotten there ahead of
them. "Stop here," said Lazar, tapping Michael
on the shoulder. He saw Simon step out of a
black sedan with Carter.

"Is it all right?" asked Michael, looking at the

girl. She nodded. When they came to a halt, Lazar got out and approached the two intruders who were walking down the driveway toward them. Michael got out. Lazar seemed to know the men, but he wasn't friendly.

"Simon, you're running with the yellow dogs. It suits you." The man he was addressing, who was apparently English, scowled.

"You're the one who ruined everything," he said accusingly.

"How? By wanting you to leave us alone?" said Lazar.

"You took something with you, remember?" said the other man, the one in Ray-Bans and a blue suit. Michael wondered how far they had come for this rendezvous and how fast.

"Ah, so Simon has convinced you of that, has he?" said Lazar. "So what's the deal? You're just here to talk to her or destroy her? No, I guess the deal is to use any means to grab her. The rest comes later." Lazar craned his neck and saw Stillano, who had emerged from one of the military vehicles and was watching impatiently. "I see the chief helmet-head is hanging back," Lazar remarked. "Did he get his hand slapped for letting the pooch off its leash? Of course, you lost it, too, Carter, but I guess you finessed the blame, eh?"

"Who is this?" asked Carter, ignoring the jab.

He took off his sunglasses and pointed toward Michael.

"I'm an innocent bystander, the kind who talks to the media," said Michael, his mind wandering anxiously toward the interior of the house. He wondered if either Beth or Marvell had spotted them yet.

"I suggest you get out of here," said Carter. "Something might explode, and innocent bystanders tend to be the ones who get hit by the shrapnel." If this was a threat, it was smoothly backed up as Carter pulled out a handgun. Michael hesitated until he remembered what had to be done.

"I'm going into the house. I'm a doctor, and someone in there needs me." In the middle of the confrontation Michael's commonplace words sounded bizarre. He saw Carter point the gun at him, and his heart began to sink. If the soldiers burst in on Marvell first, he would be dead or dying in his study. Was that going to be the ending?

"Christ, this is a load of crap," Lazar shouted. "Cut it out. That girl is not an alien. She's—" The words stuck in his throat.

"She's from God?" jeered Simon. "It's hard to say that when you aren't in your private hallucination, isn't it?"

Standing out of earshot, Stillano must have

grown too impatient. At his quiet direction a squad of soldiers was now sweeping around on the periphery, moving in on the Jeep. Michael caught this motion out of the corner of his eye. He had just enough time to sprint back to Susan and the girl.

"They're coming for you," he said, his heart pounding. "I'll try to drive us out of here."

Didi shook her head. "I'm not in danger. This is your moment."

Michael stared at her. "What do you mean? You won't go?"

"I'm never going," she said with a smile.

By then the soldiers were surrounding the Jeep, holding their rifles at the ready. A buzz-cut lieutenant was in charge. "Ma'am, step away from the car," he barked. Michael could feel the danger, breathing on him like a beast. Without thinking, he reached out and slapped away the barrel of the nearest weapon.

The lieutenant braced. "Get back, sir, or we will have to place you under arrest."

Michael was no longer paying attention. *This is your moment.* Whatever that meant, it didn't come with directions. He took Susan by the arm and pulled her away. "Come on," he mumbled. They strode past Lazar and Carter and Simon, heading for the front door. Michael thought he saw Beth's face behind the lace curtain. No one else noticed her. No one noticed anything but some kind of commotion in the direction of the Jeep. The guards at the door bolted and started running toward it, as did Stillano and the troops around the house. It was turning into pandemonium. Shots were fired. Lazar started screaming, "No!" Michael knew he shouldn't look back.

"Hurry, hurry!" Beth was calling a few feet inside the foyer. Running, she led the way down the familiar dark hallway. The air was cool. Michael felt Susan's hand trembling in his.

Beth gave a soft, timid tap at the study door. An irritated muffled voice said, "What is it? Go away."

Beth gave them a significant look. "It's been a devil of a time keeping him in there. The best way was to threaten to interrupt him." She put on her mask of dutiful wife and opened the door.

"Rhineford, darling," she said. "There's someone here to see you."

"What the hell!" But before Marvell could jump up and slam the door in their faces, Michael and Susan edged into the room. From outside there was the loud sound of gunfire. Marvell seemed oblivious to it. No details had changed around him. Every pile of papers and books was in place. A few candles were lit—not the dozens that Michael had seen on his first intrusion—and the air smelled of incense that had burned down too far.

"I know you. You're neighbors, right? Go away," said Marvell. His face looked frantic, as if he were in the last phases of a hallucinogenic trip that had gone far astray.

"We can't go away," said Michael. "We're here to show you your angel."

Marvell all but staggered. "What?" he mumbled in deep confusion.

Michael gazed at his reddening face, which looked like it was swelling. "Steady," he said. "She's waiting."

Marvell clutched at his chair. "I won't go. Who are you? What do you know about—"

"We know enough. Come on," Susan urged more gently. At first stubbornly, then like a dumb animal, Marvell allowed himself to be led away. The hall didn't seem so dark this time, and even before they reached the foyer Michael saw that the lace curtains over the door were glowing with white radiance.

"Run, now!" he shouted. "Or we'll miss it."

Dragging Marvell bodily, Michael made it to the door first. He flung it open and pushed the writer out onto the porch.

Where the Jeep had been, there was now just flat ground. A ring of soldiers stood around it, their necks craned back, weapons dropped to the ground. What they stared at appeared to be a brilliant white flare, only hundreds of times brighter. It emitted a faint hum. By rights their retinas should have been burned out, yet they weren't. The hovering light had caught them in stop-motion. If this was a holy vision, Michael had no time to notice, for in less than a second it was gone. A brilliant blue afterimage obscured his field of vision.

"My God," Marvell kept mumbling. "My God."

As his eyesight seeped back, Michael at first thought it was night. He groped to find Marvell in the darkness, to make sure he hadn't fled or fallen. In a moment everything cleared, however, and he saw that it was still afternoon. Marvell was on his knees about a yard away; Susan and Beth stood behind him. No one could say how long this freeze-frame lasted, but the tableau of soldiers remained stock-still. Marvell spoke, this time almost in a whimper.

"Make it come back. It has to come back."

Michael thought the man would break down crying. Did he have any idea that he was the center of such a storm, ground zero for events that had spread far beyond his private obsessions? Beth stepped forward, lifted her husband up, and embraced him.

"I'm sorry, Ford," she said. "This was all you

could take, all any of us could take. It's for the best." Without glancing at Susan or Michael, she led him back into the house.

The soldiers, obeying a delayed reaction, jumped into motion. Some threw themselves on the ground, others grabbed their rifles and swung them in all directions to spot the enemy, a few simply ran. In the midst of the commotion Stillano shouted for order; Lazar stood his ground, laughing wildly. He made a few loud "Whooee!" noises, then walked toward them.

When he got near the porch, he said, "You folks live near here?"

"Used to," said Susan. She was laughing, too, and hugging Michael.

"Are you planning to stick around? I would think you'd want to go home," said Michael.

"No, I can't," said Lazar. "She told me everything. I know the plan."

At that moment Michael wasn't curious about what this plan was. He put his mouth close to Susan's ear. "We're safe," he whispered. She was shaking in his arms.

"Out of the maze," she repeated, "and never going back."

Postscript

If you are a devoted reader of the back pages of the *Times,* some notice about the commotion up-state might have reached you. The county sheriff and state police investigated briefly but found no evidence of any brilliant light or explosion reported by locals. There was a minor flurry in UFO groups, which more or less guaranteed that no one else would take the story seriously. Carter and Stillano filed separate classified reports that contradicted each other wildly and placed heavy blame on outside parties for inadequate surveillance of the air space over New England. Simon Potter was promoted within the agency, without public notice, and after making sure that his pension was secure, he retired several months later. His severance package enabled him to pay cash for an isolated cottage in the Orkney Islands off the north coast of Scotland. He was never heard from again.

The mysterious light on the edge of the Milky Way originally spotted at Palomar in 1996 remains a mystery, despite the fact that its spectrum was being compared to all known galaxies and stellar bodies.

Conditions in Kosovo worsened steadily. The spark of hope that had burned when the people believed that an angel had appeared in the village of Arhangeli was gone, and the environs got swallowed up in ethnic violence that no one could prevent. Susan Aulden occasionally saw news clips of the carnage from that region and wondered if everyone really did, as she had predicted, get what they wanted.

Michael Aulden was rumored to have become a recluse after all charges against him were dropped. Few people ever encountered him or his wife, and many assumed that they moved away after their house was sold. Once, during a drenching thunderstorm, a woman with two small children ran off the road and almost slid into a swollen river. When the highway patrol showed up, the woman was hysterical, insisting that the car had plunged over the edge but then had miraculously been pulled from harm by a man. The only person who fit her description was

Aulden, but efforts to find his address proved fruitless.

The only significant repercussion of the capture took a year to appear, when Rhineford Marvell wrote a novel called *The Angel Is Near*, coauthored with a retired physicist, Theodore Lazar. The book had the ring either of revelation or of illusion, depending on who reviewed it. In the novel an angel talks for hours to a writer at his secret retreat in the Maine woods. She materializes out of the snow on Christmas Eve, taking the form of a ten-year-old girl. The angel's message had prophetic but never menacing overtones.

"God is still waiting for you to notice Him," she says at one point. "It has been a long time in coming, but he has decided that too few will wake up unless He reveals his divine plan. So that shall be done."

"What is the plan?" the writer asks.

"Let me tell you."

And the angel proceeds to unfold an astonishing script of expanding light and knowledge that gradually rises in the world until all the obvious objections to the divine plan—death and evil, uncontrollable violence and the rape of the planet—begin at last to fade away. She seems quite confident that this plan will succeed. She gives no timetable for it, however. Unlike many of Marvell's works of fiction, this one has continued to sell well after its initial flurry, and there was some talk that it was gathering a cult following. The author shows apparent indifference to its sales, although when he autographs a copy, he always inscribes the same words:

If you were born without wings, do nothing to stop them from growing.

AN UNFORGETTABLE THRILLER FROM THE MAN WHO HAS TOUCHED THE MIND AND SPIRIT OF MILLIONS.

Ancient writings tell of the 36 pure souls who can keep the world from a descent into evil. Michael Aulden, an American doctor working in the war-torn Middle East, is one of these souls. Can he and the woman he loves join forces against a destructive man known as The Prophet—and save the world from a collapse into unspeakable darkness?

DEEPAK CHOPRA'S

LORDS OF LIGHT

Created by Deepak Chopra
and Martin Greenberg

AVAILABLE WHEREVER BOOKS ARE SOLD FROM ST. MARTIN'S PAPERBACKS